WILLIAM HOWARD TAFT
SAID TO BE HIS BEST PHOTOGRAPH
Copyright 1908 by Moffett Studio

WILLIAM HOWARD TAFT
THE MAN OF THE HOUR

HIS BIOGRAPHY AND HIS VIEWS ON
THE GREAT QUESTIONS OF TO-DAY

The Control of Railroads and Corporations;
The National Currency; The Tariff;
The Rights of Labor and Capital, etc., etc.

With the Platform of the Republican Party, and a
Sketch of the Nominee for Vice President

BY

OSCAR KING DAVIS

AUTHOR OF " OUR CONQUESTS IN THE PACIFIC," " DEWEY'S CAPTURE OF
MANILA," ETC., WHO WAS WITH MR. TAFT IN THE PHILIPPINES,
IN CUBA AND IN WASHINGTON

———

Including a chapter by
Theodore Roosevelt
President of the United States

———

PHILADELPHIA
P. W. ZIEGLER CO.

CONTENTS

CONTENTS

LIST OF ILLUSTRATIONS

LIST OF ILLUSTRATIONS

INTRODUCTION

Brains and body man has from God; what he makes
of them depends upon himself. He is the driver of his
own mental engine. He advances, stands still or falls
back as he wills. Even the overcoming of natural physical limitations is often a matter of personal determination.
One of the greatest works of American historical literature is the monument to the will of a man who could devote but five minutes at a time to his task.

Work,— hard, persistent, undaunted,— is the only
means man has of progressing beyond the dead level of
mediocrity. It is the touchstone of genius, the key to
all great success. It will tell, even with poor native equipment. But when it begins with brains that are resultant
of generations of culture, and a physique of robust and
generous proportions the effect is certain. Commanding
distinction in whatever line of endeavor he chooses is always the achievement of such a man.

That is the secret of the career of William Howard
Taft. On a superb mental and physical foundation, inherited from a long line of cultivated, sturdy ancestors,
he has reared a monumental superstructure by dauntless
devotion and tireless toil. It is now thirty years since he
was graduated from Yale. During nearly all that pe-

riod he has devoted himself to the public service. It
has been a service marked by intense and constant application to duty, with utter disregard of personal reward. Recompense he has found in the accomplishment
of substantial benefits for others. His growth has been
tremendous. Above all he is an altruist. A great
fighter, his battles have been in other interests than his
own. He combines an unshakable integrity, a very high
order of courage, great executive ability and unusual
intellectual equipment, with an insight into human nature
and a knowledge of men, which, with the varied and extended experience he has had in the public service fit him
for the discharge of the duties of the presidency as probably no other man nominated for that office ever was.

When Mr. Taft first served in Washington, as Solicitor-General of the United States, Theodore Roosevelt
was also there, as Civil Service Commissioner. The two
men formed a friendship which has grown into an unusual relation of intimacy. When President McKinley
chose Mr. Taft to go to the Philippines as the first Civil
Governor, no one more heartily approved the selection
than Mr. Roosevelt, then governor of New York. Subsequently, after he had been elected Vice President, on the
ticket with Mr. McKinley, Mr. Roosevelt wrote for The
Outlook, an article about Governor Taft. Before it was
printed Mr. McKinley had perished, at the assassin's
hand, and Mr. Roosevelt had become President. This
article thus became the first public expression of President
Roosevelt concerning Governor Taft. The judgment

there set down has only been confirmed by the subsequent years of closer association with Mr. Taft which President Roosevelt has enjoyed since Mr. Taft became Secretary of War. In the last four years Mr. Taft has been the constant adviser of the President on all the important questions of policy or action that have been handled by the administration. What Mr. Roosevelt wrote seven years ago is as literally faithful to-day as it was then, and it gives a remarkably clear view of the character and abilities of the War Secretary.

GOVERNOR WILLIAM H. TAFT

BY THEODORE ROOSEVELT

Presidant of the United States

Written for The Outlook by Colonel Roosevelt in August, 1901.

A year ago a man of wide acquaintance, both with American public life and American public men, remarked that the first Governor of the Philippines ought to combine the qualities which would make a first-class President of the United States with the qualities which would make a first-class Chief-Justice of the United States, and that the only man he knew who possessed all these qualities was Judge William H. Taft, of Ohio. The statement was entirely correct. A few more difficult tasks have devolved upon any man of our nationality during our century and a quarter of public life than the handling of the Philippine Islands just at this time; and it may be doubted, whether among men now living, another could be found as well fitted as Judge Taft to do this incredibly difficult work. Judge Taft be-

13

longs to a family which has always done valuable
public service.　He graduated from Yale in 1878;
and a few years later, when Yale gave him the hon-
orary degree of LL. D., he was the youngest of her
graduates upon whom she had ever conferred this
honor.　On graduation he took up the study of the
law, and also entered actively into public life.　In
both careers he rose steadily and rapidly.　Under
President Harrison he was made Solicitor-General
of the United States, and he left this place to become
a Judge of the United States District Court.

But his weight in public life was something entirely apart from the office he at any time happened
to hold.　I dislike speaking in hyperbole; but I
think that almost all men who have been brought in
close contact, personally and officially, with Judge
Taft are agreed that he combines, as very, very few
men ever can combine, a standard of absolutely un-
flinching rectitude on every point of public duty, and
a literally dauntless courage and willingness to bear
responsibility, with a knowledge of men, and a far-
reaching tact and kindliness, which enable his great
abilities and high principles to be of use in a way
that would be impossible were he not thus gifted
with the capacity to work hand in hand with his fel-

lows. President McKinley has rendered many great services to his country; and not the least has been the clear-sightedness with which he has chosen the best possible public servants to perform the very difficult tasks of acting as the first administrators in the islands which came into our hands as a result of the Spanish war. Such was the service he rendered when he chose Assistant Secretary of the Navy Allen and afterwards Judge Hunt as Governors of Porto Rico; when he chose General Leonard Wood as Governor-General of Cuba; and finally when he made Judge Taft the first Governor of the Philippines.

When Judge Taft was sent out as the head of the Commission appointed by the President to inaugurate civil rule in the Philippines, he was in a position not only of great difficulty, but of great delicacy. He had to show inflexible strength, and yet capacity to work heartily with other men and get the best results out of conflicting ideas and interests. The Tagalog insurrection was still under full headway, being kept alive largely by the moral aid it received from certain sources in this country. Any action of the Commission, no matter how wise and just, was certain to be misrepresented and bitterly attacked here at home by those who, from whatever reasons, desired the success of the insurgents. On the other hand, the regular army, which had done and was doing its work admirably—and which is entitled to the heartiest regard and respect from every true American, alive, as he should be, to its literally inestimable services—was yet, from its very nature, not an instrument fitted for the further development of civil liberty in the islands. Under ordinary circumstances there would have been imminent danger of friction between the military and civil authorities. Fortunately, we had at the head of the War Department in Secretary Elihu Root a man as thoroughly fit for his post as Governor Taft was for his. Secretary Root was administering his department with an eye single to the public interests, his sole desire being to get the best possible results for the country. Where these results could be obtained by the use of the army, he used it in the most efficient possible manner—and month by month, almost day by day, its efficiency increased under his hands. Where he thought the best results could be obtained by the gradual elimination of the army and the substitution of civil government, his sole concern was to see that the substitution was made in the most advantageous manner possible. Neither the Secretary nor the Governor was capable of so much as understanding the pettiness which makes a certain type of official, even in high office, desire to keep official control of some province of public work, not for the sake of the public work, but for the sake of the office. No better object-lesson could be given than has thus been given by Secretary Root and Governor Taft of the immense public benefit resulting, under circumstances of great difficulty and delicacy, from the cordial co-operation of two public servants, who combine entire disinterestedness with the highest standard of capacity.

Governor Taft thus set to work with the two great advantages of the hearty and generous support of his superior, the President, and the ungrudging co-operation of the War Department. The difficulties he had to combat were infinite. In the Philippines we were heirs to all the troubles of Spain, and above all to the inveterate distrust and suspicion which Spanish rule had left in the native mind. The army alone could put down the insurrection, and yet, once the insurrection had been put down, every consideration of humanity and policy required that the function of the army should be minimized as much as

possible. Until after the Presidential election in
November last peace could not come, because both
the insurgent leaders and their supporters on this
side of the water were under the mistaken impression that a continuance of the bloodshed and struggle
in the Philippines would be politically disadvan-
tageous to the party in power in the United States.
Soon after the results of the election became known
in the Philippines, however, armed resistance collapsed. The small bands now in the field are not,
properly speaking, insurgents at all, but "ladrones,"
robbers whose operations are no more political than
those of bandits in Calabria or Greece.

The way has thus been cleared for civil rule; and
astonishing progress has been made. Wherever possible, Governor Taft has been employing natives in
the public service. Being a man of the soundest
common sense, however, he has not hesitated to refuse to employ natives, where, after careful investigation, his deliberate judgment is that, for the time
being, it is to the advantage of the natives themselves
that Americans should administer the position, notably in certain of the judgeships and high offices.
For the last few months the Filipinos have known a
degree of peace, justice, and prosperity to which they

THEODORE ROOSEVELT, PRESIDENT OF THE UNITED
STATES. HIS FAVORITE PHOTOGRAPH

ELIHU ROOT, SECRETARY OF STATE
Copyright 1908 by Harris & Ewing

have never attained in their whole previous history, and to which they could not have approximated in the remotest degree had it not been for the American stay in the islands. Under Judge Taft they are gradually learning what it means to keep faith, what it means to have public officials of unbending rectitude. Under him the islands have seen the beginnings of a system of good roads, good schools, upright judges, and honest public servants. His administration throughout has been designed primarily for the benefit of the islanders themselves, and has therefore in the truest and most effective way been in the interest also of the American Republic. Under him the islanders are now taking the first steps along the hard path which ultimately leads to self-respect and self-government. That they will travel this road with success to the ultimate goal there can be but little doubt, if only our people will make it absolutely certain that the policies inaugurated under President McKinley by Governor Taft shall be continued in the future by just such men as Governor Taft. There will be occasional failures, occasional shortcomings; and then we shall hear the familiar wail of the men of little faith, of little courage. Here and there the smouldering embers

2

of insurrection will burst again into brief flame; here and there the measure of self-government granted to a given locality will have to be withdrawn or diminished because on trial the people do not show themselves fit for it; and now and then we shall meet the sudden and unexpected difficulties which are inevitably incident to any effort to do good to peoples containing some savage and half-civilized elements. Governor Taft will have to meet crisis after crisis; he will meet each with courage, coolness, strength, and judgment.

It is highly important that we have good laws for the islands. It is highly important that these laws permit of the great material development of the islands. Governor Taft has most wisely insisted that it is to the immense benefit of the islanders that great industrial enterprises spring up in the Philippines, and of course such industrial enterprises can only spring up if profit comes to those who undertake them. The material uplifting of the people must go together with their moral uplifting. But though it is important to have wise laws, it is more important that there should be a wise and honest administration of the laws. The statesmen at home, in Congress and out of Congress, can do their best work by following the advice and the lead of the man who is actually on the ground. It is therefore essential that this man should be of the very highest stamp. If inferior men are appointed, and, above all, if the curse of spoils politics ever fastens itself upon the administration of our insular dependencies, widespread disaster is sure to follow. Every American worthy of the name, every American who is proud of his country and jealous of her honor, should uphold the hands of Governor Taft, and by the heartiness of his support should give an earnest of his intention to insist that the high standard set by Governor Taft shall be accepted for all time hereafter as the standard by which we intend to judge whoever, under or after Governor Taft, may carry forward the work he has so strikingly begun.

Governor Taft left a high office of honor and of comparative ease to undertake his present work. As soon as he became convinced where his duty lay he did not hesitate a moment, though he clearly foresaw the infinite labor, the crushing responsibility, the certainty of recurring disappointments, and all the grinding wear and tear which such a task implies. But he gladly undertook it; and he is to be considered thrice fortunate! For in this world the

one thing supremely worth having is the opportunity, coupled with the capacity, to do well and
worthily a piece of work, the doing of which is of
vital consequence to the welfare of mankind.

T. Roosevelt

*Extract from letter written by the President in July, 1907,
to a Western friend:*

"In point of courage, capacity, inflexible uprightness,
and disinterestedness, wide acquaintance with governmental problems and identification of himself with the
urgent needs of the social and governmental work of the
day, it seems to me Taft stands preëminent. He does not
think of himself. He never considers how an act or an
utterance will affect him personally save in so far as he
must consider how it will affect his power for usefulness.
His great ambition when in office is to do the job in the
best way that it can possibly be done, and he neither thinks
as to whether he is under obligations to anyone or as to
whether anyone else is under obligations to him. A number of years ago I wrote my estimate of Taft in the Outlook. Since then I have been President and I have been
very intimately associated with him in handling many great
and difficult governmental problems, and my feeling as to
his preëminent fitness for the Presidency has steadily
grown."

MR. TAFT'S GRANDMOTHER (FATHER'S MOTHER)

MR. TAFT'S FATHER (ALPHONSO TAFT)
Photo by Brown Bros.

WILLIAM HOWARD TAFT

CHAPTER I

" LIKE FATHER — LIKE SON "

" Thou shalt never find a friend in thy young years,"
wrote Walter Raleigh, " whose condition and qualities
will please thee when thou comest to years of discretion."

Human nature has not changed greatly since Sir Walter gave that advice. The case of William Howard
Taft is the exception which proves the rule. Not only
are many of Mr. Taft's youthful friendships still green
and enduring, but among his earlier playmates, of the
time when he was one of the " Mt. Auburn crowd " in his
boyhood days, there are those who have always maintained
the joyous relations then begun.

When the friends of a man's boyhood are also the
friends of his mature years there is something remarkable
about that man. Even a cursory examination of the story
of " Will " Taft reveals what it is about him that has so
held his early friends. He is a man in years, experience
and deeds, but his heart is still as light, his nature as
sunny, his laugh as free and ready, his faith as true, as it
was in the days of forty years ago when he captained the

" Gang " in its descents upon the opposition hosts of " Butchertown " and " Tailertown."

The story of the boyhood of Mr. Taft is the story of his whole life.   He is still " Will " to some of his friends, " Bill " to others, whose warming hearts are not affected by the frigidity of convention, and, best of all " Old Bill " to those whose intimacy with him began in their youth.

The first American Tafts came of the English yeomanry.   They were among the early settlers in the old Massachusetts Bay colony, whence they went, as did so many others who afterward reached distinction in the life of the new country, to Vermont.   There Peter Rawson Taft, grandfather of William Howard, lived on a farm, in the years following the establishment of our independence of Great Britain and took part in the affairs of his state both as a maker and interpreter of its laws.   He was a member of the legislature for a time, and afterward served as a judge.   On that farm his son Alphonso Taft grew to young manhood.   The distinction which the Tafts had attained in their community had not brought with it any substantial fortune.   When the time arrived for Alphonso Taft to set about a college education it was necessary for him to earn for himself the money to meet his college expenses.   He did it in part by teaching school.   The equipment for this occupation he had from the village schools and from his father.

With the money which he had saved from his teaching, put in during the intervals of farm work, Alphonso Taft quit the farm at sixteen, and prepared to enter Amherst college. His plans were changed, however, and he went to Yale, where he was graduated in the class of 1833. Then there was a further interval of work for himself, to earn money for his expenses in the law school. It took him five years to make the law course, and it was not until 1838 that he received the degree which enabled him to set up for himself as a lawyer.

In the persistency of Alphonso Taft in thus fighting his own way through the law school there is a clue to the determination of William Howard Taft in all the work that has fallen to him to perform in his nearly thirty years of public service.

The next year after his graduation in law Alphonso Taft took up the westward march in which so many of his friends and neighbors were then engaged, and went out to the great Western Reserve. He settled at Cincinnati, and began the hard struggle for a law practice. Inevitably he prospered. He was a man of determination and energy, of unremitting industry and of great intelligence. He was a student all his life, as was evidenced by his learning the German language when he was more than 70 years of age.

As he prospered the range of his interests broadened and he rose in distinction and the estimation of his fellow citizens. He took a large part in public affairs, and was foremost in work on behalf of his city. His own difficulties in securing an education made him all the more earnest on behalf of others to have the facilities for public education of the best possible. He was always a

friend-of the schools.   One of his famous legal contests
was in defense of the University of Cincinnati, which had
been attacked in such a manner as to endanger a part of
its endowment fund.   Mr. Taft was successful in saving
the fund for the University.   He was a trustee of the
Woodward High School, where his boys began their education.

The public interests of Alphonso Taft were not limited
to the schools of his city and state.   He devoted himself to everything which would make for the advancement
of Cincinnati and Ohio materially as well as intellectually.
It was the commencement of the era of railroad building.
He foresaw the wonderful advance in civilization that
was sure to come through the development of this new
means of communication and transportation, and he
worked hard to secure railroads for Cincinnati.   He became the counsel for some of the earlier roads, and a
member of their boards of directors.

The call to public service which sooner or later is almost inevitable in the life of Ohio men of distinction, took
Alphonso Taft first to the bench of the Superior Court,
in his home city, where in later years his son was to begin
his judicial career.   This is truly a case of like father
like son.   Alphonso Taft was first appointed to the judgeship, and then elected, his election being unopposed.
From the service of the city and state he was called to
that of the nation, when President Grant made him Secretary of War.   Afterward Grant transferred him from
the War Department to that of Justice, as attorney-gen-

eral. Later Mr. Taft entered the diplomatic service, and represented his government as minister to Austria and to Russia.

Alphonso Taft was a man of imposing personal presence, of dignity and refinement. In demeanor he was unostentatious, kindly and gentle, a disposition which made him enduring friendships, wherever he was known. But he was endowed with a firmness of character which made him respected and trusted universally.

So much attention has been given here to the characteristics and accomplishments of Alphonso Taft because this description of the father is but a delineation, in part, of the son. But although in William Howard Taft there are reproduced the distinguishing qualities of his father, he owes much also to his mother. She was a descendant of the old Puritan stock, who was a fit mate for such a man as Alphonso Taft. Like her husband she had broad views of life, and high ideals. Also she had that sturdy material sense which comes from Puritan ancestry, but without the acerbity and rigidity of the early New England life. She was actuated by lofty principles and a high courage, with a dignity and self-respect which gave her such an independence of character and thought as to make her an element to be reckoned with in any community where she might live.

An incident almost at the close of her long life, of 80 years, affords perhaps the best illustration of her character which can be given. She had been keenly alive to the development of the career of her son, and had followed with intimate interest his course in public life. He was in constant and confidential correspondence with her, and visited her as often as was possible. She knew the worries as well as the pleasures of his work. He discussed with her the problems that fell to him to solve. She had approved at every step his course in the Philippines, and was with him heart and soul in the great labor of altruism in which he had engaged for the sake of the Filipinos. She knew how he had won over the suspicious people of the islands, and she realized, as he did, how absolutely essential it was for him always to keep faith with them to the letter.

Mr. Taft had promised the Filipinos that he would go to Manila to make in person the formal opening of their new Assembly. This was their first concrete experience in self-government. It was the first step toward the realization of their great ideal. He was the man who had given it to them. It was in the line of fulfillment of his promises, part of the reward he had held out to them for peaceable acceptance of American supervision. It was by all means important that he should not fail to go to Manila as he had promised.

But as the time approached when it would be necessary for him to start, the health of his mother had become so precarious that it was doubtful if she would live. In fact the great probability was that if Mr. Taft left her then he would never see her again. Under those circumstances he was inclined to give up the journey, trusting to the good sense of the Filipinos and their affection for him to make them understand and sympathize with his position. But his mother forbade. She told him that his duty lay first to the people whom he had brought to the beginning of the road to liberty, and not to her. She expressed her desire to have him go in a manner that had the force of a command, and he obeyed. No one was more interested in his presidential possibilities than she, and no one understood better than she the danger to his campaign for the nomination that was almost certain to result from his prolonged absence from the country. She would not have been the noble mother that she was if she had not fondly hoped and desired to have her son chosen to the great office to which he aspired. But she would not admit that even that consideration should alter the original plan. Better lose the presidency, she felt, than fail in his obligation to the Filipinos. So Mr. Taft went. He made the long journey in the shortest possible time. But he was delayed about ten days in Manila by the necessity of settling certain questions which had arisen there and which demanded his personal consideration. That ten days made his return to the United States too late to see his mother alive. She passed away after he had taken steamer at Hamburg for New York.

Such was the parentage of William Howard Taft. The offspring of forebears like these has inevitably a good start in the race of life. His native equipment is of a character to take him as far as he wills to go. It depends only on the man himself, with such an inheritance, how far he shall progress, to what height he shall rise.

CHAPTER II

" FATHER TO THE MAN "

In point of preparation William Howard Taft is a product of the last half of the nineteenth century; his great work began with the opening of the twentieth. He was born at Mt. Auburn, a suburb of Cincinnati, on September 15, 1857. Seven or eight years later he had become " Old Bill " to his boy friends, and had given his first demonstration of leadership, as captain of the " Mt. Auburn crowd," the little group of Mt. Auburn boys of his age who made life worth living by descents upon the similar boy " gangs " of " Butchertown," on one side of the Mt. Auburn ridge, and " Tailertown " on the òther. Which shows that his beginning as a boy was healthy and normal. From the start he was of that sturdy mould which gave promise of development into the tremendous frame of the full-grown man. He was a good play-fellow, a bit too slow moving for a first class captain of baseball, but a master swimmer, and pioneer of the " plumping " game at marbles. His triple inheritance of brains, physique and disposition began early to manifest itself. He liked to play, but he had no fear of work, or inclination to shirk it. It had not then become the passion with him which developed in later years, but his first school

MR. TAFT AT ELEVEN YEARS

MR. TAFT AT SIXTEEN YEARS

days revealed the tendency. He was possessed then of a curiosity that is abnormal with boys. It was aimed at the discovery of all that was concealed between the covers of his books. Ordinarily when a boy has that curiosity it results in his becoming an object of derision among his mates. It leads to the bandying of epithets like " milksop " and " sissy," which are fighting words wherever boyhood is human. But " Old Bill " Taft was not of that kind. He was just as ready for a game as the next one, but when it was time to work he was for doing the work. And there is where his all absorbing curiosity made itself felt. He was not satisfied merely to find out something about his task, he wanted to know all about it. Now that is a characteristic which makes for thoroughness everywhere, and it has continued one of the dominant traits of Mr. Taft all his life. When first a proposition comes before him he goes to the bottom of it. Then it is his for all time. It may be stowed away in a far corner of his brain, but it is there, and the next time a call comes for that information a word is sufficient to bring it back. And that is the secret of his amazing ability to-day to get through quantities of work that would stagger most men. It might almost be called the keynote of his character. His letter to John F. Wallace, whom he dismissed in disgrace from the chief engineership of the Panama canal strikes this note with unmistakable energy.

" In my view," he wrote, " a duty is an entirety, and it is not fulfilled until it is entirely fulfilled."

Of course a boy with that disposition progressed rapidly in his school work, and traveled far.   It was inevitable that he should stand well up toward the head of his classes, and that his information should not be confined to the school book tasks.   He devoured the newspapers, and hung fascinated over historical books.   When he obtained a bit of information that was new to him he wanted to pass it along for the benefit and amusement of others. One day when he was still a chubby little chap he came to school in the morning bursting with news.   He could hardly wait until the formal opening exercises were concluded.   Then up went his hand.   When the teacher asked him what it was he stood up and solemnly informed his class that the " Imperial Yak " had passed through the canal.

Somehow that information was not as startling as it was amusing.   But skillful questioning by the teacher developed the fact that the Suez canal had been opened the day before, and the Imperial British yacht had been the first vessel to use it.

Boys are far keener to notice physical characteristics than mental.   They called young Taft " Lubber " in those days, because his movements had not the element of grace and activity which boys of less burly build possessed.   He was indifferently " Lubber," or " Lub " and " Old Bill " until his increasing prowess at wrestling, and his developing mastery over his mates gradually overcame " Lubber " and left him just " Old Bill," which he is to those boys to this day.

Here is a case where the child was truly " the father

of the man." The essential attributes of Mr. Taft to-
day are good nature, sympathy, a quick sense of justice,
slowness to wrath but a magnificent capacity for fight
when aroused, and a ready willingness for battle in case
of need. These are all qualities he displayed in boyhood.
He has added to his youthful equipment through the development of education and experience. But it has all
been built on the foundation that was laid in his early
years.

Young Taft finished the course at the Woodward High
School and then went to Andover, where he prepared for
Yale. His father had been elected to the Yale corporation, the first alumnus of the old college to be so honored.
His elder brothers had graduated from Yale, and of
course Will Taft became a son of Eli. When he entered college in the fall of '74, at the age of seventeen,
Taft was an upstanding boy of nearly six feet, and a bulk
considerably more than 200 pounds. The photographs
taken of him then show a clean-cut youngster, solid but
not fat, with a figure which showed power in every line.
He was hailed by his classmates as a certain champion in
athletics, and the football enthusiasts received him as a
tower of strength for the team. But Taft did not go in
for athletics. He was in college for the sake of an education, and he meant to make the utmost of his opportunity. The education of a young man, in Mr. Taft's
view, should be " as thorough and as useful as he himself wishes to make it." He has held that view since
his own experience in college, and in his time at Yale

he acted on it for himself. He believed in athletics. He held it to be the duty of every young man to be a " good animal " for this reason, if for no other, that it the better enabled him to do well in his work. The sound body was the foundation for sound work, and that was the main thing. He joined in the play of his fellows, worked in the gymnasium, wrestled, and played football a little. But his athletics were for exercise and recreation, not a means of winning honor or reputation.

There is a record of one occasion, however, when he joined in the class athletics for the sake of the class, and it was an altogether characteristic performance. There was a field day, and one of the events was a tug of war in which his class was pitted against another. Taft had already demonstrated his prowess against these rivals in the early rushes, when he had plowed irresistibly through their lines. But in this rope pulling contest they got the better of his classmates and he saw his team being dragged bodily down the field. That was too much for him. He grabbed hold of the end of the rope, got a good foothold and sung out:

" Now let 'em all get on the other end! "

The two classes tallied on at that, and there was a royal struggle. But Taft as the anchor for his side held fast, and his class won.

The keen appreciation of the ridiculous which is one of Mr. Taft's best known traits to-day, the cheerful good humor and hearty laugh which always distinguish him, were as much in evidence in his college days as now. His

disposition was so helpful and sympathetic, his nature so
sunny, that he was naturally about the most popular man
in his class. College boys as a rule do not take kindly
to a " grind." They do not usually form a high admiration for a man who is always poring over his books.
Young Taft was openly out for honors. He made no secret of the fact that he intended to secure as high a place
in the class as he could, and he never let anything in the
way of fun interfere with his work. But somehow he
managed to find time for participation in his class
" stunts." His whole college life was an exhibition of
clean living, clean thinking and clean working. It won
him not only the honor he coveted, but the respect and
love of all his class. He graduated second among 120 and
was made salutatorian of his class. The hold he established on his classmates he has maintained ever since. In
scores of ways in after years the love they bear him has
been evidenced. And he himself bears witness to how it
has helped him, sometimes on occasions when it was sorely
needed. Not long ago he delivered an address to the
students of the University of Wisconsin, in which he dealt
with this subject of college friendships.

" I purpose to speak of something which you can secure
nowhere else except in a college like this," he said, " the
wealth of reminiscence and friendship contracted at a time
when your character is being formed, when you have no
selfish ambitions, when life has not become hard, when
you have not run against those things that make you
pessimistic; contracted at a time when you are full of en-

3

thusiasm, when your bosoms have windows in them that show the heart that is beating in you. The friendships that you then form are friendships you can never form again. In this four years of life there is an epitome of the life to come, it is true, but it is life with a higher standard, with purer ideals than any life that is to come in the whirlwind you are to meet hereafter. It is to this that I call your attention, and tell you to enjoy it to the full. For of the two things that you will carry from here — your friendships — your college associations — and your education, I feel that everyone who has had them both to the full, will value the former more highly. Not only will your feeling toward your fellows be strong, but the fact that through that same mould, through that same experience, men of the same universities have passed, will create a bond between you and them that no freemasonry can make as strong.

"I speak with earnestness and fervor of this because I feel it to the bottom of my soul, and with an apology for going into a personal incident I may tell you something that occurred to me.

"I was in Manila as governor of the Philippines in October, 1902. I was alone in what they call the 'Palace,' with only Chinese servants, and I was on my back with a very painful illness. The government had not been going just as we all would have liked it. The newspapers were criticising, as they always do, but they seemed to have more ground for criticism at that time. The shadows of night were coming on and the day had just reached that period when everything that is burdensome or pessimistic seems to lengthen with the shadows. I was very much depressed, when a cablegram was handed me by a Chinaman.

" I ought to say that Yale had been celebrating her 200th anniversary, and all the class had gathered there to honor her in that celebration. I had forgotten it in the woes that I had, but when this cablegram was opened, I remembered. This is what it said:

" ' We love you, Bill, and we are with you in everything you are doing.

" Yale, '78.' "

" Now if the sun had returned and shone into that room it could not have given me more light. It could not have given me more strength to meet the burdens which were not light at that time than that message from those men. I could feel myself standing elbow to elbow, because I knew that they were my most generous critics, that they would bear any defect that a man might have because they knew his heart was right; that they would bring to bear in the judgment of him the charity, the love and the deep feeling of companionship which nothing but a college friendship can give."

With 120 friendships like that Mr. Taft quit college at 21, and began his career of nearly thirty years of public service.

CHAPTER III

THE BEGINNINGS OF A CAREER

There was never any hesitation over the selection of a profession by Mr. Taft. He was marked for the law from the first, and it was natural that during his course at Yale he should devote himself as far as possible to such studies as would help in laying the foundation for his subsequent technical training. The public experience of his father, with the record of his grandfather, turned him naturally to the consideration of government and public affairs. And like most college students he developed some theories which his later experience did not support. But on one essential point his after years have only confirmed his early opinion. That is the duty of every right minded and self-respecting American citizen to take part in the politics of his district, in order to advance the interests of good government. In Yale, Taft had been a believer in the laissez-faire doctrine, that appealing theory of non-interference which works so beautifully in the textbooks and acts so differently in practical application. Taft soon found out, when he went back to Cincinnati and began to apply his other belief, concerning participation in politics, that laissez-faire had a very small part to play there.

44

MR. TAFT AS A STUDENT AT YALE

MR. TAFT AND HIS BROTHER CHARLES P. TAFT, EDITOR
OF THE CINCINNATI "TIMES STAR."
Photo by Brown Bros.

True to his inclination he began at once to take an active part in the business of electing good responsible men to office. He went into ward politics and worked at the polls. By inheritance first, and then by personal conviction he was a Republican. When he made his own investigation of the practical workings of the protective tariff he got a result that did not comport at all with laissez-faire, and since then he has practiced a different let-alone theory.

Mr. Taft believes that the best thing that can happen to a young man is to have " an education as thorough and as useful as he himself wishes to make it, and then under the spur of necessity to enter upon a life of work without the temptation to lack of effort and idleness which a competency always creates." That is a fair description of his own situation when he returned to Cincinnati with his Yale diploma. His family was of excellent position in Cincinnati, but his father, although for years prominent in public life and one of the leaders of the Ohio bar was far from being a man of wealth. Young Taft had to go to work for himself at once, in order to help out on the expenses of the course in the Cincinnati Law School which he entered as soon as he got home from college. He began as a reporter on the Times-Star, owned by his half-brother Charles P. Taft. His assignment was to " cover " the courts, and after nine months he did it so well that his work attracted the attention of Murat Halstead, the veteran editor of the Cincin-

nati Commercial-Gazette. Halstead sent for Taft and
gave him a job at $25 a week, to report the courts.

While he was thus studying law and doing newspaper
work Taft was making good his theories of political activity. He believes that it is the duty of every college
graduate to spend as much time as he can in learning
the local situation, in becoming acquainted with the precinct and ward leaders and with the voters. He should
know not only the well-to-do and educated men in his
ward, but also the laborers, the workingmen, the store
keepers and even the saloon keepers, so that he may be
thoroughly informed as to the controlling influences in
the primaries and elections of his precinct and ward.

That was a practical business that he had set out upon,
and he went at it with the same thoroughness that had
characterized his work in college and as a reporter. He
believes in the " scholar in politics " but not in the accepted " scholar in politics " plan of activity. If the
scholar can be persuaded to get down to rock bottom and
meet the people of his district and associate with them
in their political activities Taft believes that the result
can only be beneficial to both sides.

His own contact with the practical politicians gave
evidence of the hardest kind of hard fisted practicality.
He was a watcher at a polling place when it was reported
to him by another watcher that one of a gang of toughs
who were hanging around was attempting to intimidate
some of the voters.

" Which one ? " asked Taft.

The man was pointed out and Taft started for him. At the same time the man walked toward Taft. He was a big stone mason, who did not appreciate the practical value of the scholar in politics. As he came up to Taft he demanded angrily to know what Taft was doing around the polls.

Taft's only answer was a boulder-fisted crack on the jaw that sent the stone mason to ground in a heap.

"Now," he said to his friends, "let's find out what the trouble is here."

But there was no more trouble. He had ended it with one blow.

The man who doesn't like to fight, but who is always ready and willing to do so when it seems necessary is usually a bad man to meet in that kind of an encounter. It is a curiously interesting part of the biography of the best natured man in the government which deals with the prowess with his fists displayed in his early days. There are not many such incidents, all of them confined to the days when he was engaged in practical politics in Cincinnati, and all of them brought on by his concern for some one else. The most celebrated of these engagements was with a man named Rose, who ran a blackmailing newspaper in Cincinnati. Rose was a plug-ugly graduated from the prize ring, who went about the city with two or three of his prize-fighting friends ready to help him in case of need. He printed a scurrilous article about Judge Alphonso Taft, which was so palpably a slander that Judge Taft's friends only laughed and gave it no serious thought.   But it didn't strike Will Taft as in any way funny.   He started for Rose's office with his face flushed and his fists doubled up.   On the street he met his man.

"Are you Rose?" demanded Taft.

Rose started an affirmative nod, but before he had half concluded it Taft had picked him up bodily and flung him down with a bang on the pavement.   He didn't deign to strike.   He simply put one knee in the small of the blackmailer's back and began cheerfully grinding his face into the paving stones.   Rose howled with pain and rage.

"I'll let up if you'll get out of town to-night," said Taft.

Between howls Rose managed to get out a promise to quit and Taft let him up.

"Now," said Taft, "I'll come down here again to-night, and if you are still here this is only a starter."

But Rose had had plenty.   He quit Cincinnati that night and his slander-monger never appeared again.

So young Taft varied his activity during the two years he was in the law school.   He got his degree in 1880, dividing the first honors with another industrious and ambitious student.   Immediately upon his admission to the bar he began the practice of law in his father's old firm.   He kept right on in politics, however, and devoted himself to opposition to gang rule.   He was sufficiently practical to see that under the American system it requires not only organization but the most persistent application to maintain headway against the bosses.   His

plan was a counter organization of young men similarly
minded, who would make it their business always to
see that only clean and able men were nominated for office.
And as far as possible he would get the offices out from
the possible reach of the bosses through a permanent civil
service.

He had been practicing law but one year when he was
called to his first public service.   A friend, Miller Outcalt,
now a leader of the Cincinnati Bar, had been elected prosecuting attorney of Hamilton county, and Taft was appointed his assistant.   The sort of prosecutor he was is
described by Joe Moses, one of the court bailiffs.

"He wanted to get every criminal into the penitentiary," said Joe.

That is a feeling which Mr. Taft has to-day.   And
he would work a decided reformation of the criminal
procedure if it were possible.   He believes that " the administration of the criminal law is a disgrace to our civilization."   In one of the ablest speeches he has made,
before the graduating class of the Yale law school two
years ago, Mr. Taft discussed very thoroughly this subject, tracing the growth of technicalities in our law, and
the increasing tendency of the courts to give heed to them.
It is a tendency, he believes, which regards the liberty of
the individual accused of crime more than it considers the
rights or the welfare or the safety of the community,
and for that reason it is dangerous.

One of his early experiences was an effort to secure a
reformation in the criminal code of Ohio.   He had been

engaged in the fight to drive a gang of shyster lawyers from the Cincinnati courts which culminated in an attempt to disbar the leader. The effort failed for the gangster was too "solid" politically, but Taft made a great speech which so convinced the public that the blackleg's business was destroyed and he left town.

Before that Taft had gained a reputation for ability, integrity and clean politics which extended outside his state. President Arthur, seeking a way out of a factional fight in Cincinnati, found it by making Taft collector of internal revenue there. Here Taft got his first business experience, a training which stood him in good stead later, when he was called to important judicial duties with almost constant supervision of large business enterprises, including railroads. That internal revenue office collected more than $10,000,000 annually on whiskey and tobacco. It carried a good salary, more than Taft had ever earned before. But it was not attractive to him, and after ten months at it he resigned, to go back to practising law.

This was his second step in a long career of resignations. He has held one office or another for nearly twenty-five years. He has occupied seven different posts, of steadily increasing importance. Each office he has resigned, to move on soon afterward, to one of greater responsibility. It has been a career of promotion as well as of resignation.

They needed a man of Taft's qualifications in the public service in Cincinnati, and he had not been long in private practice before he was brought again into active employment in the criminal law as assistant county solicitor. He had nearly two years at that, which was a long time for him in one job. Then he received a tremendous surprise. Judson Harmon, judge of the Superior Court in Cincinnati, resigned his office to take up a federal post under President Cleveland. Joseph B. Foraker was Governor of Ohio. Taft had not trained in the Foraker political camp, but he had made a mark which Foraker had not overlooked. Several friends suggested him for the appointment, and Foraker saw that it would be a good stroke. So he named Taft for the judgeship, very much to that young man's surprise as well as his delight. This was the ambition he had always held, and he recognized the appointment as a step toward his goal.

This was the only office Taft has ever held which he did not resign. He served out that term, and then was elected to succeed himself for the full five years. Taft had been in open opposition to the Governor and to George B. Cox, the boss of Cincinnati. Cox would have named another candidate, but Foraker knew what an element of strength Taft would give the ticket, and advised Cox to nominate him. So Taft won the only election at which he has thus far stood as a candidate.

One of Alphonso Taft's colleagues at the Bar in Cincinnati was John W. Herron, ex-United States district attorney, and formerly law partner of President R. B. Hayes. Mr. Herron had a daughter, Helen. The families had been close friends and Miss Herron and Will Taft were something more. She finished school about the time that Taft was graduated from Yale, and soon afterward their engagement was announced. But Taft was not then in position to marry. He had his way to make, and although his progress was sure and steady it was some time before he was able to support a family. Miss Herron was an enthusiastic and accomplished musician, and for a time taught in a private school. In 1886, Taft being then comfortably established, they were married. They spent several months in Europe on their wedding journey, and then returned to Cincinnati to begin a home life that has never grown away from the serenity and simplicity of those early days.

MRS. WILLIAM H. TAFT (NEE HELEN HERRON)

THE HOME OF JUDGE THOMPSON WHERE MR. TAFT WAS BORN

Photo by Brown Bros.

CHAPTER IV

THE STRAIGHT LINE TREATMENT

It was while judge of the Superior Court in Cincinnati that Mr. Taft first came into contact with organized labor. He was called upon then to try a case involving a boycott of the firm of Moores & Co. by Bricklayers Union No. 3. It was not a great case in itself, but it has been made important by subsequent developments, and especially by the assertion which has been made in recent years that Mr. Taft's attitude toward organized labor has lately undergone a change. The case was a suit for damages by the boycotted firm against the Bricklayers Union. It was not an injunction suit, nor did it involve a dispute between employers and employed. A jury had given Moores & Co. a verdict for $2,250, and the matter came before Judge Taft on motion for a new trial. In preparing his decision he made an exhaustive examination of the law with a special review of the English cases which had been cited by lawyers for the defense.

After a full discussion of the case at bar and the authorities, Judge Taft made a statement of the rights of labor. He asserted the right of laborers to unite in withdrawing from their employment in order to embarass their employer and thus force him to make better terms

for them.   He went further and declared the right of a
labor union to impose penalties upon its members for refusing to comply with its regulations, or to expel them for
failure to obey the union rules.

" We do not conceive that in this state or country," he
said, " a combination by workingmen to raise their wages
or obtain any material advantage is contrary to law, provided they do not use such indirect means as obscure
their original intent, and make their combination one
merely malicious, to oppress and injure individuals."

But, it was not lawful, he declared, for a union to
coerce an employer by boycotting those who dealt with
him.   Acts of this character and intent may not be action-
able when done by individuals, but they become so, he
held, when committed as a result of combination.

Judge Taft's decision was affirmed by the Supreme
Court of Ohio without opinion, and is generally accepted
as the correct exposition of the law of the secondary boycott, that is, a boycott against a stranger to the trade
dispute.

Now that is exactly the opinion of Mr. Taft to-day.
It is fully set forth in some of his most recent public
speeches, notably those at Seattle and at Cooper Union,
liberal extracts from which appear elsewhere in this volume.

Mr. Taft remained on the bench of the Superior Court
but two years after his election, when he resigned to become Solicitor General of the United States, in the administration of President Harrison.   No better commen-

tary on the reputation he had earned for himself as a lawyer could be made than this selection by the president to conduct the government's cases before the Supreme Court. Mr. Taft was then 33 years old, about fifteen years under the average age of solicitors general. This is a post where the unremitting toil of a man like Taft produces its result. Mr. Taft came into the office to be confronted by a monumental task. The old seal fisheries' question, which had agitated this country and Great Britain for years, had come up in a new and unexpected form. Diplomatic negotiation had exhausted itself in the effort to reach an amicable agreement between the two countries which would preserve the seal herd. Several Canadian sealing schooners were seized by United States revenue cutters while at work in the Bering sea. One of them, the Sayward, was condemned in the United States court, in Alaska, and ordered sold. The owner appealed to the Canadian government, which presented his claim for damages to this country through the British Foreign Office. Mr. Blaine, then Secretary of State, rejected the claim, whereupon Great Britain proposed arbitration. While that proposition was under discussion, and before a decision had been reached, the British Government suddenly adopted new tactics, and brought the case directly before our Supreme Court.

This implied a high compliment to our court, but it created a very embarrassing situation. Great Britain would not necessarily hold herself bound by the decision, if it went against her, but if it went against us we should be bound fast. It became, therefore, extremely important that the United States should win.

The case had been brought into the Supreme Court on an application on behalf of the Canadian Minister of Justice for a writ of prohibition forbidding the forfeiture proceedings against the Sayward. It was Mr. Taft's first case as Solicitor General. He was opposed by Joseph H. Choate, the Nestor of the American bar, and Calderon Carlisle, Jr., one of the ablest attorneys of the country. Now the habit formed in his boyhood, of learning all about every new problem which he attacked, stood Mr. Taft in good stead. This was all new to him, and he had not much time for its study. But he had a power of application which made most of what time he had, and he went to the bottom of the affair. When he had concluded his study of the whole fisheries' question and of the Sayward case in particular, he set forth his conclusions in a brief 300 pages long.

One of the distinguishing characteristics of Mr. Taft is clarity of expression. Perspicacity and perspicuity go hand in hand with him. The story is told of an old Filipino, who knew Mr. Taft in later years, and who had some opportunity to observe him. The Filipino could speak no English, but one day he told an American what he thought about Mr. Taft and some of the other Americans he had known in the islands. He smoothed off a little space in the sand and drew on it a series of crooked marks. They ran hither and thither, crossed and recrossed, and doubled backward and forward in the course of their general advance toward a given point. These lines the Filipino gave the names of different Americans. Finally he drew one sharp straight line from start to finish. Then he straightened up and threw away the stick with which he had been drawing.

"Taft!" he said, smiling.

That was the quality in Mr. Taft's Sayward brief, as, in fact, it is in all his transactions. It told with the court and he won his case.

There was another important case which he had to conduct as Solicitor General which he won by a simple application of common sense. It grew out of the practice revived by Speaker Reed of counting a quorum when the members of the minority in the House sat in their places and refused to vote. The McKinley tariff bill was passed by that method. A firm of importers raised this point as a reason why the law was invalid so that they would not have to pay the new high duties. Counsel for the importers argued that when a member does not vote he cannot be counted as present. To that Mr. Taft replied by asking why it was then, that the house could compel the attendance of absent members, if by refusing to vote they could break a quorum and prevent the transaction of any business. There was no answer to that question, and Mr. Taft won his case.

He developed, in fact, a habit of winning, and it is the record that not a single important case went against him while he remained Solicitor General. But he did not hold the office very long. President Harrison saw that

4

he was too good a man to keep at that work. Others
would be able to handle the government cases successfully before the Supreme Court, but this was a rare find
for the bench. So he named Mr. Taft for the vacancy
in the sixth United States circuit court, and the young
man went back to Ohio a federal judge. Now he was
on the direct road to the fulfillment of his dearest ambition, a justiceship in the Supreme Court. He was a member of the circuit bench from which time and again promotion to the highest court had been made.

It was during this service as Solicitor General that one
very important event in the life of Mr. Taft occurred,
outside the range of his official duties. He met Theodore
Roosevelt. As far apart in method as the poles the two
men are close together in ideals, and absolutely alike in
intensity of application and vast power of work. Each
had formed the great fixed habit of industry, which is
after all the largest element in any success, great or small.
Each was intensely devoted to the service of the country
and animated by lofty purpose. Naturally they became
warm friends. Roosevelt had his eye on the presidency
as his ultimate goal, Taft on the chief justiceship of the
Supreme Court. Roosevelt had not then begun to study
the question of control of interstate corporations on which
he made his great advance as President. He was only
beginning the line of investigation suggested by the dis-
satisfaction with conditions throughout the west and middle west which was then bringing the Populist movement
to its height. Taft, going almost as rapidly but with

vastly less motion and commotion, was even then form-
ing his opinions on the subject which Roosevelt has since
vitalized with all the country. He was laying the foundations for that opinion which he was to render six years
later and which was to be the first step in making Federal
control of interstate corporations a living active reality.
He was behind Roosevelt in appearance but nearly ten
years ahead in action.

CHAPTER V

TEACHING LABOR ITS RIGHTS

When Mr. Taft resigned the solicitor-generalship to return to the bench many of his friends, looking at it merely from the material point of view, thought he was making a great mistake. The reputation he had made by his handling of the government cases was worth many thousands of dollars a year to him if he should again engage in private practice. But he did not care for money any more then than he does now. If he had been a money getter he would not have resigned the lucrative internal revenue collectorship at Cincinnati to go back to a law practice that was hardly worth enough to warrant his getting married. Nearly all his life in the public service has been at a personal sacrifice, so far as his financial condition is concerned, and he is to-day poorer than when he quit the bench, eight years ago, to take up the greatest task of his career, that in the Philippines.

Financial considerations had no part in his decision to accept the place on the federal bench offered to him by President Harrison. It was a long step toward the fulfillment of his great ambition, and he had no hesitation whatever in reaching his conclusion. The sixth United States circuit includes the states of Michigan, Ohio, Ken-

MR. TAFT AS A FEDERAL JUDGE

Photo by Brown Bros.

MR. TAFT'S MOTHER (LOUISE M. TORREY)

tucky and Tennessee. Judge Taft became associated with Judge William R. Day, afterward Secretary of State and now an associate justice of the Supreme Court, and with Judge H. H. Lurton, still on the bench of that circuit. These three men made that the greatest of the United States circuit courts. Judge Taft retained his membership in it for eight years. In that time his reputation extended throughout the country as an able and upright judge who was absolutely fearless in the expression of his convictions and the performance of his duty.

Three great decisions were rendered by Judge Taft during this period which have become part of the well established law of the land. They are the cases which distinguish his service as a federal judge. All have had far reaching results, but one, the last of the three, marked an epoch in the exercise of the power of the federal government to regulate and control interstate commerce. This was the famous decision in the Addyston Pipe case. The others were in labor cases, and in both he aroused the violent opposition of organized labor by issuing injunctions which had the effect of breaking strikes. In later years labor has come to realize that Judge Taft merely expounded the law as he found it, and that in doing so while he dealt a heavy blow to the then desire and purpose of the labor unions, he did it in a way which marked out for them for all time the clear path along which they might travel unmolested and unafraid.

The first of these labor decisions has worked a great reform in the course of the organization directly affected

by it, the Brotherhood of Locomotive Engineers.   This
has long been known as one of the most conservative and
effective of the labor unions of the country.   It is com-
posed of men above the average of intelligence, and with
a fuller realization of their responsibility than is the case
with unions in some other trades where such a high degree
of intelligence or skill is not required.

There was a strike on the Toledo, Ann Arbor & North
Michigan railroad, caused by the refusal of the road to
grant the demand of the engineers for increased wages.
Three years previous to that, the Brotherhood convention
had adopted a rule which provided that thereafter it
should be a violation of obligation for a Brotherhood
engineer employed on a road where there was no strike,
to handle business from a connecting road which was
under strike.   Under this rule P. M. Arthur, grand chief
of the Brotherhood, notified eleven chairmen of adjustment committees to see that their men complied " with
the laws of the Brotherhood."   The Toledo & Ann
Arbor sued out an injunction against several other roads
forbidding them to refuse to handle its business, and
then asked Judge Taft for an injunction against Arthur,
restraining him from endeavoring to enforce this Brotherhood rule.

This case also took the form of a boycott.   The engineers ordered by Chief Arthur to observe the Brotherhood rule — known as Rule 12 — had no grievance
against their own roads, they were simply to refuse to han-

-lle the business of the Toledo & Ann Arbor in order to
force that road to an agreement with its men.

The decision of Judge Taft first took up and reviewed
Rule 12 and the acts of the engineers under it in the light
of their relation to the criminal and civil law, and then
with reference to the remedy. An exhaustive discussion
of the position of railroad employees engaged in interstate traffic led to the conclusion that the engineers in
attempting to enforce Rule 12 were violating the interstate commerce law, which provides a fine of $5,000 for
" any person acting for or employed by " an interstate
railroad who " wilfully omits or fails to do any act " required by the law, one of which is the affording of " reasonable, proper and equal facilities for the interchange of
traffic " between lines.

" The normal condition," said Judge Taft, " the
status quo, between connecting common carriers under
the Interstate Commerce law, is a continuous passage of
freight backward and forward between them, while each
carrier has a right to enjoy without interruption, exactly
as riparian owners have a right to the continuous flow of
the stream, without interruption."

The injunction already granted against the other roads,
was therefore a proper means of enforcing this continuous
flow of freight. The question then raised was whether
Arthur could be enjoined from ordering the engineers
to carry out Rule 12. If he were not enjoined, said
Judge Taft, his order would be issued and obeyed. The

interstate business of the Toledo & Ann Arbor would be interrupted and interfered with at every hour of the day. The injury would be irreparable and a judgment for damages would be wholly inadequate.   So he granted the injunction.

In the course of his examination of the position of railroad employees engaged in interstate traffic Judge Taft made it clear that the relation of the men to the companies is that of free contract, terminable at will by either party. The men had a right to combine to leave their employment and a right to enforce penalties upon the members of their organization for violation of its obligations.   The court could not compel the men to remain in personal service against their will.

" It would be impracticable to enforce the relation of master and servant against the will of either," said the Judge.   " Especially is this true in the case of railway engineers, where nothing but the most painstaking and devoted attention on the part of the employee will secure a proper discharge of his responsible duties; and it would even seem to be against public policy to expose the lives of the traveling public and the property of the shipping public to the danger which might arise from the enforced and unwilling performance of so delicate a service."

Nevertheless as Judge Taft showed, should the men combine to quit in the execution of Rule 12, in order to compel their companies to injure the Toledo & Ann Arbor they would be doing an unlawful act, because it was aimed at injuring some one else and not at benefiting their relations with their own employer. In such event they would be liable to damages, but the court could not by mandatory injunction compel personal service.

"We have thus considered with some care the criminal character of Rule 12 and its enforcement," said Judge Taft, " not only because, it will presently be seen, it assists in determining the civil liabilities which grow out of it, but also because we wish to make plain, if we can, to the intelligent and generally law-abiding men who compose the Brotherhood of Locomotive Engineers, as well as to their usually conservative chief officer, what we cannot believe they appreciate, that, notwithstanding their perfect organization and their charitable, temperate, and other elevating and most useful purposes, the existence and enforcement of Rule 12, under their organic law, make the whole Brotherhood a criminal conspiracy against the laws of their country."

Judge Taft was entirely correct. The Brotherhood had not appreciated the force and effect of Rule 12, perhaps because it was made up of engineers and not of lawyers. But the men appreciated the justice of Judge Taft's showing, and acquiesced in it. Rule 12 was abrogated, and since that time all the railway brotherhoods have been most conspicuous in their conservatism in adjusting grievances with their employers.

The effect of the decision was far reaching. It was the first judicial declaration of the duties of railroad employees engaged in interstate commerce. It was not only approved by the public generally and the railroad brotherhoods, but it was followed by the judges in other circuits and has become the established practice.

The other great labor decision of Judge Taft was in the case of F. W. Phelan growing out of the American Railway Union strike in the summer of 1894. This was the time when Eugene V. Debs undertook to cause a tie-up of all the railroads in the country in the effort to help the employees of the *Pullman Car Company to secure an increase in wages and a general betterment of conditions of labor. Again it was a boycott, Debs's scheme being by a general refusal to handle Pullman cars to force that company to agree with its employees. This was the strike in which President Cleveland sent United States troops to Chicago, to see that the mail trains were not interfered with, and out of the action of the courts in the cases of Debs and Phelan grew the cry of organized labor against " government by injunction." The phrase was coined by the late John P. Altgeld, the Illinois governor who refused to do anything to prevent violence and disorder during that strike, and who pardoned the anarchists convicted in Chicago of the Haymarket bomb throwing. But as in the Arthur case, Judge Taft's decision was acquiesced in and ultimately approved by the man whom it hit hardest at the time, so it proved in the Phelan case. When Phelan came out of jail after serving his sentence 'or contempt of court he went to Judge Taft and admitted that he had been in the wrong, and had escaped lightly.

It is a singular thing that the animosity aroused by these two decisions should be borne by others than those directly affected. But the men immediately concerned knew all the circumstances and heard the lucid reasoning of Judge Taft in pronouncing judgment, while the others for the most part have neither known what really occurred, nor read the decisions to acquaint themselves with the facts. It is safe to say that there never have been two clearer cases of the just and absolutely imperative use of the injunctive writ than these.

The Cincinnati, New Orleans and Texas Pacific railroad, known as the Cincinnati Southern, was in the hands of a receiver appointed by Judge Taft when Debs started his general strike of railroad men. Debs sent Phelan to Cincinnati to tie up all the roads there, and Phelan, disregarding the fact that this road was under the direction of the court, ordered out its men. There was no grievance on the part of the men of the road over the conditions of their own employment, and when Phelan ordered them out on a sympathetic strike, that is a boycott, receiver Felton applied to the court for an injunction, which was issued. Phelan, however, paid no attention to the injunction, and openly boasted that he would defy it.

"I don't care if I am violating injunctions," he said in a speech to the men. "No matter what the result may be to-morrow, if I go to jail for sixteen generations I want you to do as you have done."

Upon that Phelan was of course cited for contempt of court, and duly tried by Judge Taft. The intensity of feeling on the part of the men generally at that time is well remembered. They thronged the court room during the several days which the examination lasted, and there were open and free threats as to what would happen to Judge Taft in case Phelan were punished. The situation seemed so critical that friends of Taft urged him to be extremely cautious, to go armed, to have a guard, and even to send his decision to court to be read by some one else, so that he should not expose himself to the animosity of the men.

But Judge Taft only smiled at such suggestions and went on in his own way. He is blessed with a courage which is not only equal to meeting its moral obligations but does not quaver at the imminence of physical peril. In the midst of the trial he gave a characteristic exhibition of his native kindliness and thoughtfulness. One of Phelan's lawyers, a man whose standing at the Cincinnati bar did not command the greatest respect from other attorneys, was making his argument when Judge Taft looked up and saw one of the attorneys for the receiver reading a newspaper. There is nothing which stirs Mr. Taft to anger so quickly or so surely as injustice, and it matters not who or what is its victim. A flush shot up over his face as he noticed this discourtesy, and he asked the speaker to suspend. Then, as the court room became quiet, he laid one hand significantly on his desk and said, sternly:

"This is a court room, not a reading room."

The offending lawyer was one of the most distinguished members of the Ohio bar. He crushed his newspaper together and arose, flushed and embarrassed, to

MR. TAFT IN CALIFORNIA

Photo by Underwood & Underwood

MR. TAFT WITH HIS WIFE AND THEIR SON CHARLES IN
THEIR HOME IN WASHINGTON.

apologize to the court and to the opposing attorneys. From then on Phelan's lawyer was heard with the utmost respect.

When trial closed Judge Taft announced that he would render his decision on the fourth day, at noon. The intervening three days he employed in another exhaustive examination of all the authorities on such cases. He worked with his secretary all day and far into the night. It was two in the morning of the last day when the secretary went home to transcribe his notes of what Judge Taft had dictated. At 9:30 he was in court to find the Judge already there, ready to revise the decision for the last time. When 12 o'clock came Judge Taft promptly began to read. He gave a full review of the evidence brought out on the trial, and very carefully discussed its bearing, to show how clearly it proved Phelan guilty of contempt. His discussion of the law involved followed the line of the decision in the Arthur case of a year before. He showed how the employees of the road had the right to quit their employment, but that they were not right in combining merely to injure their employer, or to compel him to withdraw from a profitable business with a third party in order to injure that party when the relation thus sought to be destroyed had no bearing upon the character or reward for their own services. The purpose of the combination in which they were engaged was to tie up interstate railroads, not as a means of bettering the condition of their own employment, but solely to injure the Pullman company. That made it an unlawful combination, in violation of the anti-trust law of 1890 as well as a direct interference with interstate commerce, and therefore a violation of the commerce law.

It was in this case that Judge Taft made a singularly lucid statement of the rights of labor unions which has been invoked several times in their behalf in other courts, and with success.

"It may be conceded at the outset," he said, "that the employees of the receiver had the right to organize into or join a labor union which should take joint action as to their terms of employment. It is of benefit to them and to the public that laborers should unite in their common interest and for lawful purposes. They have labor to sell. If they stand together, they are often able, all of them, to command better prices for their labor than when dealing singly with rich employers, because the necessities of the single employee may compel him to accept any terms offered him. The accumulation of a fund for the support of those who feel that the wages offered are below market prices is one of the legitimate objects of such an organization. They have the right to appoint officers who shall advise them as to the course to be taken by them in their relations with their employer. They may unite with other unions. The officers they appoint, or any other person to whom they choose to listen, may advise them as to the proper course to be taken by them in regard to their employment, or, if they choose to repose such authority in any one, may order them, on pain of expulsion from their union, peaceably to leave the employ of their employer because any of the terms of their employment are unsatisfactory."

Having delivered this comprehensive declaration of fundamental rights for labor unions, Judge Taft followed it with a specific application to the case of Phelan. If Phelan had come to Cincinnati when the receiver reduced wages and urged a peaceable strike, or had caused a strike for an increase in wages, and had succeeded in maintaining it, " the loss to the business of the receiver would not be ground for recovering damages, and Phelan would not have been liable for contempt even if the strike much impeded the operation of the road under the order of the court. His action in giving the advice or issuing an order based on unsatisfactory terms of employment would have been entirely lawful."

But as it had been clearly shown, his advice to the men and his order to strike had nothing to do with their terms of employment. They were not dissatisfied with their service or their pay. His order was in pursuance of a boycott, and therefore clearly unlawful. So Phelan went to jail for six months.

"The punishment for a contempt is the most disagreeable duty a court has to perform," said Judge Taft, in closing his decision, " but it is one from which the court cannot shrink. If the orders of the court are not obeyed the next step is unto anarchy. It is absolutely essential to the administration of justice that courts should have the power to punish contempt, and that they should use it when the enforcement of their orders is flagrantly defied. But it is only to secure present and future compliance with its orders that the power is given, and not to impose punishment commensurate with crimes or misdemeanors committed in the course of the contempt, which are cognizable in a different tribunal or in this court by indictment and trial by jury. I have no right, and do not wish, to punish the contemnor for the havoc which he and his associates have wrought to the business of this country, and the injuries they have done to labor and capital alike, or for the privations and sufferings to which they have subjected innocent people, even if they may not be amenable to the criminal laws therefor. I can only inflict a penalty which may have some effect to secure future compliance with the orders of this court and to prevent willful and unlawful obstructions thereof."

The formal decision having been read Judge Taft added a few words which constituted the only recognition he gave to the numerous threats of personal violence which had come to him. There was a flash in his kindly blue eyes, and a sternness in his face such as is not often seen there, as he spoke, and it went home to the men who heard him that he meant every word.

"When you men leave this room," he said, "I want you to go with the conviction that if there is any power in the army of the United States to run those trains they shall be run!" And down on the desk before him hammered his hard fist.

The strikers who had come to overawe were themselves cowed. The room was as quiet as a church, and the men filed out slowly, silent and subdued. But they found out later that Judge Taft had no feeling whatever toward any of them. When the strike collapsed the receiver refused to re-employ any of those who had struck on Phelan's order. When Phelan got out of jail he went to Taft and asked to have the old men reinstated. Judge Taft promptly wrote to the receiver, and the men were taken back as fast as places could be found for them.

That is the record, and it is a record of distinguished service to the true cause of labor. When the Brotherhoods of Railroad Trainmen and Firemen were engaged in a controversy with the Wabash railroad in 1903, and had called a strike in their effort to secure higher wages and a general betterment of conditions of service, the road undertook to restrain them, and applied for an injunction in the United States circuit court at St. Louis, on the ground that their combining to strike would be a direct interference with interstate commerce. A temporary injunction was granted, whereupon Mr. Frederick N. Judson, of counsel for the men, moved to dissolve it and cited in argument Judge Taft's statement of the rights of labor already quoted from the Phelan decision. The decision of the court conformed to that statement at all points. It was found to apply exactly to the Wabash situation, and the temporary injunction was dis-

5

solved. The court said that no one had spoken more clearly or acceptably than Judge Taft on the subject of labor unions and their rights.

This was a great victory for the men, for when the railroad found that it could not prevent the strike by injunction it compromised with them and their grievances were settled. Twice Judge Taft was instrumental in stopping an unlawful boycott. In this Wabash case he furnished the means by which the men won a just strike.

In recent years there has been a great agitation among labor men for an amendment of the laws under which injunctions are granted. Some of the labor leaders have gone so far as to demand the total abolition of the injunctive writ in cases where labor is involved. In their efforts to secure a change in the procedure, so that no injunction shall be issued until the defendant has had notice and a hearing in court, except in the event of irreparable damage being imminently threatened, the labor men have the entire sympathy of Mr. Taft, and he has given them his active co-operation. He has repeatedly called attention to the fact that that was the old procedure in the federal courts, and has urged the enactment by congress of a law reviving it. But he is unalterably opposed to the complete abolition of the injunctive process, as he is to the other proposition of the labor men for the legalization of the boycott.

No labor leader has ever given to these subjects any more calm and unprejudiced consideration than has Mr. Taft. He has examined the proposition from every point of view, impartially and thoroughly.   And he has brought to the examination the trained mind of a great lawyer, familiar with the history of the development of the law and all the reasons for it.   There can be no question that his final conclusion is entitled to vastly more weight than that of the average labor leader who is not only untrained in the law but who inevitably takes a prejudiced view of the subject.   No better proof of this could be given than was furnished by the reception given Mr. Taft by an audience of labor men at Cooper Union, in New York.   He spoke to them for an hour on the subject of the relations of labor and capital, and discussed fully his views on the boycott and the use of injunctions.   They cheered him again and again.   When his set speech was concluded he took another hour to answer the questions they sent up to him, and again he set forth his ideas on both matters.   Again they cheered, and went away convinced of the justice of his judgment.

CHAPTER VI

VITALIZING THE ANTI-TRUST LAW

For nearly eight years after its enactment the Sherman anti-trust law which had been devised out of the wrath of the people at the steadily increasing power of corporate combinations, lay practically a dead letter on the federal statute books, a thing scorned and derided on all hands as utterly powerless to meet the situation for which it was intended. It was openly flouted by the corporations, which went on making their combinations in restraint of trade as gaily as if it had never been heard of. The wrath of the country at such proceedings continued to grow, and in the presidential campaign of 1896 formed one of the great arguments of the Democratic party for popular support.

Before that Judge Taft had given a clear indication, not only in his exposition of the law in the Arthur and Phelan cases, but also in an even more direct manner in his speech before the American Bar Association, at Detroit, in the summer of 1895, of the view he might be expected to take of the Sherman law should a case involving its construction ever come before him for adjudication. He had spoken significantly at Detroit of the wisdom of the framers of the Constitution in giving

MR. TAFT'S HOME IN WASHINGTON

Photo by Harris & Ewing

MR. TAFT AS A GOLF PLAYER

Photo by Brown Bros.

to the federal government complete control over interstate commerce. In the Arthur and Phelan decisions he had emphasized strongly the illegality of interference with such commerce.

Now there came to him an opportunity to make to a combination of capital an exact application of the principles he had invoked against combinations of labor in the two strike cases. Again it was a suit for an injunction, and he showed himself just as ready to employ that agent against criminal corporate wealth as he had been to use it to prevent crime by organized labor. And just as its use in the labor cases was effective to prevent a continuance of the illegality then forbidden, so its employment in this trust case broke the legs of the corporate combination and left it nothing to stand on.

This was what has come to be known as the " Addyston Pipe case " from the name of the chief factor in the combination. It was the third of the great decisions of Mr. Taft as a federal judge. It had the effect of giving life to a thing which was dead. It vitalized the anti-trust law and made it a great and powerful instrument for the control of corporate rapacity and the prevention of criminal corporate combination.

In 1897 the attorney-general brought a proceeding in equity before Judge Clark, of the sixth circuit, for the dissolution of the combination formed by the Addyston Pipe & Steel Company, of Cincinnati, with five other pipe concerns in Kentucky, Alabama and Tennessee. The defendants admitted the existence of an association among

them for the purpose " of avoiding the great losses they
would otherwise sustain, due to ruinous competition between them," but denied that their association was in
restraint of trade, state or interstate, that it was organized to create a monopoly, and that it was a violation
of the anti-trust act.   Judge Clark dismissed the petition,
and the government appealed.   Judge Taft wrote the
opinion in the circuit court of appeals.

After a statement of the case Judge Taft cited the sections of the anti-trust act invoked, the first of which declares illegal " every contract, combination in the form of
trust or otherwise or conspiracy in restraint of trade or
commerce among the several states or with foreign
nations."

" Two questions are presented in this case for our decision," said the Judge, " First, was the association of
the defendants a contract, combination or conspiracy in
restraint of trade, as the terms are to be understood in
the act?   Second, was the trade thus restrained, trade
between the states? "

The contention of the defendants had been that their
association would have been valid at common law, and
that the anti-trust act was not intended to reach any
agreements that were not void at common law.   The
United States Supreme Court had decided in the Trans-
Missouri Freight Association case that contracts in restraint of interstate transportation were within the statute,
but the defendants had argued that that case related to
public service corporations, and did not properly apply

to contracts restricting parties in sales of merchandise, purely a private business. Judge Taft brushed that point aside and went straight at the main point, saying:

"It is certain that if the contract of association which bound the defendants was void and unenforceable at common law, because in restraint of trade, it is within the inhibition of the statute if the trade it restrained was interstate. Contracts that were in unreasonable restraint of trade at common law were not unlawful in the sense of being criminal, but were simply void and were not enforced by the courts. But the effect of the act of 1890 (the anti-trust act) is to render such contracts unlawful in an affirmative or positive sense, and punishable as a misdemeanor, and to create a right of civil action for damages in favor of those injured thereby, and a civil remedy by injunction in favor of both private persons and the public against the execution of such contracts and the maintenance of such trade restraints."

The defendants also argued that their association was not a monopoly because it controlled only thirty per cent. of the output of pipe in the country and did not embrace all the states; that its restraint of trade was reasonable, aimed only at preventing ruinous competition among themselves, and that it did not fix the prices of pipe because they had to meet the competition of other manufacturers, while the public had all the benefit from competition which public policy demanded.

To meet these contentions Judge Taft went into a review of the common law as it bore upon trade agreements, from the earliest times in England. He cited a decision of Chief Justice Parker in 1711, showing the mischief that might arise from such agreements. Referring to the language used by Justice Hull, in the time of Henry V, he said:

"The inhibition against restraints of trade at common law seems at first to have had no exception." But following the subject through its later development he showed how there had gradually grown up a practice of upholding covenants in partial restraint of trade under certain circumstances, such as when the seller of a business agreed not to compete with the buyer, or a retiring partner agreed not to compete with the firm, or an assistant or agent agreed not to compete with the master before the expiration of his term of service, or in some other similar situations. In each of these cases, however, as Judge Taft showed, it was necessary to satisfy the court that the restraints attempted were reasonably necessary to the legitimate ends of the contract between buyer and seller or between partners or between master and servant.

In this discussion Judge Taft cited thirty or forty authorities covering all the classes of cases, before finally stating his conclusion, which was: "That no convention in restraint of trade can be enforced unless the covenant embodying it is merely ancillary (supplementary) to the main purpose of a lawful contract, and necessary to protect the covenantee in the enjoyment of the legitimate fruits of the contract, or to protect him from the dangers of an unjust use of those fruits by the other party."

"The very statement of the rule," continued the Judge, "implies that the contract must be one in which there is a main purpose to which the covenant in restraint of trade is merely ancillary. . . . If the restraint exceeds the necessity presented by the main purpose of the contract it is void, for two reasons. First, because it oppresses the covenantor, without any corresponding benefit to the covenantee; and second because it tends to a monopoly.

"But where the sole object of both parties in making the contract as expressed therein, is merely to restrain competition, and enhance or maintain prices, it would seem that there was nothing to justify or excuse the restraint, that it would necessarily have a tendency to monopoly, and therefore would be void. . . . There is in such restraints no main lawful purpose, to subserve which partial restraint is permitted, and by which its reasonableness is measured, but the sole object is to restrain trade in order to avoid the competition which it has always been the policy of the common law to foster."

Then Judge Taft took up the cases which had been cited by the defendants in support of their contention, and by a careful examination of them all, seriatim, showed how not one of them really applied to the case at bar. The most that they established, as he showed, was that at the common law contracts void as in restraint of trade were not criminal. "But," said Judge Taft, "the statute we are considering expressly gives such contracts a criminal and unlawful character."

Then followed an examination and discussion of some fifty more cases which had been cited as having a bearing and from them Judge Taft showed that " in recent years even the fact that the contract is one for the sale of property or of business and good will, or for the making of a partnership or a corporation, has not saved it from invalidity if it could be shown that it was only part of a plan to acquire all the property used in a business by one management, with a view to establishing a monopoly."

The extraordinary thoroughness and care of Judge Taft in this case is shown by the fact that in addition to all the authorities examined to which reference has been made he went over fifteen or twenty more cases before announcing his conclusion. Having completed this exhaustive consideration of the arguments of counsel for the defendants, and the authorities they had cited, he said:

" Upon this review of the law and the authorities we can have no doubt that the association of the defendants, however reasonable the prices they fixed, however great the competition they had to encounter, and however great the necessity for curbing themselves by joint agreement from committing financial suicide by ill-advised competition, was void at common law, because in restraint of trade, and tending to a monopoly. But the facts of the case do not require us to go as far as this, for they show that the attempted justification of this association on the grounds stated is without foundation."

Thus Judge Taft smashed to fragments the contention of the six pipe companies that they were justified in their combination. He went on then to demonstrate how the prices they had charged were unreasonable, despite the evidence they had submitted in the shape of " a great many affidavits of purchasers of pipe, all drawn by the same hand or from the same model." He showed how they had controlled the distribution of pipe throughout their territory and had been able to fix prices, and how by the use of false bids they had deceived purchasers and concealed their combination. Thus they had formed a conspiracy, within the meaning of the statute. All the scorn with which Mr. Taft never fails to greet and treat deception and dishonesty comes out in his discussion of this feature of the case.

" It would have much interfered with the smooth working of the association," he says, " had its existence and purposes become known to the public. A part of the plan was a deliberate attempt to create in the minds of the public inviting bids the belief that competition existed between the defendants. Several of the defendants were required to bid at every letting, and to make their bids at such prices that the one already selected to obtain the contract should have the lowest bid. It is well settled that an agreement between intending bidders at a public auction or a public letting not to bid against each other, and thus prevent competition, is a fraud upon the intending vendor or contractor, and the ensuing sale or contract will be set aside. The largest purchasers of

pipe are municipal corporations, and they are by law re--
quired to solicit bids for the sale of pipe in order that
the public may get the benefit of competition. One of
the means adopted by the defendants in their plan of
combination, was this illegal and fraudulent effort to
evade such laws, and to deceive intending purchasers.
No matter what the excuse for the combination by defendants in restraint of trade, the illegality of the means
stamps it as a conspiracy, and so brings it within that
term of the federal statute."

Thus the combination of the pipe companies was not
only void at common law and strictly forbidden by the
anti-trust law, it was a conspiracy in restraint of trade.
Judge Taft then proceeded to discuss the question whether
the trade restrained was interstate. It required but a
brief consideration to demonstrate that it was. He
showed that the professed object of the contract of association was to regulate sales in thirty-six states, and that
no sale or proposed sale could be suggested within the
scope of the contract "which did not restrain at least
three, often four, more often five and usually all, of the
defendants in the exercise of the freedom which but for
the contract would have been theirs, of selling in one state
pipe to be delivered from another state at any price they
might see fit to fix."

"Can there be any doubt," he asked, "that this was
a restraint of interstate trade and commerce?"

That practically concluded the review of the case and
brought the Judge to the point of his ruling. But be-

THE LIBRARY IN MR. TAFT'S HOME IN WASHINGTON

MR. TAFT ON HORSEBACK

Copyright 1906 by Clinedinst

fore he delivered the judgment, he referred thus to the affidavits submitted by the managers of the pipe companies that they did not know what interstate commerce was and therefore could not have combined to restrain it.

" They knew," declared Judge Taft, " that the combination they were making contemplated the fixing of prices for the sale of pipe in thirty-six different states, and that the pipe sold would have to be delivered in those states from the four states in which defendants' foundries were situated. They knew that freight rates and transportation were a most important element in making the price for the pipe so to be delivered. . . . It seems to us clear that the contract of association was on its face an extensive scheme to control the whole commerce among thirty-six states in cast iron pipe, and that the defendants were fully aware of the fact, whether they appreciated the application to it of the anti-trust law or not.

" We do not announce any new doctrine in holding either that contract and negotiations for the sale of merchandise to be delivered across state lines are interstate commerce, or that burdens or restraints upon such commerce Congress may pass appropriate legislation to prevent, and courts of the United States may in proper proceedings enjoin. If this extends federal jurisdiction into fields not before occupied by the general government, it is not because such jurisdiction is not within the limits allowed by the Constitution of the United States."

The decision of the circuit court was reversed and the

injunction was issued, dissolving the Pipe Trust. Thus the first great blow was struck for federal control of interstate commerce and the vitalization of the anti-trust law. Its effect has been tremendous. Judge Taft had the extraordinary honor done him by the Supreme Court, when it heard the case on appeal, of including his decision entire in its opinion. He was sustained at every point, and that deliverance upon the law of combinations in restraint of trade has become the guide of all the courts of the land. This decision was rendered in February of 1898. Mr. Roosevelt was then assistant secretary of the navy, preparing to join a regiment of cavalry for the approaching war with Spain. He had hardly begun the study of the great questions which have since become known as the " Roosevelt policies." It was this decision which marked out for him the path by which the federal government could assert itself to prevent the discrimination and monopoly which was then rapidly approaching the height of its career of oppression and suppression of trade throughout the country. Here was the weapon by which the great enemy of the true development of the country could be struck down. It was the knife with which to excise the cancer that was then fastening itself upon the commerce of the country. Mr. Roosevelt has made a wonderful use of this weapon. But it was Mr. Taft who first made it effective.

CHAPTER VII

THE HUMAN SIDE OF A JUDGE

Somewhat extended space has been given to these three decisions because in them Judge Taft made an ineffaceable contribution to the law of the country. They present him as the great judge, seeing clearly the law and the facts, and applying one to the other as the necessity arises with absolute disregard of everything but his duty, impartially, convincingly and finally. He hewed to the line, and the chips might fall where they would.

Sometimes cases came before him in which his friends were involved. That made no difference. He decided one bank case against his father-in-law, ex-district attorney Herron. Mr. Herron was tremendously angry at the decision, and was inclined to think his son-in-law had leaned over backward in his effort to stand up straight. But Judge Taft only laughed and told Mr. Herron to carry the case up. So Mr. Herron did, and Judge Taft was sustained.

After he became Secretary of War another case in which he had a personal interest came to him for decision. In fact it was thrust upon him, for it did not arise in his department but came from the State Department, at a time when he was temporarily " sitting on the lid," as President Roosevelt said. The bond existing between Mr. Taft and his classmates at Yale has been shown already, in the cablegram they sent him at Manila. One of those classmates was Herbert W. Bowen, minister to Venezuela when this incident occurred. Bowen was one of those to whom Mr. Taft was " Old Bill." But Bowen got mixed up in an affair with assistant secretary of state, Francis B. Loomis, certain charges against whom he reported to the State Department. The investigation fell to Mr. Taft. He went through the case as carefully and thoroughly as he had through that of the Addyston Pipe Company, and he found that the charges were not justified. His report drove Bowen from the diplomatic service and broke their old friendship, for as nearly always happens the man who is in the wrong regards the decision against him as injustice. It cost Mr. Taft heavily to give that decision. He struck the blow with a sore heart, but because he believed he was right he struck although it was at a friend. Not another man in the administration would have found it so great a hardship to dismiss a man from office. But Taft saw the termination of an honorable career that was involved and was as deeply pained as the man on whom the blow fell.

In the closing years of Mr. Taft's service on the federal bench several Ohio railroads were in the hands of receivers appointed by him. One of these receivers was Myron T. Herrick, his warm friend. Judge Taft heard that some of the receivers, including Mr. Herrick, had permitted rebating. He summoned them to come and see him. Mr. and Mrs. Herrick were entertained at his home. The next day Mr. Herrick and the judge went down to the court house. There in the judge's office friendship was disregarded and it became a business meeting.

"Myron," asked the Judge, "have you been rebating?"

Mr. Herrick replied by presenting a statement showing that some $80,000 had been paid to shippers by his road. Judge Taft was greatly shocked.

"If you have been permitting rebating," he said sternly, "you cannot be permitted to escape."

Fortunately for Mr. Herrick he was able to show that the money had been paid on account of contracts made before he became receiver, and which he had felt bound to fulfill. Judge Taft heard the explanation with great relief.

"These claims are undoubtedly just," he said, "and I will enter an order for their payment. But hereafter please let me settle judicial questions."

Several times while on the federal bench Judge Taft declined to grant requests made of him by ex-President Harrison, the man who appointed him. In one case the district attorney, the attorney general and Mr. Harrison were all asking for an extension of time. Judge Taft thought they had had ample opportunity to prepare their case and refused their request. Neither friendship nor

6

personal obligation ever interfered with his action on the bench.

Mr. Taft has always had a fine scorn for mere technicality, and he has not hesitated to speak in criticism even of the Supreme Court for its willingness to reverse judgments on bare technicalities. A young lawyer once filed papers in his court in a suit against a railroad on behalf of a girl whose foot had been cut off in an accident. The petition was not skilfully drawn, and the Judge saw that the clever railroad attorneys would demur to it, and the demurrer would have to be sustained. So he called the girl's lawyer to him and pointed out the defects in the petition. It was properly amended and the young woman recovered damages.

Incidents of this helpfulness are very numerous, but they all show the same quality. Before everything else, justice is his main desire. His sense of right and wrong is quick, springing and ever alert. This quality was so well recognized by the lawyers who practised in his court that Frank Loveland, the clerk of the court, who has served under twenty-five judges, declares that he never heard an attorney grumble at one of Judge Taft's decisions. Lawyers in criminal cases have often remarked that if their clients were convicted, reversal on appeal was hopeless, his rulings were so fair and correct.

Mr. Taft did not confine his interest in the law to its interpretation and exposition from the bench. In the later years of his service as a judge the old Cincinnati law school at which he had graduated, had fallen somewhat behind the times. Mr. Taft associated himself with Judson Harmon and some other eminent lawyers of Cincinnati and founded a new law school, which followed the case system of instruction. Judge Taft was dean of the school, which became, in conjunction with the old one, the law department of the University of Cincinnati. His subject was " Property." He has said that he learned more law while a teacher than as a student.

CHAPTER VIII

GODFATHER TO A PEOPLE

Greatest of the problems thrust upon the United States by the outcome of the war with Spain was that of the Philippines, what to do with the islands and the people. Very few Americans comprehended it then, very many have not comprehended it yet. The first impulse that stirred this country on receipt of the news of Dewey's victory in Manila Bay was to take possession of the Philippines and hold them. It was the natural result of the first realization of our power as expressed in that victory. The inexorable military necessity that forced the sending of troops to the Philippines to back up Dewey's achievement was attended inevitably by a wave of sentiment throughout the country that demanded the retention of the islands when it came to making the treaty of peace. It was the glamour of aggrandizement working on the imagination of a people feeling for the first time its power oversea.

Here and there about the country there were men who saw the real obligation which the unavoidable course of events had thrust upon the United States. Nearly all of them were opposed to taking permanent possession of the islands and regretful that it had been necessary. Very,

MR. TAFT MAKING A SPEECH

Photo by Brown Bros.

MR. TAFT IN DENVER. SENATOR WALSH IS HOLDING
THE UMBRELLA

Photo by Brown Bros.

very few believed that the country would ever see the duty laid upon it, or that the administration could rise to the point of meeting it fully and fairly. For this was a case of the highest leadership on the part of the administration, and under our political system such leadership without the support of the country behind it, is well nigh impossible, no matter how pure the motive or firm the intention. It is one of the highest proofs of the greatness of President McKinley that he not only saw this obligation with absolute clearness from the very beginning, but that he determined at the same time, with absolute firmness, *to meet it with all the power of the government so long as he could shape its course.* Looking back at that situation, from the point of view of our present knowledge, it is astonishing that there should have been any man in the United States able to see our true course. It was a wonderful intuition.

What Mr. McKinley saw thus in the beginning was that by our forced intervention in the Philippines we had contracted an obligation toward the Filipinos which we could not in honor or decency fail to discharge. It was the most difficult obligation that a nation could incur, for it was violently opposed by the very people solely for whose benefit it was undertaken. It put the United States in the position of compelling the Filipinos by force of arms to accept what we knew would be to their everlasting benefit and their ultimate freedom, but which they regarded only as another form of oppression. To leave the islands to themselves, upon the cessation of the war with Spain, Mr. McKinley saw would be only to abandon the Filipinos first to bloody internecine strife, and then to the domination and control of some other power which would never be actuated toward its wards by the altruistic interest which he recognized as the true attitude of the United States. This was a position already sufficiently difficult, but it was rendered infinitely more so by the demand of the Filipino leaders for immediate independence.

"You demand liberty," said Mr. McKinley, in effect. "Yes, you shall have it. But it will be the liberty of the whole Filipino people when it comes, and not of a decimal fraction of them, who, through the leadership of education and property have acquired a domination over the great mass."

It was to educate that mass in knowledge of their natural civil rights and raise them to the plane where they would be fit for liberty that Mr. McKinley consented to the possession of the islands by the United States.

The first problem that confronted him was the suppression of their insurrection. One supreme blunder had been made by all our military commanders in the Philippines. They had permitted Aguinaldo to issue repeated proclamations to the Filipinos that the United States had come to the islands to give the people their independence. Not once did an American commander protest that Aguinaldo had no right to make such a pledge on behalf of the United States, although his proclamations were issued from camps so near their own that it must unavoidably appear to the simple and ignorant Filipinos that their leader was acting with the knowledge and assurance of the Americans. It gave to Aguinaldo's proclamations the effect of an implied promise on our part. The immediate result was to make the Filipinos welcome the Americans as their saviors. Every Filipino was our friend, and he would turn his own people out of their home day or night to give an American shelter. But the ultimate result was that when the time came when Aguinaldo, in furtherance of his personal ambition for dictatorship, wanted to turn his people against the Americans, he had only to point to our failure to fulfill the promise he had made for us and we had not rejected, in order to make every Filipino our enemy.

That was the situation when the insurrection against us began in 1899. By the early part of 1900, after a year and a quarter of vexatious and strenuous campaigning, we had beaten the insurgent forces and scattered the guerrillas so that the most optimistic began to talk about the "dawn of peace." It was then that President McKinley prepared to inaugurate his real policy for the Philippines, to "lay the foundations of a superior civilization, with specific reference to the needs of the people to be governed, and with definite reference to the welfare of the islands, both material and moral." He had made a trial, in the previous year, with a civilian commission, but the time was not yet ripe. Now he prepared for another effort, and again selected a civilian commission as the medium. He needed a man in thorough accord with his own lofty conception of the American obligation to the Filipinos. Where was he to be found? In all the United States there were then probably not a score of men who shared his views of what was to be done. With the people generally the glamour that had surrounded the Philippines at first was wearing off. They were growing tired, and the advocates of the policy of scuttle were finding more and more adherents. Even among the men of influence and importance, the men in high station in public life, there was a growing opposition to our remaining in the islands. The man needed by President McKinley was very, very hard to find.

"I want a man to head the commission," he said to Secretary of State, William R. Day, one morning when they were discussing the situation, "who is strong, honest and tactful; a man of education and executive ability; a man who is fearless, but conservative, and who will get along with the army people."

"That sounds like Bill Taft," replied Mr. Day, unconsciously declaring by his remark, another of Mr. Taft's qualifications, the good-natured comradeship which keeps him "Bill" to his friends.

The result of this conversation was that Mr. McKinley asked Judge Taft to come to Washington. Mr. Taft had made no open declaration of belief concerning the Philippines, but it was known among his friends that he was opposed to their retention. He had not thought it possible that in this practical, hard-headed, self-centered country there could be held by any government an ideal so purely altruistic as that which Mr. McKinley was about to propose to him.

He came to Washington, and had a long conference with the President and Mr. Root, then Secretary of War. Mr. Root is another practical man, whose great reputation was not made for altruism. But he was heart and soul in sympathy with the purpose of the President, and he was about to demonstrate that he was capable of a far greater altruism than had ever been suspected.

Judge Taft was not only inclined to believe the United States in a false position in remaining in the Philippines, he had a life place on the United States circuit bench, where his service already marked him imperatively for promotion to the Supreme Court, in fulfillment of his life long ambition. He was practically certain that within a few years he would receive the desired appointment. But above all else Mr. Taft is an altruist, with a combativeness just as largely developed as the sunshiny good nature which keeps it hidden most of the time. He needed only the statement of the proposition the President had to make to him in order to accept it.

Mr. Root went at Mr. Taft with all the skill which has made him famous as a lawyer. He contrasted directly the two places, justice of the Supreme Court and Chairman of the Philippine Commission — one a post of dignity, honor and comfort for life; the other an office of the most extreme difficulty, filled with perplexities and harassments; its occupant risking his health and even his life from tropical disease, and certain to be assailed persistently

and malignantly by the enemies of the work he was trying to do; but with an opportunity such as no American,
surely none since the time of Lincoln, had had, the opportunity to lift a poor, ignorant and helpless people up
into the light of liberty and set them on the path to freedom and national unity.

"You will have to resign your judgeship," said Mr.
Root, " and you may never have another chance of going
on the Supreme Bench.   But we need you in the Philippines."

" All right," said Mr. Taft, " I'll go."

That was a great day for the Filipinos, and for the
United States as well.   That day Mr. Taft became god-
father to a new nation.

CHAPTER IX

THE " POLICY OF ATTRACTION "

To us in the islands who had been sweating and swearing through two years of desperate toil and hardship striving to bring about a semblance of peace the laconic cable brought the news in one bald line, that Taft was coming " to establish civil government." We read the despatch, and laughed. What was the use? Ever since we had been there Washington had persistently misunderstood and had wilfully spread about the home country a description of conditions in the Philippines which our superior wisdom told us was frightfully untrue. Civil government now? Why, it wouldn't be possible for years! And Taft would find out mighty quickly after he landed. But we didn't know Taft.

In the five months just preceding the arrival of the Taft Commission at Manila I had traveled from the north end of Luzon to the south end of Jolo. It had been my business to seek out such natives as I could persuade to stand long enough to talk to, and discuss with them their ideas of their situation, and their feelings toward the Americans. Nowhere had I found a single friend. A few because of obvious self-interest, called themselves such, but none was genuine. The army had over-run every province of the islands, and occupied nearly every town in the archipelago worth having. But there was no peace, and small sign of any. No American dared travel anywhere without a guard. Every bush concealed a hostile bullet. Negotiations for peace, declared the insurgents, must be conducted through the armed representatives of their " Republic," else the " war " would go on. They, too, didn't know Taft. I don't believe that either McKinley or Root had any adequate conception of the size of the man they were sending out to Manila, or a full comprehension of the size of the job they were giving him. They had only an impressionist view of both.

The cable announcement of what Mr. Taft was coming to do produced great elation among the Filipinos, and corresponding depression among the Americans in Manila. The Filipinos believed that because Mr. Taft had announced, in San Francisco, before sailing, that he had been opposed to retaining the Philippines, they would be able to negotiate with him at once. The Americans were much afraid of a premature attempt at civil government.

Then Taft came. His business was first of all conciliation, but almost before the official calls were over he issued a statement which was a knockdown blow to the Filipinos. It declared the definite purpose of the United States to maintain their sovereignty over the islands. This was the first authoritative announcement on that subject, and it was a crusher for the islanders. The statement also said that the Commission would not treat with men in arms, with whom it was the function of the army

MR. TAFT CROSSING THE WILD MINDINAO TRAIL

Photo by Burr McIntosh

MR. TAFT RETURNING TO THE STEAMER AFTER A HARD DAY'S WORK AT TAC-
LOBEN. ISLAND OF LEYTE

Photo by Burr McIntosh

to deal; that the military government would continue indefinitely, and that the Commissioners were prepared to stay in Manila three years to see civil government "well begun." Thus the first step in the "policy of attraction" was the destruction of every hope the Filipinos had cherished. Their only ray of comfort was in the broad promise that they should participate as far as possible in the government to be established.

There was an intransigente in Manila whom I knew well. He edited an insurgent newspaper, and was one of the founders of the Katipunan society. He talked freely and very frankly about this statement of Mr. Taft's, and assured me that it meant only a terrible prolongation of the struggle. He was a well educated man, one of the most intelligent of the Filipinos. But he did not know Taft. He was one of those "East is East and West is West, and never the two shall meet" men.

"We understand this situation," he said, soberly, "and the Americans do not. The two races can never get along peaceably together. One must be dominant and the other subject, always. Quiet can be maintained only by the strong hand. Between the East and the West there is more than a mere race difference as you Americans understand it. There is a difference of mentality, of intellectual process, such that neither will ever comprehend the other. Look here! Out there on the ocean there is an imaginary line, which divides to-day from to-morrow. One side is East, the other West. What is it separates the two? Can you mark out that line? Can you see it?

Can you pick it up, or touch it? When you can you will have brought East and West together, and they will understand each other."

But Taft not only saw and picked up my Tagalog philosopher's imaginary barrier between East and West; he rubbed it out. He destroyed even its imaginary existence. He showed those Orientals that there was one Occidental, at least, whom race difference could not keep out of their hearts. Here was a man of the West to whom the East was as open as his own land, who read their desires and purposes, and fathomed their minds as easily as he towered above their bodies. And they capitulated. He won them by the power of the most persuasive personality they had ever known. The " policy of attraction " was a great success. But it puzzled the Filipinos mightily at the start. Mr. Taft showed them from the first that there was to be no fooling with him. He followed the facer of his opening statement with a straightforward refusal to be caught in the sort of trap that Aguinaldo had sprung on the military men. The Filipinos arranged a great " peace banquet " and Pedro Paterno, one of Aguinaldo's " cabinet," was to deliver the leading speech. The military authorities approved it, despite the fact that it contained, in several places, carefully worded renewals of the old promise. Mr. Taft did not learn of this speech until a short time before the banquet was to take place. Immediately he wrote to Paterno declining, for the Commission, to attend.

" No one having any authority to speak for the United

States," he told Paterno, " has ever said one word justifying the belief that a protectorate such as this speech promises will be established. It is impossible. The discussion of a protectorate as a possibility involves a misrepresentation which may induce submission to the authority of the United States by deceit. The members of the Commission cannot be parties to any such misrepresentation."

All this was entirely characteristic of Mr. Taft. He had come out there on a mission in the fulfillment of which the first step was necessarily the conciliation of the Filipinos. If he could not win their good will he had no hope of success in anything else. Nothing could be done without that. He began by clearing away entirely all the underbrush, so that everybody could have a clear view of the field. There was to be no concealment or deception. He told them the very worst the first time he spoke to them. After that he was unhampered in his efforts to secure their friendship.

The only experience the Filipinos had had was of dishonesty and deceit. Their history was of tyranny and oppression. Their tradition taught them hatred of foreign domination. Their struggle with the Americans had left them suspicious and sullen. That was the material on which Mr. Taft had to work.

He took three months to study the condition and situation of the Filipinos before he began to put into operation the governmental policy which he intended to pursue. In that time he went to the bottom of the causes of

Filipino discontent.   He had set out to comprehend the
Filipino, and he succeeded.   No Occidental has ever given
such a complete view of the various phases of the Filipino
character as Mr. Taft has given in the different speeches
and articles he has delivered concerning them, and in his
testimony before the Senate and House investigating committees.   He completely penetrated the mask of Orien-
talism.   He began by treating all exactly alike.   High
or low could come to Mr. Taft at any time and say all
that was in his heart.   This American never ran out of
patience.   His supply was absolutely inexhaustible.   He
met the Filipinos with absolute frankness.   That was a
new experience for them.   They had been accustomed to
indirection and concealment.   Here was a man who met
them on their own level and spoke to them on any subject with an openness and freedom that was amazing.
His good humor was unfailing, and his hearty, infectious
laugh caught the Filipinos and put them at once at their
ease with him.   His quick understanding of their complaints and desires, his boundless sympathy with all their
troubles and difficulties, made them recognize in him at
once a forceful factor in their destiny.   No barrier of reserve, concealment or open hostility could withstand such
an appeal.   Mr. Taft had not been in contact with the
Filipinos three weeks before they began to yield to his influence.   This is the crowning achievement of his career
in the islands.   It was the crucial thing that he should see
into the hearts of his people.   Fail there, and no matter

how he might succeed elsewhere, his whole mission would
fail.

They tell a story in Manila of a friar who had spent
nearly his whole life in the Philippines. He was understood to be writing a book about the Filipinos, and as he
had been a close student of them his work was awaited
with great expectancy. It was not to be published until
after his death. When that occurred his brother friars
could hardly restrain their eagerness to get at the man-
uscript. At last the Superior opened the desk of the dead
man and found there a pile of papers. On the first page
was the title of the book. The next was blank. So was
the next. And so it went through the whole pile. Not
a word was written until the last page, where the friar
had made this confession:

"This is all I know of the Filipinos after forty years
of unremitting study."

When at length Mr. Taft was ready to begin the establishment of civil government in accordance with the
policy proclaimed on his arrival, he made again an announcement that brought conflicting emotions to the Filipinos and Americans in the islands. " The Philippines for
the Filipinos " he declared to be his aim and that of the
United States Government, the development of the islands
in such a manner that the natives should reap the first
benefit, and have the first consideration. The government
to be established should be devised primarily for the welfare of the Filipinos, and again he promised that as rap-

7

idly as they should demonstrate fitness for participation in it they should be permitted to enjoy that participation.

This declaration produced a prompt effect among both the Filipinos and the Americans, and other foreigners in the islands. The natives saw in it, properly, a definite and authoritative promise as to their future treatment by the United States. The foreigners saw what they properly interpreted to be the death blow to their schemes of exploitation, and mistakenly took to be a serious obstacle to their commercial development. The feelings produced by the statement on the day of Mr. Taft's arrival in Manila were now reversed. The Filipinos were happy and the Americans were angry.

But Mr. Taft was not deflected in the least from his course by the howls of protest that went up from the Americans and other business men. They assailed him with angry invective and bitter denunciation. They started a campaign against him at home, and sent letters and memorials to congressmen and senators about his "betrayal" of American interests in the Philippines. They roared in the newspapers and in public speeches, and it took them two years or more to see that they were in fact helping Mr. Taft to accomplish his object with the Filipinos. Nothing could have been a stronger proof to the Filipinos of the genuineness of Mr. Taft's labors in their behalf than this violent opposition on the part of the exploiters. And just as soon as they saw that the Washington government was behind Mr. Taft and supporting him in all he did, that the wails and yelps of the exploiters were not availing to make the least alteration in his course, they realized that the programme he had announced was in fact definitely laid down by the American government, and would be carried out.   Thus the American opposition in the end furnished the last, convincing argument for the defeat of its own purpose.

While this was going on Mr. Taft had entered upon a regular campaign to win the sympathy and confidence of the Filipinos.   In his study of the causes of their discontent he made it generally known that he desired to talk with any and every man who had any grievance to submit or suggestion to make   And he really talked with them.   He was always interested, and never betrayed the least symptom of weariness.   All alike were welcome at Mr. Taft's home or office, and each had opportunity to say all that he wished.

In all the history of the Philippines there had never been anything like that.   Here was a governor who was willing to stop and talk with a coachman or a grass cutter in the fields.   For once the Filipinos were all absolutely on the same level with the government.   There was no more of the gold lace and gaudy uniform that emphasized distance and separation.   Mr. Taft wore the same kind of clothes that the Filipinos did.   He went to them and they could come to him freely, openly and on terms of frank equality.   Nor was there anywhere the least mystery about him.   He told them the absolute truth, and he showed them that he expected just the same from them. He did not hesitate or mince words in order to conceal something that was disagreeable. But when he had an unpleasant decision to give or a disappointing announcement to make he did it in a manner that convinced the Filipinos of his sincerity and sympathy. He took the time and pains to explain in detail, and to make perfectly clear and simple the reasons for his action. It was not merely the arbitrary determination of a master that he declared, it was the convincing argument that had compelled his conclusion.

Thus full play was given to the personal element in the "policy of attraction," and with immediate and far reaching effect. Mr. Taft learned from this experience that the principal factors in the disaffection of the Filipinos were the domination of the friars who had been in charge of their churches; their enforced exclusion from any participation in the government except from such subordinate and unimportant places as they could purchase; the oppression and tyranny of an unjust and arbitrary government, their unsatisfied and forcibly repressed yearning for education, and their inability to secure title and peaceable possession of their homes. They were held largely as unwilling tenants on lands owned by the same friars who ruled their churches and dominated their lives.

It was a curious and tangled situation. The Filipinos are nearly all members of the Catholic Church, and in an exceptional degree loyal and faithful to it. It had been the instrument of their civilization, the means of bringing them from the same state of barbarism which still holds certain of the island tribes. But its administration had

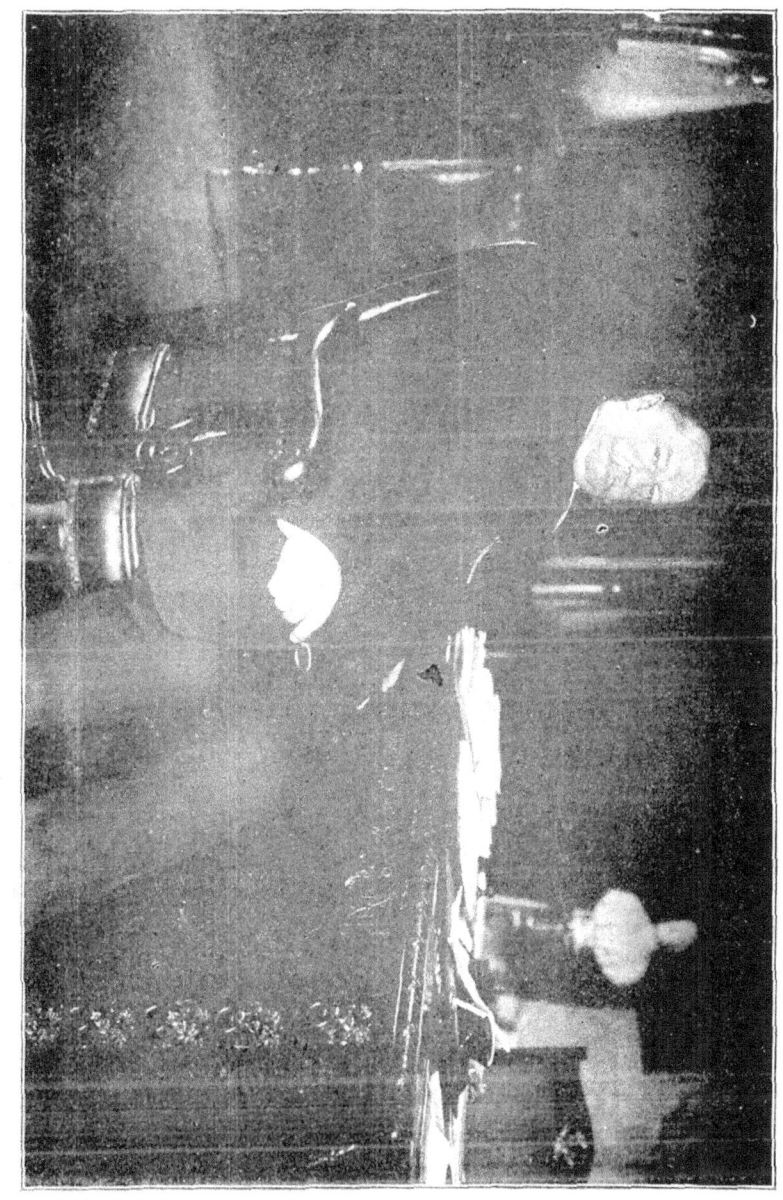

MR. TAFT AT HIS DESK IN THE WAR DEPARTMENT

Photo by Brown Bros.

THE INDUSTRIAL PARADE IN CEBU, MR. TAFT IN REVIEWING STAND AT RIGHT

Photo by Burr McIntosh

been corrupted by too great use of power. The friars had become in fact the arbiters of the lives and destinies of the Filipinos, and their rule had been accompanied by grinding oppression, injustice, corruption and immorality. Driven to desperation the Filipinos had revolted, and the Americans were confronted by the anomalous spectacle of a race of loyal churchmen in armed rebellion against the administration of their church.

This was an extremely delicate condition for an American to undertake to settle. The Filipinos had no comprehension of the separation of church and state. For them the church had been so long the government that they could not understand how the Americans could keep saying, as they did, that the government had nothing whatever to do with the church. It took a practical object lesson to give them their first inkling of the reality of the changed order of things. A well-known priest in Manila was the owner of a building which he rented to several tenants. He was ordered by the sanitary officers to clean up his premises, but did not obey. Consequently he was arrested and haled to court, just as the lowliest Filipino in the islands would have been for a similar offense. He attempted to plead his " benefit of clergy " and demanded a trial by the ecclesiastical authorities. But to his surprise he found that there were no longer any ecclesiastical authorities who had jurisdiction in civil affairs. That was a great and valuable lesson to the Filipinos.

Mr. Taft saw that the question of the friars' lands would be a perpetual menace as long as the lands were held under their then ownership. The friars held title to enormous tracts of the best agricultural lands in the most thickly populated provinces. The solution proposed by Mr. Taft was the purchase of these lands by the government, for resale to the Filipinos upon such terms as would enable the poorest of them to purchase and own their homes. To accomplish this it became necessary first to have the authority of Congress to spend the money, about $7,000,000 being involved, and next to conduct successfully the delicate negotiation with the church authorities. It was of course essential that the Vatican should see that in making the proposition the United States had no intention whatever of seeking to undermine or displace the Catholic church from its position of pre-eminence in the Philippines. Ultimately Mr. Taft accomplished it, and the lands were bought.

This attitude of the Filipinos toward the friars gives one of the clearest views of their intellectual possibilities. They had done what few much more highly educated people have ever done, differentiated conclusively between the church as an institution, and the men who were administering its affairs. In the fact that a certain friar was a bad man they saw no ground for accusing the church. They accused the friar and held him directly responsible for his own wickedness. I accompanied an expedition of our troops in southern Luzon which rescued forty-two friars from a force of Filipinos that had held them prisoners for nearly two years. These friars had been most despitefully used. One of them told me, with tears

rolling down his face, how he had been forced to his hands
and knees in the public square in front of his own church,
a bridle put on his head and a saddle on his back, and
ridden around the square by Filipino children.   He saw
in that a sacrilege, a crime against the church.   But the
Filipinos who did it saw only an act of retaliation for the
desperate cruelty of which they accused their victim.
They rode him around the square and then went inside
the church and prayed for him.   In their view he had dis-
graced his church and theirs, but that did not affect the
church itself.

The natural result of this clear view of their situation
on the part of the Filipinos was that as soon as the individuals whom they abhorred were eliminated from the
equation they were quite contented and went on peace-
fully and happily in their old church relations.   It is probable that a good many of the friars were unjustly accused.
But for the sins of some all were condemned, and there
was no guarantee of stability for any government in the
Philippines as long as this disturbing element remained
there.

Mr. Taft found very quickly that justice was something
with which the Filipino was familiar only in imagination.
He had had no concrete example of it to serve as a guide.
The fact was that only about 7 per cent. of the Filipinos
had any real education.   It had been the policy of the
friars to keep their people from education, in order the
better to maintain their complete power over them.   The
consequence was that the people had no conception of

their civil rights.   The educated among them, who had grown up under the " civil code " of Spain, had no comprehension of personal liberty as the American understands it from his childhood.   " Equality before the law " was a meaningless phrase to them, and the writ of habeas corpus they had never heard of.   Mr. Taft had been in the islands but a short time when there came to him one day an old Tagal accompanied by the lawyer who had been attorney-general in Aguinaldo's " cabinet."   The old man told a pitiful story of the arrest of his son, six years before, on a political charge.   The boy had been in prison ever since, with neither trial nor examination.   The old man wanted Mr. Taft to do something to get him out. The only means of relief of which he had any conception was a pardon by the government.

" Why don't you sue out a writ of habeas corpus? " Mr. Taft asked the former attorney-general.

" Writ of habeas corpus," repeated the puzzled lawyer. " What is that? "

The astonished Mr. Taft thereupon set to work patiently to show the old man and the lawyer what the great writ is and what it means.   When he had concluded he had prepared the form with which the lawyer went to court, and the next day not only that boy but nearly ninety others had had personal experience of its benefit.

CHAPTER X

THE PHILIPPINES FOR THE FILIPINOS

The "policy of attraction" had been working extremely well for about three months when Mr. Taft began the establishment of civil government in some of the municipalities and provinces. There again he gave the Filipinos a new view of their new governor. He had promised that they should have as large a measure of participation in their government as was possible. This involved teaching them how little equipped they were for such participation. The process was this. Mr. Taft and the Commission held open hearings wherever they went. Any and all Filipinos were welcome to attend and say all they wished. They could make suggestions and criticisms and arguments to their heart's content. Mr. Taft set no limit. He listened for hours to the long-winded discourses of men who had no conception whatever of the true principles of self-government. Once or twice some of his less patient colleagues protested at the "waste of time."

"Let 'em go on," replied Mr. Taft. "For once the Filipinos shall have a chance to say all they want to."

It was after such hearings that the municipal code and provincial law were adopted, and the Filipinos had the

satisfaction of seeing some of their suggestions incorpo-
rated in those laws.   Thus they found themselves at last
actually participating in their own government.   It was a
new and strange but delightful sensation.

When it came time to establish provincial governments
the Commission made a great tour of the provinces, visit-
ing more than thirty of them, some of them two or three
times.   Here Mr. Taft came face to face with the people
of all the islands, and won them as he had those whom
he had met in Manila.   In each province a public meeting was held for the discussion of the law.   Mr. Taft
began by reading the law and explaining each of its provisions simply and directly, so that all could understand.
He took care to show them how many matters were left to
the determination of the province itself, and how largely
they would share in their government.   Then he invited
general discussion.

Now this procedure was all new to the Filipinos, and
very often it happened that although many of them had
suggestions which they wanted to make, they were abashed
and timid in the presence of the governor.   They had
never before, in all-their lives, been invited to that sort
of a conference with the man at the head of the government of all the islands.   But Mr. Taft had a way of getting them started, a scheme that never failed.   It was
to have some one of his party propose that the location of
the provincial capital be changed.   That always precipi-
tated a discussion.   The champions of the existing location forgot their embarrassment under such a stimulus, and

when they were once started, Mr. Taft could question them generally as to local conditions, and shift the discussion into the desired channel. Thus the "school for self-government" was set working.

The Filipino is a quick-witted, good-natured chap, with a lively sense of humor. The "ilustrados" or educated, among them, have the polish of Spain's courtly manners and are pleasant men to meet. Mr. Taft's geniality and hearty good nature, with his ready, sunshiny roar of laughter, was a great agent for the "policy of attraction" with these people. His democracy was an added element of strength. He met them on the level and acted on the square, and they understood and loved him. They felt his sincerity and sympathy in his hearty handclasp. The news of his coming always preceded him and the fiesta-loving people received him invariably with display of arches and decorations. Some of the Americans grew weary of these celebrations, and at times were inclined to sneer at them. But Mr. Taft always entered enthusiastically into the entertainments. He was not deceived into thinking that they meant a sudden conversion of enemies into friends, but he knew how to make them serve his ends in bringing about a better feeling all around.

The business over there was always a banquet and a "baile." Mr. Taft made it a point always to take in at the banquet one of the leading native women. And he went religiously through the courses. At the first "baile" he surprised the members of his party by leading out the wife of the local "presidente" for the first dance. It was the old Spanish quadrille called the " Rigadon." It was a complicated figure, but Mr. Taft went through with hardly a slip, and danced as well as the lightest Filipino there, to the immense gratification of all the natives. Mr. Taft had foreseen that situation, and had had a young Filipino make him a diagram of the figures of the Rigadon, which he had studied until he was letter perfect. Throughout this tour of the Commission Mr. Taft kept up this practice. When he was describing it to the House committee, during the congressional hearings, he said:

" That entailed, I may say, a considerable effort, when the number of ' bailes ' reached twenty or more in forty days."

The personal influence of this man was irresistible. He found the Filipinos sullen, suspicious and resentful, every man our enemy. He made them all his friends, and gradually the friends of the Americans. Some things about them touched him very deeply — the eager desire, especially of the lower classes, for even-handed justice, and the quickness with which they recognized it at his hands; and the longing of the whole people for education. The chance to go to school was first of all their wants. Gray-haired old men and women craved the opportunity to learn, and when the way was opened to them went cheerfully to sit on the benches with little tots of five and six, their children and grandchildren, to learn the rudiments, the simplest matters of the elemental branches, and were glad and proud to go.

So while he worked at establishing provincial civil gov-

BANQUET GIVEN TO MR. TAFT BY THE CHAMBER OF COMMERCE IN THE GRAND
OPERA HOUSE IN MANILA.

Photo by Burr McIntosh

MR. TAFT AND THE "YALE GROUP" ON THE MANCHURIA ON THE WAY TO THE
PHILIPPINES

Photo by Barr McIntosh

ernment, Mr. Taft labored also at the problem of getting the courts to running on their new basis and schools opened at every possible point in the islands. The adaptation of the American common law procedure to their old civil law practice was a long and difficult task. It required a vast amount of labor on the part of the Commission, in the enactment of new laws. It could never have been carried through successfully but under the direction of a man like Mr. Taft, who was not only a great lawyer and a great judge but a great administrator as well. For the schools, he strove to advance the technical training of native teachers, and brought out from the States nearly a thousand American teachers, who, scattered all about the archipelago, began the work of instructing not only the Filipino children, but those who were subsequently to become teachers themselves.

There were some terribly humiliating experiences to endure in this time of hard work and trial. They came from the failure of his own people to support Mr. Taft loyally. In the organization of the provincial and municipal governments, Americans were sometimes employed. The provincial treasurer was always an American, because the Filipinos had not learned from their previous experience of government that fidelity to trust was one of the first considerations of office. It happened that a shameful number of these American officials went wrong. But the disgrace was not wholly without its beneficial lesson to the Filipinos, for in the swift prosecution of these malefactors, and the sternness of their punishment, the island people saw the readiness of Mr. Taft to mete out justice to his own people. It was another example of good faith on his part. Never in all their history had a peculating Spanish official been punished when only Filipinos were his victims.

Mr. McKinley's promise to the Filipinos, through Mr. Taft, was to fit them for popular self-government, and then give it to them. There was thus a dual problem confronting the chairman of the Commission all the time. He had to clear away the obstacles to the material development of the people and the islands, and at the same time provide for their intellectual advancement. The establishment of schools, the settlement of the vexatious question of the friars' lands, the establishment of courts in which justice should be even-handed and open to all alike; the construction of public works; the installation of a proper and effective system of public sanitation, were all matters that had to be accomplished side by side with the establishment of civil government. First of all a real peace had to be made throughout the islands, and this was a task of infinite difficulty. The years of insurrection had put in the hands of large numbers of lawlessly inclined men the arms with which they could exact a living from their more thrifty and industrious fellows by means of force. Spain had never thoroughly put down the system of brigandage which had existed pretty much all over the islands. The Americans went at it with their customary vigor, employing both their own troops and the native constabulary. The Filipinos soon found, from the thorough application by the courts of the criminal law to such cases, that there was a great difference between political revolution and organized pillage.   Sentences of from fifteen to twenty years in prison at hard labor have made a great change in the number of men who sought to live on their neighbors by force.

But while all this labor for the Filipinos was going on the American and other business men in the islands were keeping up their backfire at home, and hampering with all their ingenuity the fulfillment of the great altruistic purpose of Mr. Taft and the administration.   At last Mr. Taft made a speech in which he dealt with the subject and the men in unsparing language.   He presented to them, face to face, the true picture of their attitude.   It was at Iloilo, the principal town in the island of Panay.   There was a meeting of all the principal business men of the island, gathered to hear Mr. Taft discuss the general situation.   The islands were in a sorry condition.   Plague and famine had followed the ravages of war.   The rice crop, the main staple of the Filipino diet, had failed, and rinderpest had carried off the great majority of the work cattle.   The new government was facing the gravest crisis that could well arise.   Under these circumstances the Iloilo business men proposed to Mr. Taft that the government subsidize rice growing.   That was one of a number of suggestions by which they assumed to tell the Commission how to go about its work.   It was of a piece with the general attitude of all the Occidentals in the islands.   Intolerance and contempt marked their relations with the native, and open disgust, continually voiced in loud and vehement criticism, signaled their disapproval of the announced policy of the " Philippines for the Filipinos." To these men the Philippines were only opportunities for exploitation, and they condemned unsparingly any policy which aimed at a different object. They had sneered continuously at the work of Mr. Taft and the Commission, and were persistently busy in spreading insinuations of their certain failure.

So Mr. Taft spoke to them from the heart, and they heard the naked galling truth about themselves. As to their suggestions for subsidizing rice growing, he said:

" I can conceive of nothing which will more greatly interfere with the development of independence and self-reliance among the farming and laboring classes than to give them money out of the public treasury."

He went on to tell how the government proposed to meet the difficulty by purchasing rice in quantities and selling it to the Filipinos at cost, so that the combination which some of his hearers had formed to take advantage of the famine conditions and make large profits at the expense of the starving people should not succeed.

Then he turned to the general attitude of his hearers toward the Commission and its work. He spoke of their hostility and their criticisms, and described the effect of their sneers and insinuations. He told them they were preventing the realization of peace, and destroying the hopes of advancement of the Filipinos.

" It is your duty, as it is to your benefit," he continued,

"so long as you remain in the country, to aid and support the government, and not to place obstacles in the way of its success by encouraging sneers, criticism and suspicion directed either against the government or the Filipino officials or the people. You must take into consideration and understand, that this is a Filipino government for the benefit of the Filipinos, and if any of your number is not willing to assist it as such, but must obstruct it by creating dissension, he stands in your light. He is not obliged to stay in the islands, and if he dislikes the government he can leave."

The business men of Iloilo heard this with open-mouthed amazement. But they had sense enough to realize that Mr. Taft was speaking not only with understanding but with determination, and although they did not immediately alter their course, they found before long that it was indeed better for the man who disliked the government to keep still or go away. They were not essential to the scheme of Philippine development which had been adopted by the United States, and unhappy as it made them to find that out they had to learn it and submit. So short-sighted, very often, is the selfishness of business. Altruism has no place in its plans, and yet this is an illuminating instance of the benefits of altruism even in business. In a recent speech to an American club, in Iowa, Mr. Taft discussed this very subject.

"The prosperity of the Americans in the Philippines depends upon the prosperity of the Filipinos," he declared. "There are eight million Filipinos. The whole

8

wealth of the islands must arise from agriculture and what the Filipinos bring forth for sale in the markets of the world. Therefore it is the prosperity of the Filipinos that is to effect the prosperity of every one who has anything to do with those islands. I am not denying for one moment that the energy and enterprise and capital of Americans may aid greatly in developing the islands, but the real development of the islands, both politically and as a matter of trade, must rest finally and ultimately with the Filipino people."

The difference between Mr Taft and the men of Iloilo was that he saw that truth when he was speaking to them, but they did not. It took them years to comprehend it.

CHAPTER XI

THE GREAT ALTRUISM

One by one the other problems he had to solve advanced toward settlement, but the great question of the friars' lands still continued to baffle Mr. Taft's efforts. Everywhere but there the new government was making decided headway with the Filipinos. At home the assaults were kept up and criticism was unceasing. But in the face of it all Mr. Taft went on serenely along his course, giving the best that was in him, and even risking his life itself. Famine, plague, cholera, business depression, economic distress the Commission met and overcame. The time was approaching when Congress would take some definite action concerning the future of the Philippines. Up to then it had not moved toward exercising its authority, permitting the government to run along on the lines laid down for it by Mr. McKinley in his instructions to the Taft Commission. Mr. Taft's health was badly broken, and he greatly needed the benefit of the change which a visit home would give. But as long as that was the only consideration he refused to come. It developed, however, that there was a real and urgent need for him to come to Washington directly on behalf of the Filipinos. In both houses of Congress the insular committees were

preparing to make a general investigation of what had
been done in the islands. The administration, also, was
preparing to submit a general organic law for the island
government. Mr. Taft could help in the preparation of
the law, and in the testimony he could give before the
Congress committees he would have opportunity to meet
and put down a great deal of the unfounded criticism of
the Philippine policy and action. When this view of it
was presented to him Mr. Taft decided to come home.
It was with great misgiving that the Filipinos saw him
prepare to leave the islands. They were still suspicious
of the Americans — all but Taft — and were much afraid
that he would not return. But he made them a solemn
promise that he would come back, and they reluctantly
acquiesced in his journey. That was early in 1902.

This visit to the United States first revealed the man
Taft to his own people. He made several brief journeys
away from Washington to deliver speeches about the
Philippines, and everywhere he went he was received with
much the same sort of enthusiasm that the Filipinos felt
for him. In these speeches and in his testimony before
the Congress committees he made a showing of the American policy that practically ended the criticism, and converted the great part of the opposition. He presented to
the Americans their first clear view of the beauties of national altruism as revealed in the great work going on in
the Philippines. He made no effort at concealment of the
difficulties and burdens of the undertaking.

"We must find our reward," he said, " in the pleas-

MR. TAFT AND PARTY ON THE MANCHURIA BOUND FOR THE PHILIPPINES, MISS
ALICE ROOSEVELT AND NICHOLAS LONGWORTH AT MR. TAFT'S FEET

Photo by Burr McIntosh

MR. TAFT AND PARTY AT NUNANU PALI, 7 MILES FROM HONOLULU. THE LAND-
SCAPE IS SAID BY TRAVELLERS TO BE ONE OF THE WONDERS OF THE WORLD.
MISS ALICE ROOSEVELT IS AT MR. TAFT'S RIGHT.

ure of pushing the cause of civilization, and in increasing the opportunity for progress to those less fortunate than ourselves. We are in the Philippines to discharge the highest duty that one nation can toward another people."

Then he gave the American people some sound advice, coupled with some shrewd observations of their characteristics and shortcomings. We make of the terms "independence" and "self-government" a shibboleth, and prate about government deriving "its just powers from the consent of the governed" without once pausing to consider what we mean. Because our experience, which has been only of self-government, has been satisfying to us, we are convinced that our form of government is the very best that can be applied to any people on earth, and that all we have to do is to give it to them and they will carry it on to a glorious and free development. Mr. Taft knew better.

"Self-government does not come by nature," he said to one of the committees. "It must be taught even to the educated who are used to a different system. . . . It seems to us that the self-restraint and sense of responsibility necessary to carry out successfully the principle of free civil government can be learned, by the educated as well as the ignorant, and the practice of it in association with Americans, who understand the self-restraint necessary before self-government is possible."

Then, having set forth with almost discouraging frankness the fullness of the burden that the Philippines were bound to be to this government, Mr. Taft turned to the brighter side and showed some of the possibilities for us.

"That which makes a people happy, prosperous, intelligent, self-governing and conservative," he said, "makes them the best customers in trade. A liberal and generous colonial policy directed to the betterment of the people's condition is the quickest to justify itself, both in loyalty and profits."

His work with Congress finished, and the final authority to treat with Rome for the purchase of the friars' lands having been given, Mr. Taft prepared to redeem his promise to the Filipinos and go back to Manila, passing by way of Rome for the negotiations with the Vatican. His health was somewhat improved, but still in a precarious condition. His friends and physicians warned and urged him not to go. But he had given a promise and he never wavered about its fulfillment.

While he was here there was talk of a prospective vacancy in the Supreme Court. President Roosevelt spoke to him about it one day, and said:

"If it comes I do not see how I could possibly give the place to you, for I need you where you are."

"It has always been my dream to be in the Supreme Court," replied Mr. Taft, "but if you should offer me a justiceship now, and if at the same time Congress should deprive me of my entire salary as Governor, I should go straight back to the Philippines nevertheless, for those people expect me back and believe I will not desert them."

"I believe I have the missionary spirit," he had told the Senate committee. That was how it showed.

Still far from well, Mr. Taft started back to the Philippines. His visit at Rome did not result in the immediate sale of the friars' lands, but it paved the way for the successful completion of the negotiations later at Manila, through an agent sent out directly by the Vatican. Mr. Taft succeeded in keeping his business at Rome strictly on a business basis, so that there could be no complication of church affairs with it. He made it very clear that the United States had no objection or opposition to the Catholics retaining their church supremacy in the Philippines. But the presence of the friars provoked trouble from the members of their own church, and solely in the interests of peace, which was incidentally the best interest of the church, he advised a change.

Then he went on to Manila. On his arrival there, in August, 1902, he found the reward for all his labor and sacrifice in the reception given him by his people. It was a spontaneous demonstration of affection and confidence such as no Westerner had ever had from those people, and it confirmed Mr. Taft in his judgment of the ultimate success of the great altruistic experiment which he was conducting on behalf of his government. He plunged at once into the business of the Commission and was soon engrossed in the negotiations for the friars' lands. Then came, first a temptation, and then a command, from the President to leave his post and return to the United States to take up again the judicial career he had laid down to go to the Philippines, but this time on the Supreme Court. The prospective vacancy of which they had talked in Washington had become a reality, and the President had concluded after all to give the place to him. Thus at one stroke there was offered to him the fulfillment of his life-long ambition, and release from the suffering and distress of his situation in Manila. But he put it by. He had just had renewed proof of the feeling of the Filipinos toward him, and he saw the danger to all his work if he left them then. At the intimation that he might go the Filipinos with one accord made outcry in protest. Their experience of government had taught them loyalty not to an institution but to a man. Their respect was not so much for the law as for him who had administered it. Mr. Taft had striven to teach them that the law was a continuing force, and that the policy he had begun to develop would remain the policy of the United States for the Philippines, because it was not that of one man but of the whole American people. But the idea of a permanent government, unaffected by the change of governors, was as yet outside the range of the Filipinos, and they could not understand or accept it. So Mr. Taft offered himself again as a sacrifice to their good. He cabled to President Roosevelt that he had promised the Filipinos to stay with them, and he could not break his word.

"Great honor deeply appreciated," he said, "but must decline. Situation here most critical from economic standpoint. Change proposed would create much disappointment and lack of confidence among people.

"Two years now to follow of greater importance in

development of islands than previous two years.   Cholera, rinderpest, religious excitement, ladrones, monetary crisis, all render most unwise the change of governor.

"Nothing would satisfy individual tastes more than acceptance.

"These are sentiments of my colleagues and of two or three leading Filipinos consulted confidentially.

"Look forward to time when I can accept such an offer, but, even if it is certain that it can never be repeated, I must now decline.   Would not assume to answer in such positive terms in view of words of your despatch, if gravity of situation here was not necessarily known to me better than it can be known in Washington."

But President Roosevelt had other problems to solve than those of the Philippines alone, and he needed Mr. Taft on the Supreme Bench.   He made an effort to find another man for the place, failed, and then decided not to accept Mr. Taft's declination of the appointment.   A month after the receipt of the cable from Manila the mail carried back this letter:

WHITE HOUSE, Nov. 26, 1902.
"Dear Will: —

"I am awfully sorry, old man, but after faithful effort for a month to try to arrange matters on the basis you wanted I find that I shall have to bring you home and put you on the Supreme Court.

"I am very sorry.   I have the greatest confidence in your judgment, but, after all, old fellow, if you will permit me to say so, I am President and see the whole field.

"The responsibility for any error must ultimately come upon me, and therefore I cannot shirk this responsibility, or in the last resort yield to any one else's decision if my judgment is against it.

"After the most careful thought, after the most earnest effort to do what you desired and thought best, I have come irrevocably to the decision that I shall appoint you to the Supreme Court, in the vacancy caused by Judge Shiras's resignation, and put Luke Wright in your place as governor with Ide as vice-governor. . . .

"With affectionate regards,
"Ever yours,
"THEODORE ROOSEVELT."

Thus the temptation was followed by a command. When the word went out among the Filipinos that the President had called Mr. Taft to return to the United States permanently there was a great demonstration. They gathered in crowds about his residence and besought him not to desert them. In their view they were threatened with a terrible calamity. Taft, they knew, and none other. He was their friend. He would never desert them as long as he was in position to do anything in their behalf. It was a demonstration that went straight to the heart of the governor, and he made one more appeal by cable to the President.

"I have your letter of November 26," he telegraphed. "Recognize soldier's duty to obey orders.

" Before orders irrevocable by action, however, I presume on our personal friendship, even in the face of letter, to make one more appeal, in which I lay aside wholly my strong personal disinclination to leave work of intense interest half done.

" No man is indispensable; my death would little interfere with progress, but my withdrawal more serious.

" Circumstances last three years have convinced these people, controlled largely by personal feeling, that I am their friend and stand for a policy of confidence in them and belief in their future and for extension of self-government as they show themselves worthy.

" Visit to Rome and proposals urged there assure them of my sympathy in regard to friars, in respect of whose far reaching influence they are morbidly suspicious.

" Announcement of withdrawal pending settlement of church question, economic crisis and formative political period when opinions of all parties are being slowly moulded for the better, will, I fear, give impression that change of policy is intended, because other reasons for action will not be understood. My successor's task thus made much heavier because any loss of people's confidence distinctly retards our work here. I feel it my duty to say this.

" If your judgment is unshaken I bow to it and shall earnestly and enthusiastically labor to settle questions of friars' lands before I leave, and convince the people that no change of policy is at hand; that Wright is their warm friend, as sincere as they think me, and that we are both but exponents of the sincere good will toward them of yourself and the American people."

Mr. Taft won in his renunciation. His second cable convinced the President of the necessity of his remaining in Manila, and Mr. Roosevelt replied with this character- istic telegram:

" All right, old fellow, you can stay."

MR. TAFT AND MISS ALICE ROOSEVELT AT JOLO

Photo by Parr McIntosh

MR. TAFT IN SIBERIA

Photo by Brown Bros.

CHAPTER XII

The greatest difficulty the Americans, under the lead of Mr. Taft, had in the school for self-government which they opened in the Philippines was in teaching the Filipino that a public office was not created solely for private emolument. "The educated Filipino," says Mr. Taft, in one of his reports, "has an attractive personality. His mind is quick, his sense of humor fine, his artistic sense acute and active; he has a poetic imagination; he is courteous in the highest degree; he is brave; he is generous; his mind has been given by his education a touch of the scholastic logicism; he is a musician; he is oratorical by nature." Also he is an aristocrat by Spanish association. He prefers that his children should not be educated at the public schools. He dislikes manual labor as beneath his dignity. Young men of this class prefer working as clerks in a government office for $20 a month, to industrial occupations that would bring twice or three times that much. Up to the time of the American occupation the government had represented to the Filipino an entity entirely distinct from himself, with which he had little sympathy and which was engaged in an attempt to obtain as much money as possible from him in the form of taxes.   He regarded an office as the private property of the person holding it, who was justified in making as much out of it as he could.   The idea that public office is a public trust had never been suggested to him by experience or precept, and the conception that an officer who fails in his trust by embezzlement or otherwise was violating an obligation which he owed to every member of the community was extremely hard for him to grasp when the Americans endeavored to implant it.   He recognized the sincerity of the Americans in that belief when he saw them promptly send some of their own people to prison for long terms because of violation of such trust.   But he was apt to regard the robbing of the government by one of its officers as an affair in which he had little or no interest, and in which, not infrequently, his sympathies were with the robber.   It took the fear of inspection by the central government and sharp punishment for breach of trust to instil this idea of duty into the minds of most of the Filipinos.

The conceptions of liberty, of independence and of government which Mr. Taft found among the educated Filipinos were wholly ideal.   Their education was entirely academic, and not at all practical.   When they came to participate in actual government they were unable to realize their conceptions, and only a one-man power, or an oligarchy with class-privilege resulted.   They needed as much education in practical civil liberty as their more ignorant countrymen needed in reading, writing, and arithmetic. Some of these "ilustrados" were the only Filipinos to offer objection to the American plan of general education for all the people. They saw that it would destroy their class distinction. It was a group of "ilustrados" who argued to Mr. Taft that the Filipinos were quite capable of self-government, because, they said, they had counted up all the offices and found there were twice as many "ilustrados" as there were places. This would give two shifts, so that there could be constant changes in the office holders and make possible good government if independence were granted. But there are, or were, Americans who believe that if the Philippine government were turned over to these people it would derive "its just powers from the consent of the governed."

There is no real difference between the educated and ignorant Filipinos that cannot be eradicated by education. They are wonderfully quick to learn, and pathetically eager to make the most of their opportunities for schooling. And they are a capable people, in the sense that they can be given a normal intellectual development by the same kind of education that is given in our common school system.

At the same time that opportunity for general education was freely given to all the Filipinos, the new government undertook to teach them the dignity of labor. This was a slow process, but it is gaining constantly. Industrial schools are established, art and trade schools, with agricultural schools as well. They teach domestic science also. There is now at least one industrial school for each province, and it is the intention to increase this number as rapidly as possible.

Their practical political education the Filipinos are deriving from their participation in municipal and provincial governments and their association with the Americans. Then, under the provisions of the organic act for the island government, they have now elected their first national assembly and have held one session of it. They are learning what the privilege of the franchise means, and from their experience in the assembly and in the provincial governments they have gained wisdom and conservatism.

They have learned, too, the practical benefits of separation of church and state. That teaching, incidentally, helped the Americans out of what might otherwise have been a serious difficulty. It came through the organization of the native church by what is known as the Aglipayan schism. Aglipay was a native priest who, for some infraction of church discipline, was excommunicated. Thereupon he set up a Filipino church of his own. It purports to be a branch of the Catholic church but independent of Rome. All its leaders have been excommunicated. The Aglipayans seized a number of the church buildings at different points in the islands on the ground that inasmuch as the people had contributed of their money and labor to erect them they were entitled to hold them for their own organization. At that the representatives of the Roman church appealed to the Government to dispossess the Aglipayans.

But the Government replied that this was none of its business. There had been no breach of the peace in the occupation of the properties by the Aglipayans, and a distinct question of ownership was set up. This question it belonged to the courts to decide. Let the case be taken there and justice would be done. Marveling vastly at this attitude of the men in power the complainants went into court, and there they have threshed the matter out. In nearly every instance the Aglipayans were beaten. But so far had they progressed in their understanding of this new justice that the decisions were accepted without the resort to violence that had been greatly feared.

Thus slowly the Filipinos are progressing in general education and in practical self-government. They see for themselves now that the Americans have given them a general up-lift. The clamor for immediate independence is not so great. They are beginning to learn from personal experience that self-government is a matter of education and training, and not of gift. They are learning the meaning of civil rights. Peace prevails throughout the islands to-day in far greater degree than ever in their history under either Spanish or American occupation. Agriculture is nowhere impeded by the fear of robbery and pillage. A community of 8,000,000 people, who for four years were in open rebellion against the United States, with all the disturbances that followed in the wake of war, that has suffered from robbers and brigands and from plague, pestilence and famine, has been brought to a state of profound peace and tranquillity in which the people as a whole are loyally supporting the Government in the maintenance of law and order.

9

This is the first and greatest accomplishment of the United States in the Philippines, and it is almost wholly the work of Mr. Taft. He found in the islands a sullen and suspicious people, practically unanimous in their hatred and distrust of us, submitting to our presence there only by the force of arms. He converted them into genuine friends. He convinced them of their own limitations. He read their hearts and their minds as not even their own leaders had done. He showed them their weakness and their strength. He taught them the dignity of labor and fired them with the ambition to progress. He has lifted a people out of the slough of ignorance and superstition and set them on the true path to liberty. He has brought about a new birth of freedom. The work is not all done yet, but it has progressed so far that from the beginning there will now be no retrogression. The future is sure, the end is safe.

Distinguished honors have come to Mr. Taft in the course of his long career in the public service. There is now little doubt that he will be even more distinguished in the eyes of his fellow countrymen by their selection of him as their President to succeed Mr. Roosevelt. But when all distinctions shall have ended, his crowning achievement will be found to have been this work of lofty altruism on behalf of the poor and helpless, the ignorant and feeble Filipinos. Not often is it given to one man to bring a nation into being.

CHAPTER XIII

SECRETARY OF WAR

When, after nearly four years of intense labor for the Filipinos in the Philippines, Mr. Taft was finally persuaded early in 1904, to relinquish his direct and immediate supervision of their affairs, it was only to come home and enter the cabinet of President Roosevelt.as Secretary of War. The deciding consideration which induced him to accept the President's invitation was that at the head of this department, the Philippines would still be under his care. He was not deserting his people. Mr. Taft came to the War Department better equipped for its especial duties than most of his predecessors, for his experience in the Philippines had given him a wide acquaintance with the army and its needs. But he came to find that he was to administer not only the Philippines and the army, he was to supervise the building of the Panama Canal. The preliminaries for that vast undertaking had been concluded just as he arrived in this country from Manila. The purchase from the French company had been completed, and Secretary Hay had negotiated the treaty with the new Republic of Panama which gave us the right to build the canal. Mr. Taft had hardly been at his new

163

post long enough to get the chair warm when he was called upon to take up this tremendous task.

Now again Mr. Taft gave a demonstration of the quality of his brain. He saw the problems confronting us on the isthmus in their natural order and sequence, and there were very few Americans who did. The newspapers were teeming with cartoons of Uncle Sam, in long rubber boots and with a spade on his shoulder, setting out for Panama to " dig the ditch." We were going to show those Frenchmen who had failed how easy it was for us self-confident Americans to make a success of their failure. The public generally neither knew nor cared anything about the vast tangle of perplexities and difficulties that had to be confronted and smoothed away before a shovelful of earth could be thrown for us on the isthmus. Panama was a pest-hole, a sink of yellow fever and malaria, with a death rate that staggered the imagination. But the President and Mr. Taft knew that in Cuba there was an army surgeon who had demonstrated that he could clean up just such a pest-hole and make it safe for white men to live there. This was Col. Gorgas, who had directed the campaign that eradicated yellow fever from Cuba. So he was sent to the isthmus to clean up there, and behind him stood Mr. Taft with all the power of the administration. The next thing to do was to organize the work. That involved at the start elaborate engineering investigations and calculations. They had to know just how much work was to be done, and how and where, before they could begin to plan the machine that was to do

MR. TAFT AT ZAMBOOANGA. WATCHING GENERAL CORBIN RETURN THE BOLO WHICH THE FAMOUS "DOTTO PIANG" HAS JUST GIVEN HIM.

Photo by Burr McIntosh

SHIBA PALACE, TOKIO, JAPAN. MISS ALICE ROOSEVELT IS BETWEEN MR. TAFT
AND MR. NAGASAKI (THE EMPEROR'S REPRESENTATIVE)

Photo by Barr McIntosh

it. Here we have Mr. Taft, the judge and administrator, deeply immersed in engineering problems and mastering them as he had mastered the law to be applied to the Addyston Pipe case. The preliminary plans having been laid out, the work of organization and selection of supervising force for the great army of workmen that was to come after followed. Then there arose a host of questions with Panama concerning the relations that should exist between the new authority on the canal zone and the isthmian republic. Mr. Taft went down to Panama and in a few days had straightened those out and reached a basis for the settlement of future problems. There were matters of statecraft, of politics, of finance, of discipline and of administration. They piled up mountain high, and yet they were only a side issue of his work as Secretary of War.

Now again there came into splendid play that old habit of the thorough mastery of every question when it comes to him new. As each arose he went through it to the bottom, and thereafter it troubled him no more. His successor in the Philippines, Gov. Luke Wright, had been associated with him so long and intimately there, that that machine continued to run as he had started it almost under its own momentum. So he had time to give to the harassing direction of canal affairs.

It was not long before the inevitable began to happen. The self-confident, cock-sure American public, that had expected to see the dirt flying on the isthmus within fifteen minutes after Congress decided to build a canal there found after waiting a couple of years that still no dirt had flown, and there was the usual outcry. Whenever anything doesn't go just as the American people have figured out for themselves it will or should go the invariable conclusion is that there is either fraud or incompetency. Often the suspicion is that there are both. Now the newspapers began to want to know. The air was filled with charges, accusations and hints of disaster. But Mr. Taft had anticipated this, and was ready for it. He simply accepted a few of the invitations to speak that were always pouring in on him, and delivered some broadsides that set the people to wondering why they had not thought before of the simple and plain fact that preparation and organization must precede any task of great magnitude.

There *was* trouble about the commencement .of the work on the isthmus, plenty of it. Undoubtedly some mistakes were made. The United States had never built a canal before, and there was no experience as a guide. And there was more than trouble and mistakes to hamper and delay. There was insubordination and jealousy, and in a few cases craven desertion under fire. Mr. Taft endured it all without complaint until at last the chief engineer on the isthmus quit in the face of a panic about yellow fever. Then Mr. Taft blazed out in a splendid burst of anger. That put a permanent check on the tendency to desert. A little later a magazine writer of some note spent twenty-two hours on the isthmus and came back to tell the people of the United States more things than men who had been two years on the work had ever dreamed. Everything was wrong, said this writer, and everything was either scandalously incompetent or scandalously corrupt. Upon the publication of this wail Mr. Taft prepared a report of conditions on the isthmus which left as true only the magazine writer's signature at the close of his article. And that practically put an end to that sort of criticism. That particular magazine writer has been hammering away ever since, at intervals of a few days, but it is a safe prediction that himself and the proofreaders are the only ones who go through his screeds.

The organization of the canal work has involved tremendous labor and not a little disappointment. The effort to conduct the enterprise under the supervision of civilian engineers proved a failure after several realignments of personnel. Both the President and Mr. Taft believed at first that the work would be handled most satisfactorily if placed under railroad engineers, the men who had been accustomed to the largest construction enterprises. But it developed promptly that such men had no power of endurance under the constant heckling that attends a public work. They are good organizers and hard workers when they have their own way uninterfered with and unquestioned by the public. But when they found themselves not only constantly subjected to the questions and advice of Congress, but also the target for a steady fire from the newspapers, they grew disgruntled and quit. So at length the job was turned over to the army engineers, men who are trained to stand fire and say nothing. Since then it has gone forward with amazing strides. Each month sees an advance on that preceding. New records are constantly made, with the result that already the excavation work has reached a stage where its end can be set with practical certainty for a definite date several years earlier than was at first expected.

The sanitation of the zone has been carried to a point where the former pest-hole is actually a more healthful place of abode than the national capital. Its death rate among whites is less than almost any city of the United States. Yellow fever is unknown and malaria has been greatly reduced. The labor question that involved constant perplexities has been worked out fairly satisfactorily, and the whole organization on the zone is moving forward with energy, enthusiasm and contentment. Mr. Taft has given the canal the same sort of close personal attention that he gave to the problems of the Filipinos when in Manila. He has visited the zone at least once each year, and made careful personal inspections of the canal work. He knows the men on the job, and his personal influence with them counts.

The experience with a people trained under Spanish rule which Mr. Taft gained in the Philippines has been of great value to him in dealing with the canal problems. One of the most difficult phases of the isthmian situation has been the relation between the zone government and the Republic of Panama. By the treaty titular sovereignty of the zone remains with Panama, but the right to control there as if it were in fact United States territory belongs to us. With a people sensitive and proud, and jealous of all the outward forms and ceremonies, this has been a situation requiring infinite patience, delicacy and tact. Besides there has been the constant menace of renewed trouble between Panama and Colombia. Mr. Taft has had to be on the lookout to prevent an open outbreak between those countries, and only within the last few weeks made a special journey to the isthmus largely to settle some threatening complications which had arisen between them. Moreover he has had to serve as a special instructor in self-government for the Panamanians, as he did for the Filipinos. But here the work has required a delicacy of touch even greater than in Manila. For these people owe no governmental allegiance to him. His suggestion must come to them subconsciously or it would provoke a fiery outburst and defeat its purpose. So while his object has been accomplished in all the dealings, it has always appeared to have been the result of their initiative. Mr. Taft has been seeking only results, and not personal glorification.

The canal work has disclosed Mr. Taft in the light of a very great administrator. This has been not only a tremendous business undertaking, it has involved questions of political and diplomatic administration of the highest order. He has had the finances of the Republic of Panama to direct, in effect, and the business of the Panama railroad to run. In his office in the War Department every conceivable kind of question concerning the canal has come to him for determination or advice, from the employment of an individual steam shovel man to the proposal to let the entire work by contract. Bids for every kind of material to be used there; propositions to contract for Chinese coolies or for other foreign laborers; the vital question of the type of canal to be constructed, whether sea level or lock; an infinite variety of matters of organization and questions of accounting; the determination whether this or that man in the service should go to the isthmus or might stay in Washington, sometimes even a question as to the style of stationery to be used; all these and a thousand more have come to him for action. In no other office in the United States, except perhaps the Presidency itself, would a man gain such an equipment for the Presidency as in this War Department, with the Panama Canal as an adjunct.

But the canal is only one of a list of duties of the head of the War Department which it would take some pages of this book to give in full. For instance it fell to Mr. Taft, under an act of Congress, to determine how much water the government would permit to be diverted from the Niagara river for the use of power companies. And it fell to him under another act to determine how much money a Washington man should pay for a piece of ground on the Potomac river bank. He is a member of more kinds of commissions than could be told in half a day. Hardly a statue of a distinguished man is erected in the national capital without Mr. Taft being called upon, as a member of a commission, to say where it shall be placed. Commissions charged with the location and erection of monuments on all the battlefields of the Civil War number him in their membership. The army engineers, in charge by law of river and harbor work all over the country bring their problems to Mr. Taft for final decision and approval. He has had to give long time and careful consideration to the problem of the effect of the Chicago drainage canal upon the level of the great lakes. This paragraph may give some inkling of the range of his activities, but it can convey no adequate conception of the number of things that occupy him. No one but a man who early in life had acquired the habit of mastery of every task as it first comes before him could keep his head above this enormous mass of business for one week.

The administration of the army alone has frequently been enough to occupy the entire time of a man of good ability. Mr. Taft has the regular department work so systematized that in most cases an hour or two in the morning and another at the close of the day in his office suffice to keep all its wrinkles smoothed away. His knowledge of the army, its personnel, organization, location, doings and needs is marvelous. I was present on one occasion when he was having a conference with the assistant secretary and four generals about a question of reorganization. They submitted papers and pamphlets and documents and reports in a great pile, and Mr. Taft had them all packed in a gripsack to take with him on a trip he was about to make. The generals and assistant secretary all talked at once, and he heard each one. When he started off to catch his train the chief of staff turned to me and said:

"He's got all the papers, but he doesn't need any of them. He heard everything each of us said and he will remember it all. He has the whole matter in his head now, and all he wants is a little time to think it over. Then his decision will be made."

That is one of the great secrets of his marvelous ability to handle so much work, the phenomenal power of absorbing information and retaining it to apply to his purposes as he needs.

While serving as Secretary of War, a post that makes him in fact Secretary of the Colonies, Mr. Taft has been called upon constantly by the President as a general adviser on all important questions that have come before the administration. This was natural from his old and close friendship with Mr. Roosevelt. It comes naturally also from his firm belief in and warm support of the course of the President on the public questions which have come to be known as the "Roosevelt policies." As a matter of fact, as has been pointed out in previous chapters of this sketch, Mr. Taft was an advocate of the main items in the "Roosevelt policies" before Mr. Roosevelt had announced himself concerning them. But when it fell to Mr. Roosevelt as President to put them into operation there was never the least hint or sign of jealousy on the part of Mr. Taft. He put his shoulder

MR. TAFT WAITING FOR THE TRAIN AT THE CANTON STATION OF THE CANTON
AND HANKOW RAILWAY.

Photo by Burr McIntosh

MR. TAFT IN TOKIO, JAPAN, IN 1908. U. S. AMBASSADOR O'BRIEN IS ON MR. TAFT'S
LEFT

Photo by Brown Bros.

to the wheel manfully and did all he could to help on the work. It was as always with him, the result to be obtained which interested and attracted him, not the personality of the agent. The work is the point. His life has been a long devotion to the public service, and he is to-day a candidate for the presidency solely because he became convinced that that office presented the greatest opportunity to carry on the fight for the public good in which he had enlisted.

It has befallen Mr. Taft, on several occasions while Secretary of War, to have a hand in diplomatic matters. There was the famous time when President Roosevelt left him " sitting on the lid " during the temporary absence of himself and the Secretary of State from Washington. That was when he had to face the embarrassing and painful duty of passing upon the controversy between his old friends Mr. Bowen and Mr. Loomis.

Thus it befell him, while traveling to the Philippines last fall, to serve as the unofficial emissary of his government with Japan. His acquaintance with Japanese statesmen, gained upon former visits to the Island Empire, made it imperative that he stop in Tokio on his way to Manila to open the sessions of the first Philippine Assembly. Of course the Japanese took advantage of the occasion to discuss with him the relations between the two countries which had become more or less critical owing to the increasing immigration of Japanese laborers to this country. Mr. Taft thereupon seized the opportunity afforded by a banquet in his honor to make a great speech, in which he discussed with characteristic but amazing frankness, the folly of war between Japan and the United States. His speech had a tremendous effect in clearing the troubled atmosphere, and greatly improved the relations between the two countries.

He stopped at Shanghai, after leaving Japan, and in another speech at a banquet attended by the foreign business men there, made a great declaration of the American policy for the Far East. That speech, as did the one at Tokio, produced an immediate and beneficial effect. Incidentally he ran across some matters on this trip which were not in his department, but his observation and judgment have been of immense value in their subsequent treatment by the proper authorities.

There remain for consideration, in any full sketch of Mr. Taft, many matters which cannot be discussed here. But one affair cannot be passed over, although it will be handled only briefly. That is the second intervention in Cuba, in the fall of 1906. With characteristic happy-go-lucky confidence in ourselves we had turned the government of Cuba over to the people of the island, after we had freed them from the domination of Spain, upon what amounted to only one consideration. We required that the Cubans should adopt a constitution. Now there was nothing in the tradition, or the experience or the education of the Cubans to teach them what a constitution was, or what its uses were. They knew nothing of self-government, and were as ignorant as the Filipinos of the principles of civil and personal liberty.

Their proximity to the United States had taught them nothing of the science of free government. But that made no difference to us. Americans have always been so certain that self-government is the very best government for any and all peoples of the earth that we proceeded on the theory that all that was necessary was for Cuba to have a constitution and everything else would follow naturally and inevitably. The Cubans, anxious to grasp the reins of their own government, readily acquiesced, and adopted a constitution just as they would have builded a monument to Mars if the Americans had required it. Thereupon we sailed away from Havana and left them to their own devices.

Freed from American control the Cubans at once and of course, proceeded to govern on the only plan known to them, by the personal decree of the ruler, whom, in accordance with American command, they called president. They had a congress, too, but knew no more what to do with it than with their constitution. The will of the president succeeded the will of the old captain-general of Spanish days. His decree created the departments which should have been organized under the constitution by law of congress, and his word was the final utterance in all matters of dispute.

They were hampered by only one thing, they had to have elections, being required by the Americans to go through the form of selecting a popular government. But they had learned from observation of some boss-ridden American cities how to handle an election to suit

the party in power, and they gave an exhibition of apt-
ness in following their example which would put to the
blush the most domineering boss America ever saw.
The result was obvious and inevitable,— revolution, the
only means known to Cubans of upsetting an election
machine.   Thus the Americans saw their grand experiment in Cuba go to smash after only four years of trial,
and were obliged to intervene again by force to straighten
matters out.

It fell to Mr. Taft to direct this intervention, and
it was due to his masterly skill in handling men that
he obtained the agreement of both factions, so that we
went in without conflict.   Then Mr. Taft had to devise
a provisional government to fit the case.   He built new
from the ground up, using his knowledge of the Spanish-
taught people gained by experience in the Philippines
and Panama.   His provisional government promptly
discovered the anomaly that had resulted from the first
American folly there, and set to work to remedy it by
making a formal and legal organization of the government under the Cuban constitution.   The direction of
all this labor has fallen on Mr. Taft.   Slowly but surely
the work is progressing.   Some features of the " school
for self-government " founded by Mr. Taft in the Philippines have been adapted to the Cuban situation, and in
their municipalities the Cubans are now deriving experience in responsible control of their own affairs.   The
Americans have had another demonstration of the fact
that self-government is not a gift but a matter of educa-

tion and training. When next they sail away from Havana and leave the Cubans to govern themselves it will be with a government firmly and thoroughly organized, and running with a momentum which will give ground for the hope that it will continue to sustain itself.

Cuba thus became the third nation under the tutelage of Mr. Taft. In the Philippines, Panama and Cuba he has had similar experience. In all he is directing the people on the path to true civil liberty and the knowledge of their personal rights. The work in the Philippines was the greatest, because there he was a pioneer, and not only that, he was obliged first to overcome the suspicion and hostility of the people before he could begin their teaching. In Panama and Cuba it has been in large part only the practical application of the principles developed in the Far East. Never in the history of the United States has a man come up for the Presidency with such experience, such training and such equipment.

10

CHAPTER XIV

McKINLEY AND EXPANSION

ADDRESS AT THE TIPPECANOE CLUB, CLEVELAND,
JANUARY 29, 1908.

GENTLEMEN OF THE TIPPECANOE CLUB:

I thank you for your cordial greeting, and for the honor
of addressing you on this, the anniversary of William
McKinley's birthday, I express to you my grateful ac-
knowledgment.

I shall venture to speak to you to-night on that which
I think will ever be remembered as the great and distinguishing characteristic of McKinley's administration
— the expansion of the United States into a world power.

I have at another place and in another presence described in detail the exhibition of national altruism to
be found in the history of the United States during the
last nine years. Now, to-night, I propose to look at this
history as something other than an experiment in altruism. I propose to consider its effect on the government
of this country. When we entered upon the Spanish
war, we certainly had no intention of adding to our territory, for the self-denying provision, known as the
"Teller Resolution," left no doubt upon that point; and

182

it was not until the war carried us into other parts of
the world and we came to try to settle the issues at the
end of the war that we began to realize the responsibilities that we had assumed in taking the sword.   Then it
was that Mr. McKinley, as the head of the administration, was obliged to pioneer.   Then it was that in the
Treaty of Paris he was forced to assume responsibilities
that are likely to remain with the American government
for several generations and possibly a century.   There
were many who hoped that in the Treaty of Peace it
might be possible for us to avoid taking the Philippines
or taking Porto Rico, and that under the Teller Resolution we should part with Cuba and thus avoid adding
to our territorial jurisdiction.   Makeshift propositions
were numerous, and it was hoped that we might take
only one island in the Philippine group and abandon all
the rest.   But an examination of that proposition showed
it utterly impracticable.   The conditions of the islands
that we took from Spain were such that we must assume
control over them, and that we could not lose that control in the interest of the islanders and ourselves until
many years had elapsed.   Indeed it soon became apparent that the Teller Resolution was of doubtful utility
to Cuba herself, and that it might have been better to
prolong the guardianship of the United States over that
beautiful island; but our faith was pledged and no other
course was open but to reorganize the government of
Cuba and set her asail on the pathway of independence;
and the same plighted faith requires us, now that she has

come again under our control, to give her a new trial in her effort to fit herself for self-government.

The problem which Mr. McKinley had to face was apparently a new one. He called to his aid Elihu Root, a jurist and a statesman entitled to stand with those who framed the Constitution, to assist him in a construction of that instrument and an application of it to new conditions. I can well remember a morning at the White House in February, 1900, when I expressed my doubt of the wisdom of the acquisition of the Philippines, and my wish that we had not assumed the responsibility of their government. President McKinley replied, "I had the same reluctance you express in taking them over, but it was the only feasible course open to us. It was impossible to avoid this responsibility, and now that it has come to us, I think it the duty of all patriotic men to assist me in sharing the burden." It was only by gradual steps, only by the exercise of that clear common sense, and his wonderful political judgment, that McKinley had finally reached the conclusion that it was necessary for us to take Porto Rico and the Philippines and do the best we could with them; and when he made that determination, he turned to Elihu Root to advise him as a wise counselor, the steps that were to be taken to make our administration of those islands a credit to the government and a lawful exercise of authority by Congress and the executive. They were met at the outset with the cry, "You are perverting the Constitution, you are departing from the fundamental principles of our

MR. TAFT IN PANAMA, THE TRAINMASTER'S OFFICE
Photo by Brown Bros.

MR. TAFT AND ASSISTANT SECRETARY BACON IN CUBA. BACK OF MR. TAFT U. S.
CONSUL STEINHART. BACK OF MR. BACON U. S. MINISTER MORGAN

Photo by Underwood & Underwood

government, you are assuming imperial functions, and you are taking from Old Glory the unique distinction of waving over a free and independent and self-governing people."

So intense was the objection that it was not difficult for many to find within the limitations of the Constitution, insuperable obstacles to the policy which was adopted. It was said that within the four corners of that instrument as interpreted in the light of the Declaration of Independence, there was no room for the organization of colonies; there was no possibility by which the American people could govern another people. While I have a profound respect for the fears and qualms of those who took this political and constitutional view, because I think they were prompted by the highest motives, I must differ fundamentally from their judgment. The contention that we are not a nation with power to govern a conquered or purchased territory, robs us of a faculty most important for good to every sovereignty. Since the foundation of our government the people of the United States — that is, the States as distinguished from Territories — have been engaged in governing other people. But it is said that we have been engaged in governing them with a view ultimately to making them a part of our government. That begs the question. The question is whether we have power to govern other people for any time. We have done it for a hundred years. We did it in the case of Louisiana. We have done it in the case of every territory that was sub-

sequently admitted to the United States, and we are doing it to-day in the case of New Mexico and Arizona.
What inherent difference is there between the government of a territory and the government of a colony by
the Congress of the United States and the executive appointed in accordance with its direction? Of course I
understand and know the nice distinctions that are made
in supreme court decisions between an organized territory
under the Constitution and territory belonging to the
United States, the government of which is not brought
within the operation of certain limitations of the Constitution; but I am speaking now as man to man, as layman to layman — what, in principle, is the difference between the assertion by Congress of the right to pass a
law which shall be obeyed by men in New Mexico who
have no voice in the selection of the representatives or
the senators who vote that law, and the passing by Congress of such a law for the government of the Philippines or Porto Rico or Cuba when these Islands are
within our control? If the latter is a violation of the
Declaration of Independence, we have been violating the
Declaration of Independence for a hundred years.

The statements in the Declaration of Independence are
to be construed in the light of contemporary history.
They are to be made to apply to the embryo nation and
people which called them forth. They were uttered by
the representatives of men whose ancestors for one thousand years had been fitted for self-government by fighting for rights and liberty that fitted them to govern

themselves as well as any men that ever lived. But when that principle comes to be applied to territories settled either sparsely or with people not used to the exercise of self-government, with an illiteracy that prevents an intelligent exercise of the franchise, with a lack of experience in governmental affairs, then what the Declaration of Independence represents is an ideal toward which we should work; not a positive declaration with reference to the policy to be immediately adopted with respect to any people. That is shown in the treatment that we have given the territories of the United States before we had colonies, and now in the treatment that we are giving those colonies.

If we assume control over a people merely in the spirit of conquest and merely to extend our control and merely from the lust of power, then we may be properly denounced as imperialists; but if we assume control over a people for the benefit of that people and with the purpose of developing them to a self-governing capacity, and with the intention of giving them the right to become independent when they shall show themselves fit, then the charge that we are imperialists is utterly without foundation. A nation like that of the United States, with eighty millions of people, with resources unexampled in the history of the world, with ideals as high as those of any nation, with the earnest desire to spread the principles of liberty and of popular government, cannot maintain a position of isolation with respect to the peoples of the world when fate shall have thrust some of those peoples under our control. We must assume responsibility with respect to their development. We must exercise the power that the Lord has given us for the purpose of assisting our neighbors.

The policy of isolation, which would prevent us from exercising our influence or our direct control in matters where we are capable of doing good and advancing the world's progress, is a narrow, selfish, and altogether unjustifiable policy. The world is not a large one. The facilities of communication have increased with such rapidity as to shrink the distances and the area of the world for practical purposes into one-quarter of the size that it had in the days of Washington and when this government was organized; while at the same time our country has grown from a little fringe along the eastern Atlantic coast to a mighty empire extending from the Atlantic to the Pacific and from the Canadian border to the Gulf, a teeming, sympathetic, and highly nervous community with a population which embraces representatives from all the nations of the globe; a people that pulsates with throbs of sympathy for their most distant fellowmen.

Under such circumstances we must regard and have an interest in what our neighbors are doing, and when we can assist them, we cannot pass by on the other side as the Levite did, but we must take them up as the Good Samaritan did and bind up their wounds and prepare to send them on their way rejoicing.

This was the future which McKinley saw for his

country. This was the step which he was willing to take; this the path which, with the aid of the legal acumen and the statesmanlike foresight of a jurist like Root, he was able to work out for the confirmation and approval of Congress and the people of the United States, and of that supreme tribunal charged with the construction of the Constitution. It would have been most disastrous if the policy which was upheld by a minority of that court had prevailed, by which all the limitations of the Constitution applicable to States and Territories peopled by Americans and trained in the art of self-government, were to be made applicable to a people as untrained, as untutored in self-government, and as illiterate as the Filipinos and the Porto Ricans; and the elasticity of governmental action which the view of the court in distinguishing between territory of the United States and territory belonging to the United States gave the legislature and the executive, was of the highest importance in working out the office that the United States has been called upon to perform with certain of the less fortunate peoples of the world.

What has been the result to the United States of this so-called colonial policy? Well, it has added to her trade something over one hundred millions of dollars. I do not think that is important except as a beginning. If the government continues its friendly policy toward Porto Rico and the Philippines and opens her markets as well to the Philippines as to Porto Rico, this trade will treble and quadruple in a marvelously short time, so that merely from the standpoint of material progress, the mutual benefits for the people we are helping and ourselves will be no mean justification for the policy.

Again, our action in assuming our part of the responsibility of the world powers for the development of the world, has added to our influence the world around and has made our voice influential in all international councils. So great has been this growth that the immediate successor of William McKinley, Theodore Roosevelt, has been able to accomplish more in the preservation of the peace of the world than any President that ever administered or any monarch that ever reigned. The influence that we are exerting in South America, in Central America, in Europe, and in China, is, much of it, the result of the policy of expansion adopted under William McKinley. His administration gave notice of our intention to take our position with other nations and do our part with them in keeping the house of the world in order.

I am no blind admirer of England's colonial policies from the time she began them until the present day. The defects of those policies have been exposed from time to time by the event, and we have shown our difference of view from hers in the course that we have taken with respect to our dependencies. But no one can examine the history of England and consider the influence that she has exerted the world round, in Australia, in New Zealand, in Africa, in Canada, and among the teeming millions of India and in the Strait Settlements, and in the numerous crown colonies over which she exercises control, without recognizing the immense obligation that she has put the world under by the spread of civilization due to her colonial administration. We, as part of the world, are enjoying it. We, as part of the world, derive benefit from the peaceful and civilized conditions that prevail in those English colonies that extend into the remote corners of the world.

Shall we then, as a nation richer than England, with a vastly larger population, take our position as one which refuses to accept such responsibilities, refuses to take part in the advance of civilization except as we do it within our own borders, and say to England, to France, to Germany, and other colonizing empires:

" Go on; we will accept the benefits that may come to the world from your efforts, but we are better than you. We cannot permit ourselves to engage in this world progress, because if we take hold of a people, however ignorant, however unused to civilized control, however lacking in self-restraint or the knowledge of self-government, we must at once equip them with all the faculties that were conferred by the Constitution on our forefathers in the original thirteen states."

We have not taken that stand, although we were urged to do so, and although a bitter attack was made upon us for not doing so. Of course I do not mean to say that these nations to whom I have referred as civilizers, have been actuated by the purest motives and have been free from cruelty and oppression in the cause of what they have done. But I do mean to say that on the whole they have spread civilization wherever they have gone; they have made the people of the world on the whole happier; and they have contributed their part toward the onward spread of general civilization.

I admit, too, that such a policy leads from one step to another. Our possession of the Philippines makes us a neighbor to China. It gives us a greater interest in the development of that enormous empire which is only now rousing itself from its sleep of centuries to adopt slowly but certainly modern ideas and to make itself an empire of immense population and immense resources, and to secure an independence from foreign aggression and abuse. While it is in this half infancy, if I may call it such, we have induced the other nations to recognize with us the principle that in the trade to be extended by China to others, all shall have an equal opportunity; in other words, that the policy of the open door in China shall be maintained for the benefit of all. Can anyone deny that we are in a position now to make our voice in favor of such a policy much more effective than ever we were before? The part we have played in international politics rightly gives us this stand. The part we have assumed in developing other countries than our own and taking over for a time the control of these newly acquired dependencies, all adds to our prestige in those oriental countries in which influence follows power and territorial jurisdiction.

It is said that this policy has entailed upon us the enor-

PHILANDER CHASE KNOX, SENATOR FROM PENNA.

JOSEPH BENSON FORAKER, SENATOR FROM OHIO

mous burden of a navy. I believe that it has increased the necessity for a greater navy. I believe that a navy is the greatest insurer of peace that we could possibly have — a navy commensurate with our resources, and commensurate with our coast line, and commensurate with the number of dependencies we have, and commensurate with our population, and commensurate with our influence as a world power.

The expression "world power" has been made an occasion for ridicule and sneers, but it has a real meaning and a real significance. It means an influence throughout the world; and so long as that influence is wielded for the betterment of mankind, for the uplifting of our unfortunate fellow-creatures, for the maintenance of peace, for the encouragement of trade, for the promotion of morality and civilization, we may well be proud to have taken any part in the change of our national policy which made us a world power.

The highest claim of William McKinley for the gratitude of his countrymen is that, in spite of the abuse and contumely that was heaped upon his head for this policy, he placed our country in the forefront of nations as a civilizer and uplifter of unfortunate peoples.

CHAPTER XV

THE FEDERAL JUDICIARY

ADDRESS BEFORE THE AMERICAN BAR ASSOCIATION,
DETROIT, AUGUST 28, 1895.

Within the last four years, the governors of five or
more States have thought it proper in official messages
to declare that the Federal courts have seized jurisdiction, not rightly theirs and have exercised it to the detriment of the Republic, and to urge their respective legislatures to petition Congress for remedial action to prevent future usurpation. One legislature did present a
memorial to Congress reciting the grievances of the people of its State against the Federal judiciary and asking
a curtailment of the powers unlawfully assumed by them.

The principal charge against the Federal courts, which
an examination of these documents discloses, is that they
have flagrantly usurped jurisdiction, first, to protect
corporations and perpetuate their many abuses, and
second, to oppress and destroy the power of organized
labor.

These charges against the Federal judiciary have not
been confined to messages from State governors. They
also come from persons, who although not holding high
office, have a standing before the bar which entitles them

198

to respectful attention. Much of what is found in the official communications I have referred to concerning the treatment of corporations by the Federal courts has taken form from the articles and addresses of the editor of the *American Law Review*. This gentleman, well-known as an able and prominent law text writer, has given much attention to the Federal decisions on corporate matters and has expressed his condemnation of many of them in language that has lacked nothing in freedom, emphasis or rhetorical figure.

The opportunity freely and publicly to criticise judicial action is of vastly more importance to the body politic than the immunity of courts and judges from unjust aspersions and attack. Nothing tends more to render judges careful in their decisions and anxiously solicitous to do exact justice than the consciousness that every act of theirs is to be subjected to the intelligent scrutiny and candid criticism of their fellowmen. Such criticism is beneficial in proportion as it is fair, dispassionate, discriminating and based on a knowledge of sound legal principles. The comments made by learned text writers and by the acute editors of the various law reviews upon judicial decisions are therefore highly useful. Such critics constitute more or less impartial tribunals of professional opinion before which each judgment is made to stand or fall on its merits and thus exert a strong influence to secure uniformity of decision. But non-professional criticism also is by no means without its uses, even if accompanied, as it often is, by a direct attack upon the judicial fairness and motives of the occupants of the bench; for if the law is but the essence of common sense, the protest of many average men may evidence a defect in a judicial conclusion though based on the nicest legal reasoning and profoundest learning. (The two important elements of moral character in a judge are an earnest desire to reach a just conclusion and courage to enforce it.)   In so far as fear of public comment does not affect the courage of a judge but only spurs him on to search his conscience and to reach the result which approves itself to his inmost heart, such comment serves a useful purpose.   There are few men, whether they are judges for life or for a shorter term who do not prefer to earn and hold the respect of all, and who can not be reached and made to pause and deliberate by hostile public criticism.   In the case of judges having a life tenure, indeed, their very independence makes the right freely to comment on their decisions of greater importance because it is the only practical and available instrument in the hands of a free people to keep such judges alive to the reasonable demands of those they serve.

On the other hand, the danger of destroying the proper influence of judicial decisions by creating unfounded prejudices against the courts, justifies and requires that unjust attacks shall be met and answered.   Courts must ultimately rest their defense upon the inherent strength of the opinions they deliver as the ground for their conclusions and must trust to the calm and deliberate judgment of all the people as their best vindication.

It will be my endeavor first to show that much, if not all, of the present hostility to the Federal courts in certain parts of the country and among certain groups of the people can be traced to causes over which those courts can exercise no control, and is necessarily due to the character of the jurisdiction with which they are vested and not to injustice in its exercise; and second, that the criticisms which such hostility has engendered are in themselves without foundation.

The history of the Federal courts since their beginning is full of instances where the exercise of their jurisdiction has involved them in popular controversies and has brought down upon them the bitter assaults of those unfavorably affected by their decisions. Yet the event has justified their course and shown the injustice of the attacks.

The Federal judiciary at once became the arbiters in the first great political controversy of the United States, and one which is continually reappearing in various forms. Beginning as arbiters in a political conflict and wielding similar powers until to-day, the Federal judiciary have never enjoyed immunity from hostile attack upon their conduct or their motives. The great controversy over the fugitive slave law needs no recounting here. In the eyes of the abolitionists the Federal courts and their marshals were instruments of hell in enforcing the

11

law, and yet there could not be the slightest doubt that such a jurisdiction was plainly within the Constitution.

The change of feeling toward the Federal courts because of the change in their jurisdiction with respect to the negro race affords an apt illustration of how mere jurisdiction may affect the popular feeling toward a court. Before the war the southern people had not looked with disfavor upon courts which did so much to preserve their property, while at the same time the abolitionists regarded them with aversion. After the war, when, for the protection of the negro in his electoral and civil rights, the election and civil rights bills were passed and their enforcement was given to the Federal courts, they became at the same time the objects of hatred and condemnation at the South and the great reliance of those who had been abolitionists at the North. Now that both parties have wisely decided to let the election problem work itself out and to await the local solution which the results of fraud and violence in elections will compel, the feeling of hostility at the South against the Federal judiciary has greatly abated.

This is but one of many historical instances showing how the Federal courts may be subjected to the most severe criticism without just grounds merely because of the character of their jurisdiction.

The last two generations have witnessed a marvelous material development. It has been effected by the organization and enforced co-operation of simple elements that for a long time previous had been separately used.

The organization of powerful machines or of delicate devices by which the producing power of one man was increased fifty or one hundred fold, was, however, not the only step in this great progress. The aim of all material civilization in its hard contest with nature was the reduction of the cost of production, because thereby each man's day's work netted him more of the comforts of life. Within the limits of efficient administration the larger the amount to be produced at one time and under one management, the less the expense per unit. Therefore, the aggregation of capital, the other essential element with labor in producing anything, became an obvious means of securing economy in the manufacture of everything. Corporations had long been known as convenient commercial instruments for securing and wielding efficiently such aggregations of capital. Charters were at first conferred by special act upon particular individuals and with varying powers, but so great became the advantage of incorporation, with the facility afforded for managing great enterprises and the limitation of the liability of investors, that it was deemed wise in this country, in order to prevent favoritism, to create corporations by general laws and thus to afford to all who wished it the opportunity of assuming a corporate character in accordance therewith. The result was a great increase in the number of the corporations and the assumption of the corporate form by seven-eighths of the active capital of the country. The great saving in the cost of production brought about by mechanical inventions and the

organization of capital worked incalculable benefit to the
public, but the necessary price of it under our system of
free right of contract and inviolable rights of private
property was a division of the profit between those who
were to consume the product and those whose minds con-
ceived and whose hands executed the work of production.   The total wealth of the whole country was thus
enormously increased, but of the increase more was necessarily accumulated in some hands than others.   In the
general prosperity caused by the revolution in methods
of production, captains of industry amassed fabulous fortunes, and the aggregations of capital under corporate
management became so great as to stagger the imagination.   In the mad rush for money which previous suc-
cesses had stimulated, it is not to be wondered at that
some of the accumulated wealth was corruptly used to
secure undue business advantages from legislative and
executive sources and that many of the political agencies
of the people became tainted.   The impersonal character of corporations afforded a freedom from that restraint in the use of money for political corruption which
is often present when the would-be briber is an individual.
Men of good repute, with complacence and intentional
ignorance, acquiesced in the use of corporate funds to
buy legislators and councilmen in the corporate interest,
when they would not wish or dare to adopt such methods
in their individual business.   The enormous increase in
corporate wealth furnished the means of corruption, and
the prospect of ill-gotten gains attracted the dishonest

JOSEPH G. CANNON, SPEAKER OF THE HOUSE OF REP-
RESENTATIVES
Copyright 1908 by Harris & Ewing

CHARLES EVANS HUGHES, GOVERNOR OF NEW YORK

Copyright 1908 by Brown Bros.

trickster into politics and debauched the weak, while the honest and courageous were often driven into private life. The genie of corruption in politics which the corporations called up has lived to plague them, and although many great companies have secured all they wish from legislative bodies, they are regarded by the political blackmailers as fair game and the corruption fund is still maintained to prevent oppression. The people not unjustly have charged these public evils to the management of corporations.

Another evil has been the injustice done to the real owners of corporate property by the reckless and dishonest management of its nominal owners. The great liberality of the general laws for the formation of corporations and the entire failure to exercise any stringent visitorial powers over them have enabled the active promoters and managers of large enterprises carried on at a distance from the homes of the real owners, to increase the corporate indebtedness and capital stock so far beyond any fair valuation of their property as to put the entire control of it in the hands of the holders of worthless stock who have nothing at stake in the corporate success.

The real owners, the bondholders, are at the mercy of this irresponsible management till insolvency comes. The reckless business methods which such an irresponsibility and lack of supervision invite create an unhealthy and feverish competition in every market, wholly unrestrained by the natural caution which the real owner of a business must feel. The concern is kept going with no hope of legitimate profit, but simply to pay large salaries or to favor unduly some other enterprise in which the managers have a real interest.

Another reason for popular distrust of corporate methods is the use by corporations of great amounts of capital to monopolize and control particular industries. It is my sincere belief that no such control or monopoly can be maintained permanently unless it is buttressed by positive legislation giving an undue advantage over the public and competitors. Of course, by close business methods and by improving all the economical advantages which the manufacture of a commodity on an enormous scale affords, the cost of production may be so reduced as to discourage competition on a smaller scale, but unless the fear of it performs the same useful office for the benefit of the public by continuing the lowest profitable prices, actual competition will certainly appear. Whatever the fate such trusts may ultimately have, it has often happened that in their formation and early history, the plan adopted has been the forced buying out of every competitor or his ruin by underselling him at heavy loss so as to put the public and the market for a time at least at the mercy of one greedy corporate concern. Such methods and such a result naturally fill the people with anxious fears and a hostile feeling toward aggregations of corporate wealth.

In spite of these well-known evils nothing can be clearer to a calm, intelligent thinker than that under conditions of modern society, corporations are indispensable both to the further material progress of this country and to the maintenance of that we have enjoyed. The evils must be remedied, but not by destroying one of the greatest instruments for good that social man has devised. Nevertheless, so strong has the hostility to corporations become, especially in certain of the southern and western States where the agricultural community is large, life is hard and wealth is rare, that any plan which can be contrived to diminish the property of corporations or to cripple their efficiency seems to meet with favor. The feeling is especially directed against the railway corporations, although without their aid and presence these very communities would be helpless and poor indeed.

Under the Fourteenth Amendment the question whether legislation and State action deprive any person of his property without due process of law has become a Federal one, and by the Act of 1875 it is cognizable by the Circuit Courts of the United States.

The prejudices above adverted to have led to much legislation hostile to corporations both resident and non-resident. It takes the forms of discriminating taxation, of the regulation of rates to be charged by those companies engaged in *quasi* public business, and sometimes, of the direct deprivation of vested rights. In all such cases resort is at once had to the inferior Federal courts by the corporations injuriously affected, to test the validity of the State's action, and it not infrequently happens that it becomes the duty of such courts to declare void the legislation involved and to enjoin State officers from seizing or injuring the property of corporations under its provisions. Such a decision in a corporation-hating community at once tends to mark the Federal courts as friends and protectors of corporations.

The repeated efforts of different State legislatures to impose restrictions upon interstate commerce to secure some apparent advantage to their own constituents, evidence the profound wisdom of the framers of the Constitution in vesting complete control thereof in the national government, but the tribunals whose jurisdiction is constantly invoked judicially to declare void all such legislation do not for the time commend themselves to the favor either of those who urged its passage or of those who were to profit by its operation, and the fact that the complainant in such litigation is frequently a railroad or transportation company only confirms the view of the undue favor of these courts to such litigants.

Corporate corruption cannot be directly punished in the Federal courts, because the bribery of which many corporations are guilty is most difficult of legal proof, and crimes of this character are usually committed against the State, so that Federal courts have no cognizance of them. The abuses which *too liberal* charters and insufficient visitorial power permit, are either for the State legislatures or for the State executive and courts, by *quo warranto*, to correct and remedy. State laws which should forbid the issue of stock or the issue of bonds by any corporation until after an examination by a State board of supervision into the affairs of the company and a certificate that the assets justify it, would do much in this direction. The Federal courts can do nothing to prevent such abuses, and their action is not usually invoked until the evil is done and only a bankrupt estate is left to administer.

The main public evil of corporate growth, the corruption of politics, must be reformed by the people and not by the courts. Courts are but conservators; they cannot effect great social or political changes. Corporations there must be if we would progress; accumulation of wealth there will be if private property continues the keystone of our society; the temptation to use money to corrupt legislatures and other political agencies will remain potent as long as undue privilege for corporations can be thus secured. The only real remedy is in the purification of the politics of the country and the selection of incorruptible public servants. The mad rush for wealth, the fevered condition of business and the opportunity for making sudden fortunes have taken the attention of the more intelligent people from politics and made them blind or callous to political abuses. But there are many signs of a quickened public conscience and of a willingness on the part of the intelligent and the pure to interest themselves in politics for their country's good.

The present successful use of corrupt methods by corporations is directly due to the neglect of the people to exercise the eternal watchfulness which is the price of pure government; but those whose interest it is to secure popular support and who are willing to secure it by appeals to prejudice do not tell the people unpleasant truths, and are glad to find a scapegoat for the people's sins in the Federal judiciary. It well rounds a rhetorical period to point to the Federal judiciary as an irresponsible and irremovable body, wholly out of touch with the people and conniving at corporate abuses.

To an impartial observer it must seem remarkable that judges should conceive a love for soulless corporations and unduly favor them. Living as most of these judges do on their salaries and deriving no profit from corporate investments, they would seem to find little in their lives to blind them to the injustice of any claim or defense which a wealthy corporation may make.

If it were conceded that greed of power is an incentive so strong that Federal judges have yielded to it and have extended their jurisdiction over corporations beyond the lines marked by the Constitution and the laws, this is far from establishing that justice has not been meted out to corporate suitors with impartial hand. The fact is that when we come to examine in detail the charges against the Federal courts, the burden of them is that they have assumed jurisdiction over corporate litigation without constitutional and legal right, and not that, in the hearing on the merits, corporations have been unduly favored. The latter is always assumed as a granted premise when the former is deemed to be established.

These are some of the reasons why the jurisdiction of the Federal courts in respect to corporations, be it exercised never so impartially, must under existing conditions arouse deep prejudice against them, and call forth severe assaults upon their conduct and motives.

If it is true that citizens of one State organize corporations under the laws of another State to do business in the former State, and thereby carry controversies with their fellow-citizens into the Federal courts, this is an abuse which should be remedied by Congress, as other frauds upon the jurisdiction have been provided against.

The Federal courts have also been severely arraigned for undue amplification of their powers in the matter of receivers of railroad companies, due as it is charged to their leaning toward such corporations and a desire to protect them.

The appointment of receivers to operate railroads pending suits in foreclosure and creditor's bills, instead of being an abuse of authority by the Federal courts, was a most commendable use of an ordinary equitable means of preserving the *status quo* with respect to a new kind of property and in a pressing emergency. Generally no one but the parties are interested in preserving the subject matter of the suit as a going concern till it can be sold, but in the case of a railroad the public are even more interested than the parties in having this done. The disastrous consequences to the whole country, were these great arteries of the nation to cease to flow, can hardly be overstated; and yet, unless in the course of liquidation sale and reorganization, they could, when insolvent, be withdrawn from liability to seizure and dis-

memberment by ordinary executions in the various juris-
dictions which they traverse, their operation would become impossible. The ordinary insolvent laws of each
State, even if their procedure had been at all adapted to
the running of railroads, as it was not, would have sup-
plied in such case but a poor substitute for the present
receivership. Most railroads are to-day interstate, and
the advantage of an *ad interim* management under practically the same jurisdiction on both sides of State lines
is apparent. In the absence of statutory provision for
such an exigency, the flexible procedure of a court of
equity is fitted to meet it, and although the remedy was
adopted soon after the building of railroads more than
forty years ago and has been applied with increasing
frequency ever since, it has not been deemed necessary
by Congress or State legislatures to provide any other
means for bridging the undoubted difficulties presented
by the insolvency of railroad companies. The fact is,
that no possible system of managing railroads could be
better adapted to a summary investigation of the details
of the management than that by a court of equity in which
the court will always and at once entertain complaints by
anyone in interest against its receiver and examine the
facts upon which they rest. This may account, in part,
for the very few instances of official corruption among
Federal receivers.

On the other hand, if any other and better way can
be devised for the temporary management of insolvent

CHARLES WARREN FAIRBANKS, VICE-PRESIDENT OF THE
UNITED STATES

GEORGE BRUCE CORTELYOU, SECRETARY OF TREASURY

Copyright 1908 by Harris & Ewing

railroads pending their sale, it may be conceded that there are substantial reasons for relieving Federal courts of equity from the duty. I sympathize heartily with every effort to impose a practical limitation upon the duration of receiverships. The use of the courts as a harbor of refuge from creditors during a financial storm may be abused, and doubtless has been. The temptation to this resort is greatly increased, if, as is too often the practice, the controlling officer of the company is continued in the management as receiver. The patronage incident to the jurisdiction is one of its evils. Recognizing this and wishing to avoid a disagreeable race for office, courts usually acquiesce in the appointment of a person recommended by the parties, who is not infrequently the president or manager of the company, and whose failure to oppose the receivership, it may be, has been secured by such a recommendation. Consent applications for receiverships would be much less common if it were provided by statute that, wherever a case is made on preliminary application for the immediate appointment of a receiver, . . . no one connected with the previous management of the railroad or interested in its bonds or stock should be eligible, even with consent of the parties. In any event, until some new way is devised for the temporary operation of railroads, pending insolvency or foreclosure and sale, courts must assume it, and it ill becomes any one to criticise their action in doing so, and to charge it to their greed of power, when any other course would result in disastrous consequences to the parties in interest and the country at large.

On the whole, when the charges made against Federal courts of favoritism toward corporations are stripped of their rhetoric and epithet, and the specific instances upon which the charges are founded are reviewed, it appears that the action of the courts complained of was not only reasonable but rested on precedents established decades ago and fully acquiesced in since, and that the real ground of the complaint is that the constitutional and statutory jurisdiction of the Federal courts is of such a character that it is frequently invoked by corporations to avoid some of the manifest injustice which a justifiable hostility to the corrupt methods of many of them inclines legislatures and juries and others to inflict upon all of them.

THE FEDERAL COURTS AND LABOR.

We come finally to the relation of the Federal courts to organized labor. The capitalist and laborer share the profit of production. The more capital in active employment the more work there is to do, and the more work there is to do, the more laborers there are needed. The greater need of laborers, the better their pay per man. It is clearly in the interest of those who work that capital shall increase more rapidly than they do. Everything, therefore, having a legitimate tendency to increase the accumulation of wealth and its use for production, will give each workingman a larger share of

the joint result of capital and labor, and it is in a large
measure because this country has grown more rapidly in
capital than in population, that wages have steadily increased. But while it is in the common interest of labor
and capital to increase the fruits of production, yet in
determining the share of each their interests are plainly
opposed. Though the law of supply and demand will
doubtless, in the end, be the most potent influence in fixing this division, yet during the gradual adjustment to
the changing markets and the varying financial conditions, capital will surely have the advantage, unless labor
takes united action. During the betterment of business
conditions, organized labor, if acting with reasonable discretion, can secure much greater promptness in the advance of wages, than if it were left to the slower operation of natural laws, and, in the same way, as hard times
come on, the too eager employer may be restrained from
undue haste in reducing wages. The organization of
capital into corporations with the position of advantage,
which this gave in a dispute with single laborers over
wages, made it absolutely necessary for labor to unite
to maintain itself. For instance, how could workingmen, dependent on each day's wages for living, dare to
take a stand, which might leave them without employment if they had not by small assessments accumulated
a common fund for their support during such emergency?
In union they must sacrifice some independence of action,
and there are bad results from the tyranny of the majority in such cases, but the hardships which have fol-

lowed impulsive resort to extreme measures have had a good effect to lessen these. Experience, too, will lead to classification among the members so that the cause of the skilled and worthy shall not be leveled down to that of the lazy and neglectful. Like corporations, labor organizations do great good and much evil. The more conservatively and intelligently conducted they are, the more benefit they confer on their members. The more completely they yield to the dominion of those among them who are intemperate of expression and violent and lawless in their methods, the more evil they do to themselves and society.

The employees of railroad companies and others engaged in transportation of freight and passengers generally have well organized unions, and the controversies arising over wages have been many. A vast majority of these have been settled without a resort to extreme measures, through the conservative influence of level-headed labor leaders and railroad managers, but in the last twenty years there have been some very extended railroad strikes, accompanied by the boycotts and open violence with which society has now become familiar. The fact that many railroads have been operated by Federal receivers, the non-residence of railway corporations in the States where the strikes occur, and the interstate commerce feature of the business, have brought some of these violations of property and private and public right within the cognizance of Federal courts. Because the participants in such contests have been spread more widely over the country than in similar contests with which State courts have had to deal, the action of the Federal courts in these cases has attracted more public attention and evoked more bitter condemnation by those who naturally sympathize with labor in every controversy with capital.

The efficacy of the processes of a court of equity to prevent much of the threatened injury from the public and private nuisances which it is often the purpose of the leaders of such strikes to cause, has led to the charge, which is perfectly true, that judicial action has been much more efficient to restrain labor excesses than corporate evils and greed. If it were possible by the quick blow of an injunction to strike down the conspiracy against public and private rights involved in the corruption of a legislature or a council, Federal and other courts would not be less prompt to use the remedy than they are to restrain unlawful injuries by labor unions. But I have had occasion to point out that the nature of corporate wrong is almost wholly beyond the reach of courts, especially those of the United States. The corporate miners and sappers of public virtue do not work in the open, but under cover; their purposes are generally accomplished before they are known to exist, and the traces of their evil paths are destroyed and placed beyond the possibility of legal proof. On the other hand, the chief wrongs committed by labor unions are the open, defiant trespass upon property rights and violations of public order, which the processes of courts are well adapted both to punish and prevent.

12

The operation of the interstate commerce law is an illustration of the greater difficulty courts have in suppressing corporate violations of law than those of trade unions. The discrimination between shippers by rebates and otherwise, which it is the main purpose of the law to prevent, is almost as difficult of detection and proof as bribery, for the reason that both participants are anxious to avoid its disclosure. But when the labor unions, as they sometimes do, seek to interfere with interstate commerce and to obstruct its flow, they are prone to carry out their purposes with such a blare of trumpets and such open defiance of law that the proof of their guilt is out of their own mouths. The rhetorical indictment against the Federal courts, that from what was intended as a shield against corporate wrong, they have forged a weapon to attack the wage earner, is in this way given a specious force which a candid observer will be blind to ignore. Thus are united in a common enmity against the Federal courts the populist and the trade unionist with all those whose political action is likely to be affected by such a combination. And yet their enmity has no other justification than the differing and unavoidable limitations upon the efficacy of judicial action in respect to corporate and labor evils.

As a matter of fact there is nothing in any Federal decision directed against the organization of labor to maintain wages and to secure terms of employment otherwise favorable. The courts so far as they have expressed themselves on the subject recognize the right of men for a lawful purpose to combine to leave their employment at the same time, and to use the inconvenience this may cause to their employer as a legitimate weapon in the frequently recurring controversy as to the amount of wages. It is only when the combination is for an unlawful purpose and an unlawful injury is thereby sought to be inflicted, that the combination has received the condemnation of the Federal as well as of State courts.

The action of the Federal courts all over the country in the recent American Railway Union strike in issuing injunctions to prevent further unlawful interference by the strikers with the carrying of the mails, and the flow of interstate commerce, followed by the commitment for contempt of the strike leaders who defied the injunction served on them, is what has called out the official protests of the Governors of Illinois and Colorado, and the phrase " government by injunction " has been invented to describe the alleged usurpation of power by the Federal tribunals in this crisis. The Federal courts did not assume executive powers any more than they do so when they issue any process to the marshal, and the marshal as the subordinate of the President executes it. The extent of the actual and threatened injury and the possible resistance to lawful process required the marshal to call to his assistance much aid, but it is a latter day doctrine that a court is usurping the executive function, in calling upon the executive to use additional force to avoid a possible defeat of its lawful process. The conservative course of the President and the Attorney-General in first applying to the courts for process and the subsequent firmness exhibited by those officers in executing that process by all the means available, will cause the country to hold them always in grateful remembrance. The duty of the courts to act on this initiative was so plain that while it does not entitle them to any especial commendation, it would seem that it should protect them from serious attack.

The real objection to the injunction is the certainty that disobedience will be promptly punished before a court without a jury. It is hardly necessary to defend the necessity for such means of enforcing orders of court. If the court must wait upon the slow course of a jury trial before it can compel a compliance with its order, then the efficacy of its process would be seriously impaired. The argument seems to be that because many men are determined to violate the rights of the public and their fellow-citizens in spite of the lawful orders of the Federal court restraining them from so doing, they should, on account of their number and popular strength, have a right which no Anglo-Saxon has hitherto ever enjoyed, to interpose a jury trial between them and the enforcement of a court's order. If the criticisms under discussion are directed against the existence of courts, then their weight depends on different considerations from those which apply on the assumption that courts are to be maintained for the purpose of remedying wrongs. But they are professedly based on the Constitution of the United States, and that certainly contemplates courts,

JOHN A. JOHNSON, GOVERNOR OF MINNESOTA
Copyright 1908 by Harris & Ewing

GEORGE GRAY, JUDGE U. S. CIRCUIT COURT
Photo by J. Paul Brown

whose decrees shall be enforced, however much resisted, and which shall not be merely advisory councils whose efficacy depends on their powers of persuasion.

It will not be surprising if the storm of abuse heaped upon the Federal courts and the political strength of popular groups, whose plans of social reform have met obstruction in those tribunals, shall lead to serious efforts through legislation to cut down their jurisdiction and cripple their efficiency. If this comes, then the responsibility for its effects, whether good or bad, must be not only with those who urge the change, but also with those who do not strive to resist its coming.

The earliest assaults upon the Federal judiciary and their harmless character in the light of the event, reconcile one to much of the fiery invective and blood-curdling epithets hurled at men who, equally with their accusers, are American freemen, impressed with the absolute necessity for maintaining sacred the guaranties of life, liberty and property, and who are probably not more in love with corruption and greed, or more disposed to crush the humble and worthy, than the average of their fellow-citizens.

The saving grace of American humor, which delights in the contemplation of grotesque exaggeration, has often saved us from domestic turbulence, which the turgid exuberance of denunciatory language might otherwise have excited against lawfully-constituted authority; and it may be that the same useful trait will prevent the success of the present agitators against the Federal courts.

But whatever fate betide the Federal judiciary, I hope that it may always be said of them, as a whole, by the impartial observer of their conduct, that they have not lacked in the two essentials of judicial moral character, a sincere desire to reach right conclusions and firmness to enforce them.

CHAPTER XVI

THE WORK OF THE UNITED STATES IN THE PHILIPPINES

ADDRESS ON THE OPENING OF THE FIRST SESSION OF THE PHILIPPINE NATIONAL ASSEMBLY, OCTOBER, 1907

GENTLEMEN OF THE ASSEMBLY: President Roosevelt has sent me to convey to you and the Filipino people his congratulations upon another step in the enlargement of popular self-government in these Islands. I have the greatest personal pleasure in being the bearer of this message. It is intended for each and every member of the Assembly, no matter what his views upon the issues which were presented in the late electoral campaign. It assumes that he is loyal to the government in which he now proposes, under oath of allegiance, to take part. It does not assume that he may not have a wish to bring about, either soon or in the far future, by peaceable means, a transfer of sovereignty; but it does assume that while the present government endures, he will loyally do all he lawfully can to uphold its authority and to make it useful to the Filipino people.

I am aware that, in view of the issues discussed at the election of this Assembly, I am expected to say something regarding the policy of the United States toward these Islands. Before attempting any such task, it is well to make clear the fact that I can not speak with the authority of one who may control that policy.

The Philippine Islands are territory belonging to the United States, and by the Constitution, the branch of that Government vested with the power, and charged with the duty, of making rules and regulations for their government is Congress. The policy to be pursued with respect to them is, therefore, ultimately for Congress to determine. Of course, in the act establishing a government for the Philippine Islands passed by Congress July 1, 1902, wide discretion has been vested in the President to shape affairs in the Islands, within the limitations of the act, through the appointment of the Governor and the Commission, and the power of the Secretary of War to supervise their work and to veto proposed legislation; but not only is the transfer of sovereignty to an independent government of the Filipino people wholly within the jurisdiction of Congress, but so also is the extension of any popular political control in the present government beyond that conferred in the organic act. It is embarrassing, therefore, for me, though I am charged with direct supervision of the Islands under the President, to deal in any way with issues relating to *their ultimate disposition.* It is true that the peculiar development of the government of the Islands under American sovereignty has given to the attitude of the President upon such issues rather more significance than in most matters of exclusively Congressional cognizance. After the exchange of ratifications of the Treaty of Paris in April of 1899, and until the organic act of July 1, 1902, Congress acquiesced in the government of the Islands by the President as Commander in Chief of the Army and Navy without interference, and when it passed the organic act it not only confirmed in every respect the anomalous quasi-civil government which he had created, but it also made his instructions to the Secretary of War part of its statute, and followed therein his recommendation as to future extension of popular political control. This close adherence of Congress to the views of the Executive in respect to the Islands in the past gives ground for ascribing to Congress approval of the Philippine policy, as often declared by President McKinley and President Roosevelt. Still, I have no authority to speak for Congress in respect to the ultimate disposition of the Islands. I can only express an opinion as one familiar with the circumstances likely to affect Congress, in the light of its previous statutory action.

The avowed policy of the National Administration under these two Presidents has been and is to govern the Islands, having regard to the interest and welfare of the Filipino people, and by the spread of general primary and industrial education and by practice in partial political control to fit the people themselves to maintain a stable and well-ordered government affording equality of right and opportunity to all citizens. The policy looks to the improvement of the people both industrially and in

self-governing capacity.   As this policy of extending control continues, it must logically reduce and finally end
the sovereignty of the United States in the Islands, unless
it shall seem wise to the American and the Filipino peoples, on account of mutually beneficial trade relations and
possible advantage to the Islands in their foreign relations, that the bond shall not be completely severed.

How long this process of political preparation of the
Filipino people is likely to be is a question which no one
can certainly answer.   When I was in the Islands the last
time, I ventured the opinion that it would take considerably longer than a generation.   I have not changed my
view upon this point; but the issue is one upon which
opinions differ.   However this may be, I believe that the
policy of the Administration as outlined above is as definite as the policy of any government in a matter of this
kind can safely be made.   We are engaged in working
out a great experiment.   No other nation has attempted
it, and for us to fix a certain number of years in which the
experiment must become a success and be completely realized would be, in my judgment, unwise.   As I pre-
mised, however, this is a question for settlement by the
Congress of the United States.

Our Philippine policy has been subjected to the severest
condemnation by critics who occupy points of view as
widely apart as the two poles.   There are those who say
that we have gone too fast, that we have counted on the
capacity of the Filipino for political development with a
foolish confidence leading to what they regard as the dis-

astrous result of this election. There are others who assert that we have denied the Filipino that which is every man's birthright — to govern himself — and have been guilty of tyranny and a violation of American principles in not turning the government over to the people of the Islands at once.

With your permission, I propose to consider our policy in the light of the events of the six years during which it has been pursued, to array the difficulties of the situation which we have had to meet and to mention in some detail what has been accomplished.

The Civil Government was inaugurated in 1901 before the close of a war between the forces of the United States and the controlling elements of the Philippine people. It had sufficient popular support to overawe many of those whose disposition was friendly to the Americans. In various provinces the war was continued intermittently for a year after the appointment of a Civil Governor in July, 1901. This was not an auspicious beginning for the organization of a people into a peaceful community acknowledging allegiance to an alien power.

Secondly, there was, in the United States, a strong minority party that lost no opportunity to denounce the policy of the Government and to express sympathy with those arrayed in arms against it, and declared in party platform and in other ways its intention, should it come into power, to turn the Islands over to an independent government of their people. This not only prolonged the war, but when peace finally came, it encouraged a sullen-ness on the part of many Filipinos and a lack of interest in the progress and development of the existing government, that were discouraging. It offered the hope of immediate independence at the coming of every national election by the defeat of the Administration at the polls. This was not of assistance in carrying out a policy that depended for its working on the political education of the people by their cordial participation, first, in the new municipal and provincial governments, and finally in the election of a National Assembly. The result has been that during the educational process there has been a continuing controversy as to the political capacity of the Filipino people. It has naturally been easy to induce a majority of the electorate to believe that they are now capable of maintaining a stable government. All this has tended to divert the people's attention from the existing government, although their useful participation in that must measure their progress toward fitness for complete autonomy.

The impatience of the popular majority for further power may be somewhat mitigated as the extent of the political control which is placed in the hands of the people increases, and as they become more familiar with the responsibilities and the difficulties of actual power. The difference between the attitude of an irresponsible critic who has behind him the easily aroused prejudices of a people against an alien government, and that of one who attempts to formulate legislation which shall accomplish a definite purpose for the good of his own people is a healthful lesson for the ambitious statesman to learn.

Other formidable political obstacles had to be overcome. There still remained present in the situation in 1901 the smoldering ashes of the issues which had led the people to rebel against the power of Spain — I mean the prospective continuance of the influence of the regular religious orders in the parochial administration of the Roman Catholic Church in the Islands and their ownership of most valuable and extensive agricultural lands in the most populous provinces. The change of sovereignty to a Government which could exercise no control over the Church in its selection of its agents made the new régime powerless, by act or decree, to prevent the return of the friars to the parishes, and yet the people were disposed to hold the Government responsible whenever this was proposed. It would have been fraught with great danger of political disturbance. It was also essential that the religious orders should cease to be agricultural landlords in order to eliminate the agrarian question arising between them and sixty thousand tenants which had played so large a part in the previous insurrections against Spain. These results were to be attained without offending, or infringing upon the rights of, the Roman Catholic Church, the influence of which for good in the Islands could not be denied. Other political difficulties attending the transfer of a sovereignty from a Government in which the interests of the State and the Church were inextricably united to one in which they must be absolutely separated, I need not stop to elaborate. The religious and property controversies arising out of the Aglipayan schism, and the disturbances caused, added much to the burden of the Government.

The novelty of the task for the United States and her people, the lack of the existence of a trained body of colonial administrators and civil servants, the dependence for *a time upon men as government agents who had come out* in a spirit of adventure to the Islands and some of whom proved not to be fitted either by character or experience for the discharge of responsible public duties, gave additional cause for discouragement.

Another great difficulty in working out our policy in these Islands has been the reluctance of capitalists to invest money here. Political privileges, if unaccompanied by opportunities to better their condition, are not likely to produce permanent contentment among a people. Hence the political importance of developing the resources of these Islands for the benefit of its inhabitants. This can only be done by attracting capital. Capital must have the prospect of security in the investment and a certain return of profit before it will become available. The constant agitation for independence in the Islands, apparently supported by the minority party in the United States, and the *well-founded fear that an independent* Philippine government now established would not be permanent and stable have made capitalists chary of attempting to develop the natural resources of the Islands. The capital which has come has only come reluctantly and on terms less favorable to the public than would have been exacted under other conditions.

Another difficulty of the same character as the last in preventing material progress has been the failure of Congress to open the markets of the United States to the free admission of Philippine sugar and tobacco. In every other way Congress has shown its entire and generous sympathy with the policy of the Administration; and in this matter the popular branch of that body passed the requisite bill for the purpose by a large majority. Certain tobacco and sugar interests of the United States, however, succeeded in strangling the measure in the Senate committee. I have good reason for hope that in the next Congress we may be able to secure a compromise measure which shall restore the sugar and tobacco agriculture of the Islands to its former prosperity, and at the same time by limitations upon the amounts of importation allay the fears of injury on the part of the opponents of the measure. Still, the delay in this much-needed relief has greatly retarded the coming of prosperous times and has much discouraged supporters of our policy in America who have thought this indicated a lack of national purpose to make the present altruistic policy a success.

But the one thing that interfered with material progress in the Islands, more than all other causes put together, was the rinderpest which carried away from 75 to 80 per cent. of the cattle that were absolutely indispensable in cultivating, reaping, and disposing of the agricultural products upon which the Islands are wholly dependent. The extent of this terrible disaster can not be exaggerated and the Islands have not yet recovered from it. Attempts to remedy the evil by the importation of cattle from other countries have proved futile, and the Islands can not be made whole in this respect except by the natural reproduction of the small fraction of the animals that escaped destruction. This is not a matter of a year, or of two years or of three years, but a matter of a decade. Then, too, there were in these years surra, locusts, drought, destructive typhoons, cholera, bubonic plague and small-pox, ladronism, and pulajanism. The long period of disturbance, of guerrilla warfare and unrest, which interfered for years with the carrying on of the peaceful arts of agriculture and made it so easy for those who had been used to work in the fields to assume the wild and loose life of predatory bands claiming to be liberating armies, all made a burden for the community that it was almost impossible for it to bear.

When I consider all these difficulties, which I have rehearsed at too great length, and then take account of the present conditions in the Islands, it seems to me that they present an occasion for profound satisfaction and that they fully vindicate the policy which has been pursued.

How have we met the difficulties? In the first place, we have carried out with entire fidelity the promises of Presidents McKinley and Roosevelt in respect to the gradual extension of political control in the Government as the people should show themselves fit. In 1901 the Commission adopted the Municipal Code, which vested complete autonomy in the adult male citizen of every municipality in the Islands, except that of Manila, which for special reasons, like those which have prevailed with respect to the government of the city of Washington, was preserved for control by the Central Government. The electorate was limited to those who could speak English or Spanish, or who paid a tax of £15 a year, or who had filed municipal office under the Spanish régime, and did not exceed 20 per cent. of the total adult males of the population. Very shortly after this a form of provincial government was established in which the legislative and executive control of the province was largely vested in a provincial board consisting of a governor and treasurer and supervisor. Provision was made for the election of a governor and the appointment under civil-service rules of a treasurer and supervisor. Subsequently it was found that the government was too expensive and the office of supervisor was finally abolished, and after some four years the board was made to consist of a governor and treasurer, and a third member elected as the governor was, thus effecting popular autonomy in the provincial governments. And now comes the Assembly.

It is said by one set of critics, to whom I have already referred, that the franchise is the last privilege that ought to be granted in the development of a people into a self-governing community, and that we have put this into the hands of the Filipinos before they have shown themselves

13

to be industrially and in other ways capable of exercising
the self-restraint and conservatism of action which are
essential to political stability.   I can not agree with this
view.   The best political education is practice in the exercise of political power, unless the subject is so ignorant as
to be wholly blind to his own interests.   Hence the exercise of a franchise which is conferred only on those who
have qualifications of education or property that prove intelligence and substance, is likely to teach the electorate
useful political lessons.   The electorate under the Philippine law are sufficiently alive to their own interests to make
the exercise of political power a useful training for them,
while the power to be exercised is subject to such limitation
as not to be dangerous to the community.   More than this,
the granting of the franchise was most useful in producing
tranquillity among the people.   The policy has been vindicated by the fact.

The importance of the agency of the Army of the
United States in suppressing insurrection I would not
minimize in the least; but all who remember clearly the
succession of events from 1901 to 1903 will admit that
the return to peace and the acquiescence of the Filipino
people in American sovereignty were greatly influenced
and aided by the prospect held out to the Filipinos of
participation in the government of the Islands and a gradual extension of popular self-control.   Without this and
the confidence of the Filipino people in the good purposes
of the United States and the patience with which they
endured their many burdens that fate seemed to increase,

the progress which has been achieved would have been impossible.

Let us consider in some detail what progress has been made:

First. To repeat what I have said, the Islands are in a state of tranquillity. On this very day of the opening of the National Assembly, there has never been a time in the history of the Islands when peace and good order have prevailed more generally. The difficulties presented by the controversies arising with and concerning the Roman Catholic Church have either been completely settled or are in process of satisfactory adjustment on a basis of justice and equality.

Second. Most noteworthy progress has been made in the spread of general education. One of the obstacles to the development of this people speaking half a dozen or more different native dialects was a lack of a common language, which would furnish a medium of sympathetic touch with modern thought and civilization. The dense ignorance of a very large proportion of the people emphasized the necessity for a general educational system. English was the language of the sovereign power, English was the business language of the Orient, English was the language in which was thought and written the history of free institutions and popular government, and English was the language to which the common people turned with eagerness to learn. A system of education was built up, and to-day upward of half a million children are being taught to read, write, and recite English. It is not an exaggeration to assert that now more native Filipinos speak English than Spanish, although Spanish was the language of the ruling race in these Islands for more than two hundred and fifty years. English is not so beautiful as the Spanish language, but it is more likely to prove of use to the Filipinos for the reasons I have given. The strongest basis for our confidence in the future of the Filipino people is the eagerness with which the opportunities extended for education in English have been seized by the poor and ignorant parents of these Islands for their children. It is alike pathetic and encouraging.

I am not one of those who believe that much of the public money should be expended here for university or advanced education. Perhaps one institution merely to form a type of higher education may be established at Manila or at some other suitable place in the Islands, and special schools to develop needed scientific professions may be useful, but the great part of the public funds expended for education should be used in the spread of primary education and of industrial education — that education which shall fit young men to be good farmers, good mechanics, good skilled laborers, and shall teach them the dignity of labor and that it is no disgrace for the son of a good family to learn his trade and earn his livelihood by it. The higher education is well for those who can use it to advantage, but it too often fits a man to do things for which there is no demand, and unfits him for work which there are too few to do. The enlargement of opportunity for higher education may well await private beneficence or be postponed to a period when the calls upon the Island Treasury for other more important improvements have ceased.   We have laid the foundation of a primary and industrial educational system here which, if the same spirit continues in the Government, will prove to be the most lasting benefit which has been conferred on these Islands by Americans.

Third. We have introduced here a health department which is gradually teaching the people the necessity for sanitation.   In the years to come, when the great discoveries of the world are recited, that which will appear to have played as large a part as any in the world's progress in the current hundred years will be the discovery of proper sanitary methods for avoiding disease in the Tropics.   The introduction of such methods, the gradual teaching of the people the simple facts affecting hygiene, unpopular and difficult as the process of education has been, will prove to be another one of the great benefits given by Americans to this people.

The efforts of the Government have not been confined to preserving the health of the human inhabitants of these Islands, but have been properly extended to doing what can be done in the matter of the health of the domestic animals which is so indispensable to the material progress of the Islands.   The destruction by rinderpest, by surra, and by other diseases to which cattle and horses are subject, I have already dwelt upon.   Most earnest attention has been given by men of the highest scientific attainment to securing some remedy which will make such widespread disasters in the future impossible.   Much time and effort and money have been spent and much has been accomplished in this matter.   The people are being educated in the necessity for care of their cattle and for inviting in public aid at once when the dread rinderpest shows its presence.   Serums have been discovered that have been effective to immunize cattle, and while the disease has not disappeared, it is not too much to say that such an epidemic as that which visited the Islands in 1900, 1901, and 1902 is impossible.

Fourth. A judicial system has been established in the Islands which has taught the Filipinos the possibility of the independence of a judiciary.   This must be of enduring good to the people of the Islands.   The personnel of the judges is divided between Americans and Filipinos, both for the purpose of aiding the Americans to learn and administer civil law and of enabling the Filipinos to learn and administer justice according to a system prevailing in a country where the judiciary is absolutely independent of the executive or legislative branches of the Government. Charges have been made that individual judges and particular courts have not been free from executive control and have not been without prejudices arising from the race of the particular judge who sat in the court, but on the whole an impartial review of the six years' history of the administration of justice will show that the system has been productive of the greatest good and that right has been sustained without fear or favor.   It is entirely natural that a system which departs from the principles of that in which one has been educated should at times attract his severe animadversion, and as the system here administered partakes of two systems, it is subject to the criticism of those trained in each.

Another agency in the administration of justice has been the Constabulary. When I was here something more than two years ago, the complaints against that body were numerous, emphatic, and bitter. I promised, on behalf of the Philippine government and the Washington Administration, that close investigation should be made into the complaints and that if there was occasion for reform, that reform would be carried out. It gratifies me on my return to the Islands now to learn that a change has come, that the complaints against the Constabulary have entirely ceased, and that it is now conceded to be discharging with efficiency the function which it was chiefly created to perform, of sympathetically aiding the provincial governors and municipal authorities of the Islands in maintaining the peace of each province and each municipality, and that there is a thorough spirit of co-operation between the officers and men of the Constabulary and the local authorities.

In respect to the administration of justice by justices of the peace, reforms have been effected, but I am not sure that there is not still great room for improvement. This is one of the things that come home close to the people of the country, and is a subject that will doubtless address itself to the wise action and consideration of the National Assembly.

Fifth. We come to the matter of public improvements. The port of Manila has been made into a harbor which is now as secure as any in the Orient, and which, with *the docking facilities that are now being rapidly con-structed, will be as convenient and as free from charge* and burden as any along the Asiatic coast. The improve-ments in Iloilo and Cebu harbors, the other two important ports of the Islands, are also rapidly progressing. Road building has proceeded in the Islands, both at the instance of the Central Government and through the agency of the provinces. The difficulties of road building and road maintaining in the Philippines are little understood by those not familiar with the difficulty of securing proper material to resist the enormous wear and tear caused by the torrential downpours of the rainy season. Progress in this direction must necessarily be gradual, for the Is-lands are a poor country, comparatively speaking, and roads are expensive.

Early in the history of the Islands we began the con-struction of a road from Pangasinan to the mountains *of Benguet in order to bring within reach of the people* of the Islands that healthful region where the thermom-eter varies from 40 to 80 degrees, and in which all the diseases of the Tropics are much more easily subject to cure than in the lowlands. Had it been supposed that the road thus to be constructed would involve an ex-pense of nearly two millions of dollars, the work would not have been begun, but, now that the road has been constructed, I would not undo what has been done even if it were possible. As time progresses, the whole Province of Benguet will be settled; there will be made the homes of many educational institutions, of many sanitariums, and there will go, as transportation becomes cheaper, the Filipino people to obtain a change of air and acquire a renewed strength that is given to tropical peoples by a visit to the temperate zone.

When the Americans came to the Islands there was one railroad 120 miles long, and that was all. In spite of circumstances, which I have already detailed, making capital reluctant to come here, contracts have now been entered into, that are in the course of fulfillment, which in five years will give to the Islands a railroad mileage of 1,000 miles. The construction of these roads will involve the investment of twenty to thirty millions of dollars, and that in itself means an added prosperity to the country, additional demands for labor, and the quickening of all the nerves of trade. When the work is finished, it means a great additional profit to agriculture, a very great enlargement of the export capacity of the Islands, and a substantial elevation of the material condition of the people.

In the matter of municipal improvements, which directly concern the people, that which has taken place in Manila is most prominent. The improvement of the streets, the introduction of a satisfactory street railway system 35 miles in length, the improvement of the general appearance of the city and its hygienic condition, the construction of new waterworks and a new sewage system, all strike one who knew the city in 1900. The improvements of other municipalities in the Islands have not kept pace with those in Manila, and of course they were not so imperatively needed; but the epidemics of cholera and plague and smallpox which have prevailed have convinced those in authority of the necessity of bettering the water supply of all municipalities and for improving this by the sinking of artesian wells and other means, so that bad water, that frightful source of the transmission of disease, should be reduced to a minimum.

The government now maintains and operates a more complete system of posts, telephones, and telegraphs than ever before in the history of the Islands. Seventy-five per cent. of the 652 municipalities now established in these Islands have post-offices, in 235 of which there are now opened for business postal savings banks. The telegraph or telephone now connects all of the provincial capitals with Manila and more than 90 offices are now open for business. Appropriation has been made to provide for a system of rural free delivery. In less than one year of operation the Postal Savings Bank has deposits exceeding £600,000, and the number of Filipino depositors now exceeds 1,000, and the proportion of their deposits is steadily increasing.

Sixth. We have inaugurated a civil service law for the selection of civil servants upon the merit system. On the whole it has worked well. It has grown with our experience and has improved with the disclosure of its defects.

One of the burning questions which constantly presents itself in respect to the civil service of a Government like this is, how far it shall be American and how far Filipino. In the outset it was essential that most of the civil servants of the government should be Americans. The government was English speaking, and the practical difficulty of having subordinates who did not speak that language prevented large employment of Filipinos. Then their lack of knowledge of their American governmental and business methods had the same tendency. The avowed policy of the government has been to employ Filipinos wherever, as between them and Americans, the Filipinos can do equally good work. This has given rise to frequent and bitter criticism, because it has been improperly assumed that every time that there has been a vacancy, it could be filled by a Filipino.

There are two great advantages in the employment of Filipinos — one is that this is the government of the Filipinos and they ought to be employed where they can be, and the other is that their employment is a matter of economy for the government, because they are able to live more cheaply and economically in the Islands than Americans and so can afford to receive less salary. There has therefore been a constant reduction of American employees and an increase of Filipinos. This has not been without its disadvantage, because it makes competent American employees feel an uncertainty of tenure, and materially affects their hope of promotion and their interest in the government of which they are a part. This disadvantage I believe can be largely obviated.

There are many American civil servants in this government who have rendered most loyal, difficult, and efficient service, in season and out of season, through plague and epidemic, in sickness and in health, in full sympathy with the purposes and policy of the government. Without them our government would have been a complete failure. They will never receive adequate reward. Their interest in their work has prevented their return to their native land, where the same energy and efficiency would have earned them large return. They are most valuable public servants who have done a work that, had they done it in the English colonial service or at home, would have been certain to secure to them a permanent salary and entire freedom from anxiety as to the future. I would be glad to see adopted a system of permanent tenure and retirement on pensions for the small and higher classes of civil employees. Their continuance in the government indefinitely is a public necessity. I sincerely hope the Philippine Assembly will exhibit its spirit of justice and public interest to the point of concurring in such a measure even though this, at present, will be of benefit to more Americans than Filipinos.

Seventh. In the progress which has been made, I should mention the land system, the provision for homestead settlement, for free patents, and for perfecting of imperfect titles by land registration. The homestead settlements under the law were very few for several years, but I am delighted to learn that during 1907 they reached 4,000 and the free patents applied for were 10,600. It is probable that the machinery for land registration, though necessary, is too expensive, and it will be for you to decide whether, in view of the great public benefit that good land titles will bring to the country, it may not be wise to reduce the cost of registration to the landowner and charge the expense to the government. Capital will not be advanced to the farmer unless his title is good, and the great benefit of an agricultural bank can never be realized until the registration of titles is greatly increased.

This naturally brings me to the subject of the Agricultural Bank. After much effort Congress was induced to pass an act which authorizes the Philippine Government to invite the organization of such a bank with private capital by guaranteeing an annual income of a certain percentage on the capital invested for thirty years. Negotiations have been opened and are pending with some American capitalists in the hope of securing the establishment of such a bank.

The condition of agriculture in the Islands while generally much improved in the last three years is still unsatisfactory in many parts of the Islands, due not only to the continued scarcity of cattle but also to the destructive effect of the typhoon of 1905 upon the hemp culture. This has properly led to the suspension of the land tax for another year and the meeting of half the deficit in provincial and municipal treasuries thus produced, out of the central treasury.

The production of rice has, however, materially increased. It is also a source of satisfaction to note that the exports from the Islands, which are wholly agricultural, are larger in value by half a million gold dollars than ever in the history of the Islands. One of the chief duties of this Assembly is to devote its attention and practical knowledge to measures for the relief of agriculture.

Eighth. The financial condition of the Philippine government is quite satisfactory, and so, too, is the state of the money and currency of the Islands. There is a bonded indebtedness for the purchase of the friar lands amounting to $7,000,000, for the waterworks and sewage of Manila of $3,000,000, and for public works amounting to $3,500,000. Sinking funds have been established for all of these. The price paid for the friar lands was a round one and may result, after the lands are disposed of, in some net pecuniary loss to the Government, but the political benefit of the purchase was a full justification. The lands will be disposed of to the tenants as rapidly as the public interest will permit. The only other permanent obligation of the Government is the contingent liability on the guaranty of interest for thirty years on the bonds issued to construct 300 miles of railroad in the Visayas. We may reasonably hope that this obligation will soon reduce itself to nothing when the roads come into successful operation. The Governor-General reports to me that the budget for 1908 will show an income and surplus from last year, without any land tax, from which it will be possible to pay all the interest on the bonds and guaranties, all the insular expenses, the proper part of the expenses of Manila, $2,000,000 in permanent improvements, and still have on hand for contingencies $1,000,000. I am further advised that the condition of most of the provinces is excellent in respect to income and surplus.

It has been necessary to reduce the silver in the Philippine peso to keep its intrinsic value within the value of 50 cents, gold, at which it is the duty of the Government to maintain it, and this change is being rapidly carried through without much difficulty. The benefit to the people, and especially the poorer and working classes, in the establishment of the gold standard is very great. It eliminates a gambling feature from the business of the Islands that always worked for the detriment of the Philippine people. We are just carrying through a settlement with the Spanish-Filipino Bank which I hope will provide a means of safely adding to the currency of the country and increasing its elasticity.

In recounting these various evidences of progress in the last six years I am not unmindful that the business of the Islands is still far from prosperous. Indeed, it is noteworthy that so much progress has been made in the face of continued business depression due to the various causes I have elsewhere enumerated; but it is a long lane that has no turning and I look forward to the next decade in the history of the Islands as one which will be as prosperous as this one has been the reverse. Business is reviving, the investment of foreign capital is gradually increasing, and only one thing is needed to insure great material improvement, and that is the continuance of conservatism in this Government. I feel confident that the inauguration of this Assembly, instead of ending this conservatism as the prophets of evil would have it, will strengthen it.

Before discussing the Assembly, I wish to give attention to one report that has been spread to the four corners of the globe, and which, if credited, might have a pernicious effect in these Islands. I refer to the statement that the American Government is about to sell the Islands to some Asiatic or European power. Those who credit such a report little understand the motives which actuated the American people in accepting the burden of this Government. The majority of the American people are still in favor of carrying out our Philippine policy as a great altruistic work. They have no selfish object to secure. There might be a grim and temporary satisfaction to those of us who have been subjected to severe criticism for our alleged lack of liberality toward the Filipino people and of sympathy with their aspirations, in witnessing the rigid governmental control which would be exercised over the people of the Islands under the colonial policy of any one of the powers to whom it is suggested that we are about to sell them; but that would not excuse or justify the gross violation, by such a sale of the implied obligation which we have entered into with the Filipino people. That obligation presents only two alternatives for us — one is a permanent maintenance of a popular government of law and order under American control, and the other, a parting with such control to the people of the Islands themselves after they have become fitted to maintain a government in which the right of all the inhabitants to life, liberty, and property shall be secure. I do not hesitate to pronounce the report that the Government contemplates the transfer of these Islands to any foreign power as utterly without foundation. It has never entered the mind of a single person in the Government responsible for the Administration. Such a sale must be the subject of a treaty, and the treaty power in the Government of the United States is exercised by the President and the Senate, and only upon the initiative of the President. Hence an Executive declaration upon this subject is more authoritative than an Executive opinion as to probable Congressional action.

Coming now to the real occasion of this celebration, the installation of the National Assembly, I wish, for purposes of clearness, to read the section of the organic act under which this Assembly has been elected:

That two years after the completion and publication of the census, in case such condition of general and complete peace with recognition of the authority of the United States shall have continued in the territory of said Islands not inhabited by Moros or other non-Christian tribes and such facts shall have been certified to the President by the Philippine Commission, the President upon being satisfied thereof shall direct said Commission to call, and the Commission shall call, a general election for the choice of delegates to a popular assembly of the people of said Territory in the Philippine Islands, which shall

14

be known as the Philippine Assembly. After said Assembly shall have convened and organized, all the legislative power heretofore conferred on the Philippine Commission in all that part of said Islands not inhabited by Moros or other non-Christian tribes shall be vested in a legislature consisting of two houses — the Philippine Commission and the Philippine Assembly. Said Assembly shall consist of not less than fifty nor more than one hundred members, to be apportioned by said Commission among the provinces as nearly as practicable according to population: *Provided,* That no province shall have less than one member: *And provided further,* That provinces entitled by population to more than one member may be divided into such convenient districts as the said Commission may deem best.

Public notice of such division shall be given at least ninety days prior to such election, and the elections shall be held under rules and regulations to be prescribed by law. The qualification of electors in such election shall be the same as is now provided by law in case of electors in municipal elections. The members of Assembly shall hold office for two years from the first day of January next following their election, and their successors shall be chosen by the people every second year thereafter. No person shall be eligible to such election who is not a qualified elector of the election district in which he may be chosen, owing allegiance to the United States, and twenty-five years of age.

The Legislature shall hold annual sessions, commencing on the first Monday of February in each year and continuing not exceeding ninety days thereafter (Sundays and holidays not included) : *Provided,* That the first meeting of the Legislature shall be held upon the call of the Governor within ninety days after the first election: *And provided further,* That if at the termination of any session the appropriations necessary for the support of the Government shall not have been made, an amount equal to the sums appropriated in the last appropriation bills for such purposes shall be deemed to be appropriated; and until the Legislature shall act in such behalf the Treasurer may, with the advice of the Governor, make the payments necessary for the purposes aforesaid.

The Legislature may be called in special session at any time by the Civil Governor for general legislation, or for action on such specific subjects as he may designate. No special session shall continue longer than thirty days, exclusive of Sundays.

The Assembly shall be the judge of the elections, returns, and qualifications of its members. A majority shall constitute a quorum to do business, but a smaller number may adjourn from day to day and may be authorized to compel the attendance of absent members. It shall choose its Speaker and other officers, and the salaries of its members and officers shall be fixed by law. It may determine the rule of its proceedings, punish its members for disorderly behavior, and with the concurrence of two-thirds expel a member. It shall keep a journal of its proceedings, which shall be published, and the yeas and nays of the members on any question shall, on the demand of one-fifth of those present, be entered on the journal.

I can well remember when that section was drafted in the private office of Mr. Root in his house in Washington. Only he and I were present. I urged the wisdom of the concession and he yielded to my arguments and the section as then drafted differed but little from the form it has to-day. It was embodied in a bill presented to the House and passed by the House, was considered by the Senate, was stricken out in the Senate, and was only restored after a conference, the Senators in the conference consenting to its insertion with great reluctance. I had urged its adoption upon both committees, and, as the then Governor of the Islands, had to assume a responsibility as guarantor in respect to it which I have never sought to disavow. I believe that it is a step and a logical step in the carrying out of the policy announced by President McKinley and that it is not too radical in the interest of the people of the Philippine Islands. Its effect is to give to a representative body of the Filipinos a right to initiate legislation, to modify, amend, shape, or defeat legislation proposed by the Commission. The power to obstruct by withholding appropriations is taken away from the Assembly, because if there is not an agreement as to appropriations between the Commission and the Assembly, then the appropriations of the previous year will be continued; but the power with this exception, absolutely to veto all legislation and initiate and shape proposed laws is a most substantial one. The concurrence of the Assembly in useful legislation can not but command popular support for its enforcement; the discussion in the Assembly and its attitude must be informing to the Executive and to the other branch of the legislature, the Commission, of what are the desires of people. The discharge of the functions of the Assembly must give to the chosen representatives of the Philippine electorate a most valuable education in the responsibilities and difficulties of practical government. It will put them where they must investigate not only the theoretical wisdom of proposed measures, but also the question whether they can be practically enforced and whether, where expense is involved, they are of sufficient value to justify the imposition of a financial burden upon the people to carry them out. It will bring the members of the Assembly as representatives of the people into close relations with the Executive, who will be most anxious to preserve a harmony essential to efficient government and progressive, useful measures of reform.

Critics who do not sympathize with our Philippine policy, together with those who were reluctant to grant this measure of a legislative assembly to the Philippine people at this time, have not been slow to comment on the result of the election as an indication that we are going too fast. I differ entirely from the view of these critics as to the result of this election and the inferences to be drawn from it.

The small total vote as compared with the probable number of the total electorate shows that a considerable majority of those entitled to vote did not exercise the

privilege.   This indicates either an indifference or a timidity that we would not find in a people more used to the
wielding of political power; but it affords no reason for
supposing that as the Assembly proves its usefulness and
important power, the ratio of votes to the total electorate
will not rapidly increase.

The election was held without disturbance.   In many
districts there were bitter controversies, but the complaints of fraud, violence, or bribery are insignificant.
Although the Government was supposed to favor one
party, and was subject to much criticism in the campaign,
no one has been heard to say that the power of the
Executive was exerted in any way improperly to influence
the election.   This furnishes a good object lesson.

A popular majority of those who exercise the franchise have voted for representatives announcing a desire
for the immediate separation of the Islands from the
United States.   This majority is a small one when the
returns are carefully considered and is much less than the
ratio between the party representatives in the Assembly
would lead one to suppose.   However, assuming a decided majority for immediate independence, the result
is one which I thought possible even while I was urging
the creation of the Assembly.   It is not a disappointment.
If it indicated that a majority of the representatives
elected by the people were a body of irreconcilables determined to do nothing but obstruct the present government,
it would indeed be discouraging, but I am confident from
what I know and hear of the gentlemen who have been

elected that while many of them differ from me as to the
time in which the people of the Islands will become fit for
complete self-government, most of them have an earnest
desire that this government shall be carried on in the interests of the people of the Philippines and for their benefit, and shall be made for that purpose as effective as possible. They are thus generally conservative. Those
whose sole aim is to hold up the government to execration,
to win away the sympathy of the people in order to promote disturbance and violence, have no proper place in
this Assembly. Had the Filipino people sent such a majority, then I should have to admit that the granting of
the Assembly was a mistake and that Congress must abol-
ish it.

It has been reported in the Islands that I was coming
here for the purpose of expressing, in bitter and threatening words, my disappointment at the result of the election.
Nothing could be further from my purpose, nothing could
be less truly descriptive of my condition of mind. I am
here, filled with a spirit of friendship and encouragement
for these members, who now enter upon a new field in
which they have much to learn, but where everything
can be learned and this duty most efficiently discharged if
they are led by an earnest desire to assist and guide the
government in aiding the people. I have no right to appeal to the members of this Assembly to conduct themselves in the discharge of their high duties in a manner to
vindicate me in the responsibility I assumed in urging
Congress to establish this Assembly, because they should

find a stronger reason for so doing in their sworn duty; but it is not inappropriate for me to touch on this personal feature of the situation, because my attitude has been misconstrued and my sympathetic interest in, and hope for, the success and usefulness of this National Assembly have not been properly stated.

I venture to point out a number of things that you will learn in the course of your legislative experience. One is that the real object of a legislature is to formulate specific laws to accomplish specific purposes and reforms and to suppress specific evils; that he makes a useful speech who studies the question which he discusses and acquires and imparts practical information by which the remedies offered can be seen to be applicable to the evil complained of; that the office of a legislator for a great country like this is one that can be discharged conscientiously only by the use of great labor, careful, painstaking investigation and hard work in the preparation of proposed measures. One of the most necessary traits in a successful legislator or executive is patience. Where the sudden change in that which is regarded as a wrong system may paralyze a necessary arm of the government, ways and means must be devised to bring about the change gradually. There will be a temptation to take up measures which will invite the support of popular prejudice rather than measures which will really accomplish good for the body politic. Such a temptation exists in older legislative bodies than this, and we cannot hope that it will be absent from here; but, in the end, the man who exerts the most influence in

this body and among the people will be the man who de-
votes most conscientiously his time to acquiring the information upon which legislation should be based and in explaining it to his colleagues and his people. The man who
is seeking to put his adversary or the government in an embarrassing situation may win temporary triumph; but the
man who himself feels responsibility of government, and
who, while not concealing or failing to state the evils which
he considers to exist in the government, is using every
effort to reform those evils, will ultimately be regarded
as the benefactor of his country.

I have not the time and doubtless not the information
which would justify me in pointing out to the Assembly
the various subjects-matter to which they may profitably
devote their attention with a view to the formulation of
useful legislation. They will properly feel called upon
to devote their attention to public economy in the matter
of the numerous governmental bureaus which have been
made the subject of criticism. It is quite possible that
they may find in their investigations into these matters
reasons for cutting off officers and bureaus, but I sincerely
hope no such effort will be made until a full investigation
is had into the utility of the functions which the bureau
performs and the possibility of dispensing with them. I
can remember that while I was Governor there was much
outcry against the extravagance of maintaining certain
bureaus which in subsequent crises in the public welfare
proved their great usefulness beyond cavil. Of course we
shall encounter in this investigation and discussion a rad-

ical difference between legislators and others as to the function which a government in these Islands ought to perform. It is entirely easy to run an economical government if all that you do is to maintain order and if no steps are taken to promote health, to promote education, and to promote the general welfare of the inhabitants. It is of course the object of the person charged with the duty of governing a country to reach the golden mean— that is, to make governmental provisions for the welfare of the people without imposing too great a tax burden for the purpose. The taxes in this country are imposed partly by the Legislature and partly by Congress. The former will constantly have your attention. In so far as the welfare of the country is affected by the latter, to-wit, the customs duties, and can be improved by a change of them, it would be wise for the Legislature to devote much time and thought to recommendations to Congress as to how they should be changed, for I doubt not that Congress will be willing and anxious to take such steps as may commend themselves to the people of the Islands in the matter of adjustment of duties, having regard to the raising of sufficient revenue on the one hand and to as little interference with useful freedom of trade as possible on the other.

As you shall conduct your proceedings and shape your legislation on patriotic, intelligent, conservative, and useful lines, you will show more emphatically than in any other way your right and capacity to take part in the government and the wisdom of granting to your Assembly and to the people that elected you, more power. There are still many possible intervals or steps between the power you now exercise and complete autonomy. Will this Assembly and its successors manifest such an interest in the welfare of the people and such clear-headed comprehension of their sworn duty as to call for a greater extension of political power to this body and to the people whose representative it is? Or shall it, by neglect, obstruction, and absence of useful service, make it necessary to take away its existing powers on the ground that they have been prematurely granted? Upon you falls this heavy responsibility. I am assured that you will meet it with earnestness, courage, and credit.

In closing, I can only renew my congratulations upon the auspicious beginning of your legislative life in a fair election, and to express to you my heartfelt sympathy in the work which you are about to undertake, and my confidence that you will justify in what you do, and do not do, the recommendations of those who are responsible for that section in the organic act that has given life to this Assembly.

CHAPTER XVII

THE ARMY OF THE REPUBLIC

ADDRESS AT THE UNION LEAGUE CLUB, CHICAGO, FEBRU-
ARY 22, 1906

Among the many important political topics which the
birthday of George Washington suggests is the Army of
the Republic. Many of the years of his life which were
most valuable to his country were spent in the command
of an army which won for us our independence from
Great Britain and which was the immediate predecessor of
the army of the United States. During all his long career
he gave great attention to the public need there was for
the maintenance of a small but efficient regular army, and
the last office which he held under the government of the
United States that he had done so much to create and
maintain, was the office of Lieutenant-General and
Commander-in-Chief of the army of the United States,
which he held from the 3d of July, 1798, until his life
went out with the century on the 14th of December, 1799.

The first question which suggests itself is — Does the
Republic need an army? There is an indefinite, elusive
but influential impression in the minds of many that there
is something in a regular army inconsistent with the purposes of a republic. It derives its force from the uses

266

to which regular or standing armies have been put in maintaining governments over unwilling people. The organization of a republic, however, does not prevent the possibility of war, as our history has already clearly shown. . . . Making every concession which history justifies in favor of the peaceful character and the peaceful tendency of a republic, he is a very unwise statesman who urges upon the people a policy which will reduce the efficiency and size of the army below that which the experience of the republic has taught was necessary for its safety and progress.

In this republic we need an army for three purposes: first, as essential to any satisfactory system of national defense; second, as an indispensable instrument in carrying out our established international policy; third, which I may say is the least important function, the suppression of insurrection and civil strife. Taking up these in their order, let us quote from Washington. In 1793, while he was still President, he used these words:

" Offensive operations, oftentimes, are the surest, if not in some cases, the only means of defense."

.   .   .   .

" It has been, very properly, the policy of our government to cultivate peace. But, in contemplating the possibility of our being driven to unqualified war, it will be wise to anticipate, that frequently, the most effectual way to defend is to attack."

Again he said:

" I cannot recommend measures for the fulfillment of

our duties to the rest of the world without pressing the necessity of placing ourselves in a condition of complete defense and of exacting from them the fulfillment of their duties toward us."

.   .   .   .

" To be prepared for war is one of the most effectual means of preserving peace."

Again:

" A free people ought not only to be armed but disciplined. To this end a uniform and well digested plan is requisite."

In his Farewell Address he advised his countrymen to remember " that timely disbursements to prepare for danger, frequently prevented much greater disbursements to repel it," and also advised them to take " care always to keep themselves, by suitable establishments, in a respectable defensive posture."

John Adams, his successor as President, said that " the national defense is the cardinal duty of a statesman."

Secondly, we have taken the position with respect to the republics established in this country in Central and South America and the West Indies, which is approved by both the great national parties and which has been repeatedly announced as the policy of the government by various Presidents and Secretaries of State. I allude to the Monroe Doctrine. This is not a doctrine sustained by any principles of international law; it is a governmental policy which this government believes to be essential for its own interests and well for the interests of the countries whose integrity it protects.   Whatever the motive, whatever the purpose, the assertion involved must rest for its sanction, not upon international law acquiesced in by all civilized nations, but rather upon the power to enforce it of the nation which asserts it.   How could we maintain such a doctrine if it should ever be questioned in the strenuous race for trade and for colonization that now is rife among the European powers?   Could we do it otherwise than by an expeditionary force to the country invaded for the purpose of assisting the local forces in repelling the invader?   It is true that our navy, enlarged as it is, would discharge a most useful function in the defense of the invaded country, but it could make but little headway against hostile forces landed therein, and after that, the only method of asserting our international policy would be by the use of the army of the United States.

Third, in the matter of the suppression of insurrection and civil strife; during the great Rebellion, of course the necessity for raising an immense army for this purpose was shown, but I do not conceive that under present conditions in this country there is any probability of domestic insurrection which will require more than the use of the improved National Guard of the States, by the State authorities themselves.

In the popular consideration of the necessity for an army there enters a feeling, illogical as it may seem, that an army in time of peace is not maintained and administered to be used for a war.   There seems to be an impression that it exists merely for show, like the mace which is carried before the Speaker of the House of Commons, or the truncheon of a field-marshal, or the scepter of a king, that it is to be regarded only as a symbol of power, the real instrument of which is to be created after the war shall begin. This conception of an army in time of peace has in the past led a usually practical and hard-headed people like the Americans to the most absurd military policy. An army is not for ceremony; an army is not a mere symbol of future power to be developed. If there were no possibility of war; if we could be guaranteed a continuous peace, the army should be disbanded and its great cost to the government should cease. But it is because peace cannot be guaranteed; it is because we must secure peace by being ready for war that we have an army, and therefore the army is not to be looked at — it is to make war. Now if an army is to make war, if that is the sole ground for its maintenance, then does it not seem a mere truism that the expenditure should be adapted to make it useful in war? Of course no one desires war. "War is hell" and should be avoided — not at all cost, but by making every honorable concession possible to escape its disastrous consequences. But the conditions which surround national life as between nations have not reached a point in the progress of civilization when war and the fear of war do not play a large part in determining the policies of governments. The voice of the United States in favor of international justice is much more weighty when it is known to have a good navy and good army to enforce its views and defend its rights.

If, now, an army exists only to make war, the people whose army it is, if they are a practical people, should bring that army to a state of the greatest efficiency possible to vindicate its existence when occasion arises, and accomplish the purpose of its creation. The existence of an *efficient army may prevent war without actual hostilities,* by convincing the threatening power of the futility or seriousness of a contest.

The history of this country since the beginning of the Revolutionary War shows that during at least one-fourth of the life of the country the Government has had a war on its hands in some part of its dominions. It is therefore most unwise to prophesy as to what may happen in this respect in the future. *The only lamp by which our steps can be guided is the lamp of experience,* and a prudent nation should accept the recurrence of wars in our history as an evidence of the wisdom of Washington's advice in respect to the preparation of the national defense. But the people of this country and the government of this country down to the time of the Spanish War had pursued a policy which seemed utterly to ignore the lessons of the past. By the exercise of national parsimony and a prejudice against the efficiency of an army, the making of proper plans for the organization of national volunteers, and the drill and mobilization of the militia, the government and the people were compelled to assume the responsibility for great losses of life and the expenditure of immense treasure, a large part of which might have been avoided, had proper and economical

15

measures been adopted for the maintenance of a small but efficient regular army and the due preparation in time of peace for the speedy organization and mobilization of a volunteer and militia force.

Take the War of 1812. The regular army at the outbreak in June, 1812, was 6,744 strong. Great Britain had in Canada less than 4,500 regulars. If our military force had been adequate to the country's needs, we could have stepped into Canada and possessed ourselves of that country easily and at first. But because of our weakness we were for a time disgracefully beaten, and the war was drawn out so that before its conclusion we could reckon, in addition to the humiliation suffered, that we had put in the field from first to last, 527,000 men; and that while in the twenty-one years preceding the aggregate cost of the War Department was but $35,669,000, it was for the five years following $82,627,000, and in addition thereto we have paid to pensioners on account of that war a sum approaching $50,000,000. An adequate force of regulars, if it had not prevented the war entirely, would have cut it short and saved life, money and humiliation. Illustrations from every war in which this country has been engaged, and notably the great Civil War, would enforce the principle even more strongly than the War of 1812.

It is a fact, whether the American citizens realize it or not, that time is indispensable to the making of good soldiers. Our own sad experience proves this proposition. The lessons of history should forbid us to stand in an atmosphere of illusion respecting the remoteness of

war and the efficacy of a brave but unorganized people
to grapple successfully with another nation equally brave
but better organized.   We must have forces trained and
ready to enable us to meet a possible foe with some chance
of success.   We cannot and should not maintain a large
regular army, but for a nation of eighty millions, or,
counting in the people who live in our dependencies, nearly
ninety millions of people, a regular army of 100,000 men
is a small force, considering especially the fact of the remoteness of the Philippines, the Isthmus of Panama, Porto
Rico and Alaska.   It is a less percentage of the population than was the army in Washington's time, in Jeffer-
son's time, or indeed in Madison's time.   In addition to
the regular army, there should be a provision for an efficient reserve of national volunteers, and such a plan for
the co-operation of the militia forces of the States with the
Federal Government and its military establishment as to
make that force able to repel invasion and constitute an
effective part of our national defense.

How has it come about that the people in America,
strong, intelligent, practical, masterful and warlike, have
adopted such a military policy, or lack of policy, in times
past as to have brought about the enormous loss of life
and money which might have been avoided by the adoption of merely reasonable precautions to secure an adequate military force in case of national emergency?   The
reasons are not far to seek, and are continually manifesting themselves at every stage of our political life.   In the
first place there are strong Anglo-Saxon traditions against

a standing army. The abuses which have been perpetrated against a people by such an army, our people do not forget. So deeply impressed are they that they even object to the maintenance of a force so small in proportion to the size of the country that the suggestion of its use to subjugate the people would be ridiculous.

Again, our geographical position, three thousand miles from the European shores, and six or seven thousand miles from the Asiatic shores, has given us a sense of security against foreign attack, which was much more justified in Washington's time than it is to-day, because the perilous and slow navigation of the ocean has now been succeeded by the quick transportation of great ocean liners which could land an army corps on our shores, if undefended by army and navy, in less than ten days after it had left its home port. Nevertheless, while this magnificent isolation does greatly reduce the necessity for elaborate preparation for war by a large standing army, it does not dispense with the necessity for having " a small but a good army," as Washington once phrased it.

Another reason for our failure to make proper preparation has been our confidence in ourselves and in our power of quickly adapting circumstances to meet any national emergency. So far has that carried some of our public men that they have been deliberately blind to the commonest and most generally accepted military principles and they have been misled by the general success or good luck which has attended us in most of our wars. They have maintained, and properly maintained, that the army of the Union, at the close of the Civil War, was as thoroughly drilled, seasoned and as brave as any army that ever marched. Were they not volunteers? Were they not the outgrowth of militia, and did they not finally bring peace to this country and subdue civil strife of proportions which the world had never before seen? Most of the men who constituted that army were called volunteers and bore the name of the States in which they were enlisted. As it was then, so it will be in the future wars, and the Republic will have at its back millions of freemen who can be depended upon to rise to its defense in case of emergency. If we once raised such an army as we did raise, could we not do it again? In the enthusiasm of these glowing questions and periods, the awful sacrifice of life and money which we had to undergo during the four years in order to train our Civil War veterans and to produce that army is entirely forgotten, and the country is lulled into the utterly unfounded assurance that a volunteer enlisted to-day, or a militiaman enrolled to-morrow, can in a week or a month be made an effective soldier. More than this, the fact that in the Civil War each side labored under the burden of having to use raw levies at first, while in any foreign war we might have, our troops would have to encounter at once a trained and disciplined force, is entirely ignored.

A fourth reason for our failure to prepare in times past has been the cost of our armies, whether regular or volunteer. Our regular army to-day amounts in effective force to about 60,000 men, and it costs us in round numbers about $72,000,000 to sustain our military establishment. In addition to this we are carrying a load of pensions for our Civil War veterans, and our Spanish War veterans, amounting to about $150,000,000. It is entirely natural for the representatives of the people in Congress to hesitate to increase a military establishment so expensive as compared with other nations. The lesson from the pension fund, however, instead of being, as it naturally is, a restraint upon expenditure to secure an efficient army, ought, if historically and critically considered, to be a warning against the lack of preparation, for the extent of that pension roll is itself the greatest exponent of the fatuity of a policy of insufficient national defense. The preparation of an army, except in times of threatening war, is the preparation for a contingency supposed to be remote. There are no advocates of the army, no strong popular feeling in favor of it. It thus has happened that instead of an intelligent economy, a short-sighted parsimony has been too often practiced in respect to it. After the emergency arises, and when it is too late for economical preparation, then the legislature opens the treasury by appropriations and provisions of the greatest liberality to meet the necessities which only time and thorough preparation could properly and economically meet. . . .

In 1901 was enacted the new Army Bill which gave us the present army organization of 15 regiments of cavalry, a corps of artillery amounting to about 18,000 men, and 30 regiments of infantry, together with such Philippine scouts, not exceeding 12,000, as the President might feel

justified in enlisting in the Philippine Islands. The act
provides that the total enlisted force of the line of the
army, together with such native force, shall not exceed
at any one time 100,000. Since the passage of the act
the regular army has been reduced so that it now does
not exceed, including the Philippine scouts, 65,000; but
it is much the most efficient regular army and is organized
on much the most efficient plan that we have ever had in
this country. The reduction in the total has not been by
cutting off regiments, but by reducing the size of the companies. In other words, by making the army more or less
a skeleton of what it will be, should occasion arise for
its enlargement. By the rapid recruitments of the skele-
tonized companies of this force so as to increase the total
to 100,000, by the organization of a reserve force of men
who have served regular terms of enlistments, we should
have a force with trained troops of 150,000 in a short
time, and to this might be added at least 100,000 and
probably 150,000 of the organized militia of the States,
armed, equipped and drilled according to the regulations
of the regular army. This would be a much more formidable and better trained force than the United States was
ever able to put in the field on such short notice before.

The cavalry regiments, if increased to their full strength,
would be enough for an army of 180,000, for the ordinary proportion of cavalry to infantry in a fighting force
need not be more than 10 per cent. It would seem wiser
for us to increase our field artillery and our coast artillery,
because the needed additional troops in these branches of

the service, like the cavalry, it would take a much longer
time to train than the infantry.   In other words, the regular army should be regarded as only a skeleton, and those
parts which it would take long to organize and train
should be much larger in proportion on the peace establishment than they would be in time of war.   The infantry of course is the most important part of every army,
but infantry regiments can be prepared in one year where
it takes two or three to prepare cavalry and artillery.
I am glad to say that we have now as fine small arms and
as efficient coast guns and field artillery as there are in
the world.   Plans have been matured for the further improvement of our coast defenses, the completion of which
will involve the expenditure of about $50,000,000 more
for the defenses of the United States proper, and $22,-
000,000 for the defenses of the Philippines, Hawaii,
Panama and Porto Rico.   Of course these new defenses
will not be built all at once.   It suffices to say that we
have a definite plan towards which we are working, and
which we may be hopeful will ultimately be treated by
Congress as a proper plan to pursue.

I think it is true that there is no general military school
in the world covering all the branches necessary for the
foundation of a military education more satisfactory and
thorough than the Military Academy at West Point.
This is now supplemented in the army by garrison schools
in which the younger army officers are instructed in the
fundamental principles of the art of war and their efficiency is noted.   From these schools are selected men to

enter the General Service and Staff College at Fort Leavenworth, the School of Application for Cavalry and Field Artillery at Fort Riley, the Artillery School at Fort Monroe, or the Ordnance School at Sandy Hook, and finally, after an exceptional excellence has been shown at any of these schools, candidates are selected for the War College, which exercises general supervision over all the graduate education of the army, and in which the students are made to co-operate and assist the General Staff in the duty of working out the military problems for defense and attack by our military forces. The office of the General Staff is not to command the army. It is chiefly advisory. It has to work out the plans of campaign both for defense and attack in accordance with the possibilities of future development. Its function is to advise the President and Secretary of War and to propose plans for improvement of the present military establishment, toward which we may constantly work in the perfection of our military machine. The General Staff will necessarily give continuity and consistency to the policies of the War Department, and that cannot but exercise the most healthful influence on both the executive and legislative course with respect to the army.

We have on the whole a very fine body of regular army officers. No man who has had to come in contact with them, to know their high sense of duty, to know their interest in their profession, and the earnestness with which they are pursuing its studies, can have but the greatest respect for them. We have had to supplement the gradu-

ates of West Point with a large number appointed from
civil life, but the garrison schools and the graduate schools
in the various courses have done wonders in fitting the
non-graduates of West Point as officers. There are no
better officers, no better men, in any army than we can
raise in America. We are a warlike people. Most pri-
vates have an independence and a self-reliance that fit
them to adapt themselves to different situations, and there
are no braver men. But they must know how to shoot
straight, they must know how to move at the word of
command, they must understand all the duties of a
soldier which grow more complicated with modern
guns and modern methods. They can not know
it intuitively. We have no right as a nation to ask our
citizens to expose themselves as enlisted men in battle without reducing the chances of disaster and death by proper
military education of their officers and proper military
training of the men.

The great deficiency among the commanding officers of
our army is in their lack of experience in the management
of large bodies of troops. The major-generals and the
brigadier-generals under the present system command territorial divisions and departments and are not learning
needed lessons in handling and maneuvering troops in
large bodies. This can only be attained by the concentration of our troops in a comparatively small number of
large posts, so that brigadiers, instead of commanding
departments, shall command brigades, and major-generals,
instead of commanding territorial divisions, shall com-

mand tactical divisions. . . . The establishment of summer camps and the union for maneuvers of the regular soldiers with the militia will add another means of drilling our general officers in grand strategy and the art of war.

I hope we may never have another war. But our experience in the past does not justify such a hope. It is our duty, therefore, if we would be wise in our generation, to make provision for a comparatively small regular army and efficient reserve of volunteers, and an adequate and co-operating force of State militia. In this way we shall follow closely the advice of Washington, given while he was President, in saying:

"The United States ought not to indulge a persuasion that, contrary to the order of human events, they will forever keep at a distance those painful appeals to arms with which the history of every nation abounds.

" There is rank due to the United States among nations, which will be withheld, if not absolutely lost, by the reputation of weakness.

" If we desire to avoid insult, we must be able to repel it.

"If we desire to secure peace, one of the most powerful instruments of our rising prosperity, it must be known, that we are, at all times, ready for war."

. What the Father of his Country said in 1793, at the end of his first administration, is even truer of the situation of the country to-day, for we are very much nearer than the country was in his day to other nations of the world, and we have a rank which will certainly be withheld and lost by the reputation of weakness. Readiness for war is quite as effective an instrument to secure peace to-day as it was more than a century ago.

CHAPTER XVIII

OUR FAR EASTERN POLICY

ADDRESS AT SHANGHAI, OCTOBER, 1907

Americans interested in Oriental and Chinese trade naturally look to the Philippine policy of the government as having a bearing upon the attitude of America toward the Oriental in general. Reports have been circulated with an appearance of authority throughout this part of the world that the United States intends to sell the Philippines to Japan or some other country. Upon that point, I do not hesitate to express a decided opinion. The Philippines came to the United States by chance, but that government assumed a duty with respect to them and entered into an implied obligation affecting them, with the people of the Philippines, of which it would be the grossest violation to sell the Islands to any other power. The only alternatives which the United States can in honor pursue with respect to the Philippines are either permanently to retain them, maintaining therein a stable government in which the rights of the humblest citizen shall be preserved, or after having fitted the people for self-government, to turn the Islands over to them for the continuance by them of a government of the same character. It is enough to say here that there is not the

283

slightest danger of a sudden cessation of the present relation of the United States to the Philippines, such as
would be involved in a sale of those Islands, and that for
our present purpose the attitude of the United States toward China must be regarded not alone as a country interested in the trade of China, but also as a power owning territory in China's immediate neighborhood.

THE POLICY OF THE OPEN DOOR.

The policy of the government of the United States
has been authoritatively stated to be that of seeking the
permanent safety and peace of the Chinese, the preservation of China's territorial and administrative entity, the
protection of all rights guaranteed by her to friendly
powers by treaty and international law, and, as a safeguard for the world, the principle of equal and impartial
trade with all parts of the Chinese Empire.   This was the
policy which John Hay made famous as that of the " open
door."   By written memorandum, all the great powers
interested in the trade of China have subscribed to its wisdom and declared their adherence to it.   The government of the United States has not deviated in the slightest way from its attitude in this regard since the policy
was announced in 1900.

I am advised that the trade, both export and import,
between China and the United States is second only to
that of Great Britain.   It is certain, therefore, that the
American Chinese trade is sufficiently great to require the
government of the United States to take every legitimate

means to protect it against diminution or injury by the
political preference of any of its competitors. It can
not of course complain of loss of trade effected by use
of greater enterprise, greater ingenuity, greater attention
to the demands of the Chinese market and greater business acumen by its competitors; but it would have the
right to protest against exclusion from Chinese trade by
a departure from the policy of the open door.

The acquiescence in this policy by all interested nations
was so unhesitating and emphatic that it is hardly worth
while to speculate as to the probable attitude of the United
States were its merchants' interests injured by a violation
of it. How far the United States would go in the protection of its Chinese trade no one of course could say.
This much is clear, however, that the merchants of the
United States are being roused to the importance of their
Chinese export trade, that they would view political obstacles to its expansion with deep concern, and that this
feeling of theirs would be likely to find expression in the
attitude of the American government.

Domestic business in the United States has expanded
so enormously and has resulted in such great profits as
to prevent American business men from giving to the foreign trade that attention which it deserves and which they
certainly would give, but for more profitable business at
home. As the population of the United States increases,
as its territory fills and its vast manufacturing and agricultural interests become greater, its interest in foreign
trade is certain to increase. The manufacturers now take

little care to pack their goods or to give them the sizes desired by Chinese purchasers, but this stiff necked lack of business sense is disappearing. We shall soon find the same zeal and the same intense interest on their part to induce purchasers in foreign markets that now characterize the manufacturers of other nations whose home business is not so absorbing as is that of the manufacturers of the United States. While we have been slow in rousing ourselves to the importance of a trade which has grown without government encouragement and almost without business effort to its present important proportion, I feel sure that in the future there will be no reason to complain of seeming government indifference to it.

The United States and others who favor the open door policy sincerely will, if they are wise, not only welcome, but will encourage this great Chinese Empire to take long steps in administrative and governmental reform, and in the development of her natural resources and the improvement of the welfare of her people. In this way she will add great strength to her position as a self-respecting government, may resist all possible foreign aggression seeking undue, exclusive or proprietary privileges in her territory, and without foreign aid, enforce an open door policy of equal opportunity to all. I am not one of those who view with alarm the effect of the growth of China with her teeming millions into a great industrial empire. I believe that this instead of injuring foreign trade with China would greatly increase it, and while it might change its character in some respects, it would not diminish its profit.

A trade which depends for its profit on the backwardness of a people in developing their own resources and upon their inability to value at the proper relative prices that which they have to sell and that which they have to buy is not one which can be counted upon as stable or permanent.

WHAT CHINA FOR CHINESE MEANS.

For the reasons I have given, it does not seem to me that the cry of " China for the Chinese " should frighten anyone. All that is meant by that is that China should devote her energies to the development of her immense resources, to the elevation of her industrious people, to the enlargement of her trade and to the administrative reform of the Empire as a great national government. Changes of this kind would only increase our trade with her. Our greatest export trade is with the countries most advanced in business methods and in the development of their particular resources. In the Philippines, we have learned that the policy which is best for the Filipinos is best in the long run for the countries who would do business with the Islands.

It is a pleasure to know that the education of Chinese in America has had much to do with the present steps toward reform begun by the Government in China. It is not to be expected that these reforms shall be radical or sudden. It would be unwise if they were so. A nation of the conservative traditions of China must accept changes gradually, but it is a pleasure to know and to say that in

16

every improvement which she aims at, she has the deep
sympathy of America, and that there never can be any
jealousy or fear on the part of the United States due to
China's industrial or political development, provided always that it is directed along the lines of peaceful prosperity and the maintenance of law and order and the rights
of the individual, foreign or alien.   She has no territory
we long for, and can have no prosperity which we would
grudge her and no political power and independence as an
empire justly exercised, which we would resent.   With
her enormous resources and with her industrious people
the possibilities of her future cannot be overstated.

It is pleasant to note a great improvement in the last
two years in the relations between the United States and
China.   In the first place, through the earnest efforts of
President Roosevelt, the administration of the Chinese immigration laws of the United States has been made much
more considerate.   The inquisitorial harshness to which
classes properly admissible to the United States under
treaty between the two countries were at one time subjected, has been entirely mitigated without in any way im-
pairing the effectiveness of the law.   The boycott which
was organized ostensibly on the ground of such harshness
of administration proved in the end to be a double-edged
knife which injured Chinamen even more than Americans
and other foreign countries quite as much.   Happily that
has now become a closed incident, a past episode.

Again the United States has exhibited its wish to do
full justice to China by a return or waiver of the in-

demnity awarded to it for injuries and expenses growing out of the Boxer trouble. It has been said that we have done only what we ought to do. This may be so, but a nice sense of international obligation is not so universal that it may not justly increase the friendly feeling between the parties to the transaction.

I do not think it too much to say that the consular representatives in China within the last decade have not been up to the standard which the importance of the business interests of the United States in China demanded. Aware of this, the administration at Washington has within the last three years given especial attention to the selection of Consuls in China. It is a new sensation for an American to come to a Chinese city and find as its consular representative one who knows the Chinese language and who understands the Chinese Empire as few Chinamen understand it.

Finally another great step has been taken by the government of the United States to improve its relations to China. In the last Congress, a law was passed which properly recognizes the dignity and importance of the power conferred by the Chinese treaty upon the government of the United States to administer justice in respect of citizens of the United States commorant in China by creation of a United States Circuit Court for China. I sincerely hope and believe that the establishment of this court will make much for the carrying out of exact justice in the controversies that arise in the business between Chinamen and Americans. There is nothing for which

the Oriental has a higher admiration than for exact justice, possibly because he is familiar with the enormous
difficulty there is in attaining such an ideal.   If this court
shall lead the Chinese to believe, as it ought to do, and
will do, that the rights of a Chinese are exactly as secure
when considered by this tribunal as the rights of an American, and that there is no looking down upon a Chinese
because he is a Chinese, and no disregard of his business
rights because he is an oriental, it will make greatly for the
better relations between the two countries.

And now what else is needed?   It goes without saying.   What you need is a great government building here
to be built by the expenditure of a very large sum of money
so that your court and your consulate shall be housed in
a dignified manner.   Our government should give this
substantial evidence of its appreciation of the importance
of its business and political relation to the great Chinese
Empire.   In the Orient, more than anywhere else in the
world, the effect upon the eye is important, and it must
be very difficult for Chinamen to suppose that the government of the United States attributes proper importance
to its trade with China when it houses its consulate and
its judges in such miserably poor and insufficient quarters
as they now occupy.   All over the United States, Congress
has provided most magnificent court rooms for the administration of Federal justice.   Will it, now that it has
created a court whose jurisdiction is coextensive with the
Chinese Empire, be less generous in the erection of a building which shall typify its estimate of the importance of its
relation to Chinese trade and the Chinese people?

CHAPTER XIX

OUR RELATIONS WITH JAPAN

ADDRESS AT TOKIO, SEPTEMBER, 1907

The growth of Japan from a hermit country to her present position in the last fifty years is the marvel of the world. In every step of that development, even at the very beginning we Americans are proud to record the fact that Japan has always had the cordial sympathy and at times the effective aid of the United States. The names of Commodore Perry, of Townsend Harris, of John A. Bingham, of General Grant and of Theodore Roosevelt will be inseparably connected with the history of the advance of Japan to the front rank among the world powers.

But now for a moment, and a moment only, a little cloud has come over the sunshine of a fast friendship of fifty years. A slight shock has been felt in the structure of amity and good will that has withstood the test of half a century. How has it come about? Well, in the first place it took a tremendous manifestation of nature to bring it about. Only the greatest earthquake of the century could have caused even the slightest tremor between such friends. I do not intend to consider the details of the events in San Francisco. I cannot trespass on the jurisdiction of the Department of State, to discuss them. But this I can say that there is nothing in these events of injustice that cannot be honorably and fully arranged by ordinary diplomatic methods between the two governments conducted as they both are by statesmen of honor, sanity and justice, and representing as they do two peoples bound together by half a century of warm friendship.

It is said that there is one word that is never allowed to creep into the diplomatic correspondence between nations, however hostile, and that word is "war." But I am not a diplomat and am not bound by diplomatic usage. I can talk war. I am not one of those who hold that war is so frightful that nothing justifies a resort to it. We have not yet reached the millennium and there are international grievances that can be redressed and just international purposes that can be accomplished in no other way. But, as one of our great generals has said, "War is hell" and nothing but a great and unavoidable cause can justify it.

War between Japan and the United States would be a crime against modern civilization. It would be as wicked as it would be insane. Neither the people of Japan nor the people of the United States desire war. The governments of the two countries would strain every point to avoid such an awful catastrophe.

What has Japan to gain by it? What has the United States to gain by it? Japan has reached a point in her history when she is looking forward with confident hope to great commercial conquests. She is shaking off the effects of war and is straining every nerve for victories of peace. With the marvelous industry, intelligence and courage of her people there is nothing in trade, commerce and popular contentment and enlightenment to which she may not attain. Why should she wish a war that would stop all this?

She has undertaken with a legitimate intent in so close a neighbor to reform and rejuvenate an ancient kingdom that has been governed or mis-governed by fifteenth century methods. His Majesty, the Emperor, has shown his appreciation ·of the difficulty of the task by sending to Korea Japan's greatest statesman who has exhibited his patriotism by accepting the heavy burden when by his years and his arduous labors for his country in the past he.has earned a right to rest. No matter what reports may come, no matter what criticism may be uttered, the world will have confidence that Prince Ito and the Japanese Government are pursuing a policy in Korea that will make for justice and civilization and the welfare of a backward people.

We are living in an age when the intervention of a stronger nation in the affairs of a people unable to maintain a government of law and order to assist the latter to better government becomes a national duty and works for the progress of the world. Why should Japan wish a war that must stop or seriously delay the execution of her plans of reform in Korea?

Why should the United States wish war? War would change her in a year or more into a military nation and her great resources would be wasted in a vast equipment that would serve no good purpose but to tempt her into warlike policies. In the last decade she has shown a material progress greater than the world has ever before seen. To-day she is struggling with the abuses which accompany such material development and is engaged in an effort by process of law to retain the good for her people and to suppress the evil. Why should she risk war in which all the evils of society flourish and all the vultures fatten? She is engaged in establishing a government of law and order and prosperity in the Philippine Islands and in fitting the people of those Islands by general education and by actual practice in partial self-government to govern themselves. It is a task full of difficulty and one which many Americans would be glad to be rid of.

It has been suggested that we might relieve ourselves of this burden by a sale of the Islands to Japan or some other country. The suggestion is absurd. Japan does not wish the Philippines. She has problems of a similar nature nearer home. But, more than this, the United States could not sell the Islands to another power without the grossest violation of its obligation to the Philippine people. It must maintain a government of law and order and the protection of life, liberty and property itself or fit the people of the Islands to do so and turn the government over to them. No other course in honor is open to it.

Under all these circumstances then, could anything be more wicked and more infamous than the suggestion of war between nations who have enjoyed such a time honored friendship and who have nothing to fight for. . . . In each country, doubtless there are irresponsible persons that war would aid or make prominent who try to give seriousness to such a discussion, but when one considers the real feelings of the two peoples as a whole, when one considers the situation from the standpoint of sanity and real patriotism in each country, it is difficult to characterize in polite or moderate language the conduct of those who are attempting to promote misunderstanding and ill-feeling between the two countries.

It gives me pleasure to assure the people of Japan that the good will of the American people toward Japan is as warm and cordial as ever it was and the suggestion of a breach of the amicable relations between them finds no confirmation in the public opinion of the United States.

CHAPTER XX

NATIONAL ISSUES

ADDRESS BEFORE THE BUCKEYE REPUBLICAN CLUB,
COLUMBUS, OHIO, AUGUST 19, 1907

I have been invited by your body to discuss the national issues. Some of these involve the abuses over which the public conscience has been aroused, and the proper remedies for their removal. The first, and possibly the greatest, abuse has been in the management of the arterial system of the country which the interstate railroads form. Any unjust discrimination in the terms upon which transportation of freight or passengers is afforded an individual or a locality, paralyzes and withers the business of the individual or the locality exactly as the binding of the arteries and veins leading to a member of the human body destroys its life.

The result of twenty years' operation under the interstate commerce act of 1887, passed to restrain abuses of unjust discrimination and unreasonableness of rates, was that the railroads came to regard the action of the commission it created as of no importance. The delays, due to the necessity of resorting to the courts to try out the merits of every order of the commission, before it became effective, made the remedy of the complaining shipper or locality so slow and burdensome that in contested cases, it was no remedy at all. The commission was not, under the old act, authorized to fix reasonable rates. It could only say that a particular rate was unreasonable and order a railroad to change its rate and make it reasonable. The railroad might fix a new rate at anything

296

less than the rate declared to be unreasonable, and if the reduction made was not sufficient, a new action had to be brought to decide that the new rate was also unreasonable.

. . .

The new act enables the commission to fix rates and give efficacy to all of its orders by providing that they shall go into effect thirty days after they are made, unless suspended by an order of court, and failure to comply with them is punishable by a fine of $5,000 a day during the delinquency. Express companies, sleeping car companies, and oil pipe-line companies are brought under the jurisdiction of the commission as common carriers. The act gives the commission power to fix the rates for the various incidental services performed by railways at terminals and on the journey, and to require them to be performed for every shipper. By withholding such services from one, and extending them to another, and by imposing varying charges for them, companies have been able in the past to make them a convenient instrument for discrimination. The new law requires the publication of rates charged for such incidental services. Railroads are compelled to furnish cars without discrimination for the movement of traffic. They are confined in their business strictly to transportation by a provision forbidding them to transport for themselves anything but what is intended for their use as common carriers. Experience has shown that the railroads cannot be trusted to deal fairly in matters of transportation between themselves and their competitors in an outside business. The new law makes radical changes in the matter of the publication of rates. Under the old law, by means of what was called the "midnight tariff," a railroad company gave favored shippers advance information of a contemplated reduction of rate and immediately restored the old rate when these shippers had profited by it. Thirty days' notice is now required of any change in the rates unless the commission, for good cause, modifies the requirement.

UNIFORM ACCOUNTS REQUIRED.

Again, the new law enables the commission to prescribe a uniform system of accounting for railroads. Under the old law the commission could call for a report of the railroads and might ask questions of railroads, but it had no way to compel a compliance with its request, and no penalty was provided in the law for failure to make the full report. Under the new law, annual reports must be made under oath, and penalties are prescribed for failure to file them with the commission within a certain time. The commission can call for monthly or special reports. It may prescribe the bookkeeping methods of the carrier and has access at all times through examiners to the carrier's books. The carrier is forbidden to keep any other books than those prescribed. The commission's authority, under the new law, over interstate commerce railroads is thus in many respects like that of the Comptroller of the Currency over National Banks, which has the approval and confidence of the country.

Never before was there such a united opposition by the railroad interests to any National measure as they instituted against the Rate Bill. A campaign of education was entered upon, speeches were made in every part of the country, and literature was showered upon the members of every community, with the hope of convincing the public that the bill was a dangerous innovation.

The great objection was that the law was invalid in that Congress was thereby delegating its legislative power to another body, and was violating the general constitutional rule that legislative power cannot be delegated. The rule has an exception. There may be delegation of legislative power where the purpose in the original conferring of the power can be subserved only by its delegation to an agent. It is admitted that the Constitution gives Congress the power to fix rates. Obviously, however, it is impossible for Congress as a body to spend the time and labor to do so. If the power is to be exercised at all, practically it can be done only through a tribunal or an agency like that of the interstate commerce commission. Hence Congress may delegate the power under proper legislative limitations and rules of decision. A similar conclusion has been reached by a number of State courts with reference to the power of legislatures under State constitutions presenting the same question, and while the case has not, with respect to a Federal commission, been brought directly before the Supreme Court of the United States, there is a plain dictum in one decision in favor of the validity of such delegation of legislative power.

The Rate Law has not been in operation a year, and the beneficial results from its operations, though clear, are not ready to be presented in statistical array. Moreover, the chief benefit of the act is likely to be its influence in discouraging attempts to renew the old abuses and such benefits do not appear in statistics. The immediate effect of the act has certainly been to compel railroads to regard the commission now as the important tribunal whose views they must follow. They are manifesting every outward disposition strictly to comply with the law and to avoid prosecution or complaint. The time has gone by in which the action of the commission can be ignored or laughed at. The commission itself has taken up its duties with renewed energy, has proceeded, without awaiting the intervention of the railroads or the filing of complaints, to construe the act by administrative rulings, in order to assist the railroads in complying with the law. With the large powers for correcting evils, which the commission now has, we may reasonably expect a marked improvement in the conduct of the railways of the country.

The Rate Law does not go far enough. The practice under it has already disclosed the necessity for new amendments and will doubtless suggest more. Such is the true method — the empirical and tentative method — of securing proper remedies for a new evil. The classification of merchandise for transportation is a most important matter in rate fixing, for by a transfer from one class to another, the rate is changed and may work injustice. With the power of rate fixing, it would seem, should go the power in the commission to classify and to prescribe rules for uniform classification by all railroads.

AMENDMENT NEEDED TO PREVENT OVER-CAPITALIZATION.

Recent revelations have emphasized the pernicious effect of the so-called over-capitalization of railroads which aids unscrupulous stock manipulators in disposing of railway securities at unreasonably high prices to innocent buyers. This evil would not of itself justify Federal restraint or control because such stock and bonds are usually issued under State charters. The practice, however, has a tendency to divert the money paid by the public for the stock and bonds which ought to be expended in improving the road bed, track and equipment of railways into the pockets of the dishonest manipulators and thus to pile such an unprofitable debt upon a railway as to make bankruptcy and a receivership probable in the first business stringency. This result in an interstate railway, necessarily interferes with, and burdens, interstate commerce, and justifies the exercise of the regulative power of Congress to stop the practice. A railroad company engaged in interstate commerce should not be permitted, therefore, to issue stock or bonds and put them on sale in the market except after a certificate by the interstate commerce commission that the securities are issued with the approval of the commission for a legitimate railroad purpose. The railroads that are honestly conducted would accept the certificate of the commission as a valuable one in the markets of the world, and only railway stock manipulators who look to the floating of watered securities as their best source of profit, would have reason to complain.

A much used means of eliminating competition among interstate lines serving the same territory is the acquisition by one company of the stock in another and the election of directors to represent that stock. This process is facilitated by the uncontrolled power to issue securities beyond the needs of the company for its legitimate business and would be curbed by the restriction proposed. The evil ought further to be directly restrained by making it unlawful for an interstate railway to acquire stock in a competing line. This is a simpler remedy of meeting the evil than by recourse to the anti-trust law under the Northern Securities case. In addition to this, competing lines should be prohibited from having common directors or officers.

These suggestions of additional legislation in respect to the supervision and control of interstate railways have been made by the interstate commerce commission, and I heartily concur in them. They are plainly within the Federal jurisdiction under the interstate commerce clause. I do not think that in order to accomplish a good which the Federal Government with its greater resources and wider geographical reach can bring about more quickly and efficiently, the constitutional limits upon Federal action should be blurred out or an undoubted Federal power should be expanded by doubtful construction into a field which really belongs to the State. But the right of Congress to take any action, not confiscatory, in the most rigid of interstate commerce cannot be denied.

The measures taken and proposed are radical perhaps, viewed from the standpoint of the *laissez faire* doctrinaire whose ideas have been allowed to prevail in respect of railroad management down to the present; but no one can read the report of the commission on the history of the union of the Southern Pacific and Union Pacific systems with the Illinois Central system without trembling at the enormous power that one man, by the uncontrolled use of the stock and bond issuing power of interstate railways under State charters, has acquired in respect of a vital part of the country's business and without looking for some means of remedying such a dangerous tendency which, if not stopped, will lead to the absorption of all the railroads of the country into one hand.

THE ANTIDOTE OF SOCIALISM.

The contention on behalf of the railroads, already noticed, that such supervision as the Rate Bill and these suggested amendments afford, is socialistic and tends to government ownership, is utterly without basis. Efficient regulation is the very antidote and preventative of socialism and government ownership. The railroads, until now, have been permitted to wield without any real control the enormously important franchise of furnishing transportation to the entire country. They have constructed 230,000 miles of road. In certain respects they have done a marvelous work and have afforded transportation at a cheaper rate, per ton, per mile and per passenger, than in any country in the world. They have, however, many of them, shamefully violated the trust obligation they have been under to the public of furnishing equal facilities at the same price to all shippers. The watering of stock and bonds and the over-capitalization of some of them for the profit of their managers have prevented the needed improvement of their railroads in construction and equipment. The tremendous demand for increased facilities due to the enormous growth of business shows the inadequacy of their equipment and construction. While they might not have been expected to meet in full such an extraordinary demand, the obligations some of them have assumed in the form of stocks and bonds leave no doubt that, had the money they represented been put into the roads in good faith, the shortage of cars and equipment and inadequacy of road bed and track would not be so great. They discharge a public function. They have been weighed in the balance and found wanting. The remedy for the evils must be radical to be effective. If it is not so, then we may certainly expect that the movement toward Government ownership will become a formidable one that cannot be stayed.

OBJECTIONS TO GOVERNMENT OWNERSHIP.

I am opposed to Government ownership —

First, because existing Government railways are not managed with either the efficiency or economy of privately managed roads and the rates charged are not as low and therefore not as beneficial to the public;

Second, because it would involve an expenditure of certainly twelve billions of dollars to acquire the interstate railways and the creation of an enormous national debt.

Third, because it would place in the hands of a reckless executive a power of control over business and politics that the imagination can hardly conceive, and would expose our popular institutions to danger.

RAILWAY RATE AGREEMENTS.

The movement of competing railway companies to consolidate arose originally from fear that the anti-trust act forbade them to make agreements as to uniform tariffs. If they were now permitted to make such agreements subject to the approval of the interstate commerce commission, such a tendency would lose much of its force. It is impossible to prevent competing railways from seeking to make their tariffs uniform in order to prevent an unending and disastrous tariff war, and though such agreements are against the law, it is perfectly apparent that tacit arrangements for uniformity exist. These arrangements do not prevent the operation of competition, from time to time, as one company finds that it may acquire new business without loss by a reduction of rate and insists on it, but they do prevent a tariff war which helps

17

neither the public nor the railway by violent fluctuations
in rates.   As the public now asserts the right to fix maximum rates and thus, to eliminate one phase of competition, it is logical to permit an agreement on rates, if approved by the Interstate Commerce Commission, the tribunal appointed to fix rates.   In this way, there would
be restored that respect for law which many railroad men
in the last decade seem to have lost.   Moreover, every
company under such a system would be a policeman to see
to it that every other company obeyed the agreement and
the law and strictest obedience would be secured.

EMPLOYEES' LIABILITY.

The frightful loss of life and limb among the railway
employees of this country, reaching more than 4,000
killed and 65,000 injured in one year, has properly attracted the attention of Congress and the Legislatures.
It makes apparent that service in connection with trains
of a railway is an extra hazardous business and may well
call for Government supervision and exceptional rules to
secure the safety of the passengers and reduce the danger
to employees.   Congress, years ago, passed stringent laws
for the adoption of safety devices to protect both employee and passenger on interstate railways.   With the
same purpose, it has recently limited the hours of continued service for which employees on such railways may
be engaged.

Finally, it has regulated the rules for the liability of
an interstate railroad company to an employee injured in
its service.   This is a most important measure, for an unfortunate lack of uniformity has existed heretofore in respect to the rules of liability in such cases, dependent on
the court in which the case has been tried.   The new
statute makes everything uniform as to interstate railroads.   It has introduced into Federal law what is called
the comparative negligence theory by which, if an employee is injured, proof of negligence on his part does

not forfeit his claim for damages entirely unless the accident was due solely to his negligence. If there was negligence by the company, the jury is authorized to apportion the negligence and award compensation for the proper part of the damage to the employee, and the question of negligence is always for the jury.

The most important provision of this law, however, is that abolishing what is known as the fellow-servant rule, by which an employee injured cannot recover from his employer for injury sustained through the negligence of a co-employee. The abolition of the exemption certainly furnishes a strong motive to the railroad companies for the exercise of greater care in the selection, supervision and control of all of their employees, which tends not only to the safety of their employees, but also to the safety of their passengers. The validity of this law is under consideration by the Supreme Court. The only serious doubt in regard to the constitutionality grows out of some carelessness of language in limiting its application to interstate railways and, therefore, even if the present law should fail, there will be no difficulty in re-enacting it in proper form.*

TRUSTS.

I pass now to the evils which have grown out of combinations existing in private business, and so come to the subject of Trusts. The combination of capital in large plants to manufacture goods with the greatest economy is just as necessary as the assembling of the parts of a machine to the economical and more rapid manufacture of what in old time was made by hand. The Government should not interfere with the one any more than the other. In the proper operation of competition the

---

* Since this speech was delivered the Supreme Court has declared the law unconstitutional, on the ground referred to here by Mr. Taft. But as he here predicted a new law has been passed, correcting this fault.

public will soon share with the manufacturer the advantage in lowered prices. When, however, such combinations not only lower the cost to themselves, but are able to control the market and maintain or raise the old prices, the public derives no benefit and is helpless in the hands of a monopoly.

Fear of the existence of such an abuse led to the passage of the anti-trust law, in 1890. It recognizes two forms in which this evil may be maintained. One is by an agreement among a number of different manufacturers of an article for the maintenance of the price of the article and the suppression of competition. This is denounced when the contract is in restraint of interstate trade as a criminal offense against the United States, punishable by fine and imprisonment, and a conspiracy which may be restrained by injunction in a civil suit. The other form is denounced, with similar remedies against it, as a monopoly of interstate trade, and covers the union of the conspiring companies into one company which, by owning all the plant or nearly all the plant, engaged in the manufacture of the product and by use of other devices, controls the prices. The Supreme Court of the United States has not defined what a monopoly under this section of the anti-trust law is.

DEFINITION OF UNLAWFUL MONOPOLY.

I conceive that it is not sufficiently defined by saying that it is the combination of a large part of the plants in the country engaged in the manufacture of a particular product in one corporation. There must be something more than the mere union of capital and plant before the law is violated. There must be some use by the company of the comparatively great size of its capital and plant in extent of its output, either to coerce persons to buy of it rather than of some competitor, or to coerce those who would compete with it, to give up their business. There must, in other words, be an element of duress in the conduct of its business toward the customers in the trade and its competitors before mere aggregation of plant becomes an unlawful monopoly.   It is perfectly conceivable that in the interest of economy of production, a great number of plants may be legitimately assembled under the ownership of one corporation.   In such a case it is either not a trust, if the term involves unlawfulness, or it is a lawful trust, if a trust merely means a company which has assembled a large part of the manufacturing plant of one product.

It must be borne in mind that in a country like this, where there is an enormous floating capital awaiting investment, the time within which competition by construction of new plants can be introduced into any business is comparatively short, rarely exceeding a year, and usually is even less time than that.   Many enterprises have been organized on the theory that mere aggregation of all or nearly all existing plants in a line of manufacture, without regard to economy of production, destroys competition.   They have most of them gone into bankruptcy. Competition in a profitable business will not be excluded by the mere aggregation of many existing plants under one company, unless the company thereby effects great economy or takes some illegal method to avoid competition and to perpetuate a hold on the business.

ILLEGAL DEVICES BADGES OF UNLAWFUL TRUSTS.

Frequent contracts have been made with customers by which they are required to deal exclusively with the Trust, on the threat that if there is not this exclusive dealing, then at a time when they most need the product, it will not be sold to them at all, or only at a very high price, and one prohibitive of profit on their part.   Again, the tremendous wealth and resources of the Trust are exerted to destroy a rival in a particular locality by selling at a very low price in that neighborhood and driving him out of business, and then raising the prices.   This can be easily detected by the inequality of the prices which the Trust asks for the same commodity in different localities under the same conditions. Such or like methods bring the company within description of a monopoly, at which the anti-trust law is directed. I am inclined to the opinion that the time is near at hand for an amendment of the anti-trust law defining in more detail the evils against which it is aimed, making clearer the distinction between lawful agreements reasonably restraining trade and those which are pernicious in their effect, and particularly denouncing the various devices for monopolizing trade which prosecutions and investigations have shown to be used in actual practice. The decisions of the courts and the experiences of Executive and prosecuting officers make the framing of such a statute possible. It will have the good effect of making much clearer to those business men who would obey the laws the methods to be avoided.

Another and perhaps the most effective method in the past for an unlawful trust to maintain itself has been to secure secret rebates or other unlawful advantage in transportation, by threat of withholding business from the carrier. This is undoubtedly what has enabled the Standard Oil Company and the Sugar Trust and other great combines, to reap an illegal harvest and to drive competitors from the field. If by asserting complete Federal control over the interstate railways of the country, we can suppress secret rebates and discriminations of other kinds, we shall have gone a long way in the suppression of the unlawful trust.

Mr. Bryan asks me what I would do with the trusts. I answer that I would restrain unlawful trusts with all the efficiency of injunctive process and would punish with all the severity of criminal prosecution every attempt on the part of aggregated capital through the illegal means I have described to suppress competition.

There has been great activity in the Department of Commerce and Labor and in the Department of Justice in an effort to investigate and restrain the continuance of such unlawful methods, and the success which has attended this effort in the dissolution of a number of such trusts where they consisted of several companies or partnerships united by a contract in restraint of trade has been gratifying. In the case of those who have made themselves into one corporation, their restraint is more difficult. It involves enormous labor on the part of the Government to prosecute such a combination because the proof of the gist of the offense lies underneath an almost limitless variety of transactions. In the outset, it can be very much more easily reached by bill in equity than in a criminal prosecution and the questions of law arising may be more quickly settled. When the law is declared so that the corporation understands exactly the limits upon its action, and it then pursues its previous illegal methods, nothing but criminal prosecution ought to be resorted to.

Mr. Bryan is continually asking why some of the managers of unlawful trusts have not been convicted and sent to the penitentiary. I sympathize with him in his wish that this may be done, because I think that the imprisonment of one or two would have a most healthy effect throughout the country; but even without such imprisonment I believe that the prosecutions which are now on foot and the injunctions which have already been issued have had a marked effect on business methods. One reason for the small number of sentences of imprisonment in trust prosecutions is that the revelations of unlawful trust methods and dishonesty have been chiefly made known in secret rebates and as I have already said, the Elkins act, until amended by the Rate Bill, only prescribed fines as a mode of punishment in such cases.

Again it is difficult to induce juries to convict individuals of a violation of the anti-trust law, if imprisonment is to follow. In the case of the Tobacco Trust, the Government declined to accept a plea of guilty by the individual defendants, offered on condition that only the penalty of a fine be imposed, and the result was that the jury did not hesitate to stultify itself, by finding the corporation guilty and acquitting the individual defendants, who had personally committed the acts upon which the conviction of the corporation was based. In the early enforcement of a statute which makes unlawful, because of its evil tendencies, that which has been in the past regarded as legitimate, juries are not inclined by their verdicts to imprison individuals. The course which the Government has pursued of resorting to civil process first, and clarifying the meaning of a general statute which needs definition, is probably the best course to pursue. As the criminal prosecutions go on (and many such prosecutions have now begun), if the violations of the trust law are continued, undoubtedly some shining marks will be hit, but the vigor with which these prosecutions have been continued, has created an anxiety among those engaged in doubtful enterprises that has either driven them out of the business or made them careful not to give occasion for further complaint.

EVIL OF SWOLLEN FORTUNES.

One of the results of the conditions and evils which I have been describing has been the concentration of enormous wealth in the hands of a few men. I do not mean to say that all the large fortunes are to be traced to unlawful means, but it is quite clear that many of those, described as swollen, are due to rebates, or to some form of unlawful monopoly, or to over-capitalization. Of course, great enterprises organized and managed by men of transcendent ability should result in great profit to them. It is proper compensation when they share with the people the profit from the economies that they introduce in the business by reducing the price. The captains of legitimate industry, therefore, are entitled to large reward, and it is impossible to impose a fixed limitation upon the amount which they may accumulate.

On the other hand, it is not safe for the body politic that the power arising from the management of enormous or swollen fortunes should be continued from generation to generation in the hands of a few, and efforts by laws, which are not confiscatory, to divide these fortunes and to reduce the motive for accumulating them are proper and statesmanlike and without the slightest savor of socialism or anarchy. The law of primogeniture was abolished in States where it had been adopted, merely for the purpose of securing a division of the land among the children of the man who owned the land. Many of the provisions of our public land laws are drawn to discourage the union of large tracts in one ownership, and to encourage small holdings.

The State legislatures have complete control of what shall be done with a man's property on his death. He has no right to leave it by will and his children or heirs have no right to receive it which the legislatures may not modify or take away. The States, therefore, can best remedy the dangers of too great accumulation of wealth in one hand by controlling the descent and devolution of property and they ought to do so. Many of the States have already and properly adopted a graduated inheritance tax which not only reduces the great fortune but lessens the motive for its accumulation.

Federal action for a Federal end may legitimately have an indirect effect to aid the States in reforms peculiarly within their cognizance. When, therefore, the Government revenues need addition, or readjustment, I believe a Federal graduated inheritance tax to be a useful means of raising government funds. It is easily and certainly collected. The incidence of taxation is heaviest on those best able to stand it, and indirectly, while not placing undue restriction on individual effort, it would moderate the enthusiasm for the amassing of immense fortunes.

INCOME TAX.

A graduated income tax would also have a tendency to reduce the motive for the accumulations of enormous wealth, but the Supreme Court has held an income tax not to be a valid exercise of power by the Federal Government.   The objection to it from a practical standpoint is its inquisitorial character and the premium it puts on perjury.   In times of great national need, however, an income tax would be of great assistance in furnishing means to carry on the government, and it is not free from doubt how the Supreme Court since its membership has been changed, would view a new income tax law under such conditions.   The Court was nearly evenly divided in the last case and during the Civil War, great sums were collected by an income tax without judicial interference, and as it was then supposed within the Federal power.

DOES NOT FAVOR IMMEDIATELY SUCH FEDERAL LEGISLATION BUT ON NEXT READJUSTMENT OF REVENUES.

I do not favor Federal legislation now to reduce such fortunes either by a constitutional amendment to permit an income tax or by a graduated inheritance tax, but whenever the Government revenues need an increase or readjustment, I should strongly favor the imposition of a graduated inheritance tax and, if necessary for the revenues, a change in the constitution authorizing a Federal income tax, with all the incident influence of both measures to lessen the motive for accumulation.

The suppression of monopolies and the abolition of secret rebates and discriminating privileges by the railroads, will lessen the possibility of such enormous accumulations as those which have already taken place.   The evils of too great concentration of money or of any kind of property in a few hands are to be best remedied by the gradual effect of a long course of legislation and not by means having an immediate and radical effect that are apt to involve injurious consequences to the general business community.

MR. ROOSEVELT'S POLICIES.

Critics of President Roosevelt denounce his policies as socialistic and likely to impair the institution of private property. The institution of private property next to that of civil liberty is the most important factor in all that is good in modern society. It is indispensable to individualism and is one of the two chief means by which man raised himself from a low estate near to that of the beasts of the field to his present condition. But if the people are not convinced that it is possible to eradicate the evils and abuses arising from the unscrupulous use of wealth and corporate combination under the system of private property, the movement toward its abolition and the adoption of socialism in some form will gain in great strength. President Roosevelt would stop this movement by a demonstration that it is possible under the system of private property, by efficient Government regulation, supervision and prosecution, to stamp out the evils which have created our social unrest. He knows what a futile remedy socialism will prove to be. Socialism looks to a dead level of life, to an absence of all motive for material progress, to a stagnation in everything. It involves a lack of individual freedom and requires an official tyranny to carry out its system that finds no counterpart in modern Government. It offers no real remedy for the evils that appear from time to time as the accompaniment of our progress. And yet, President Roosevelt knows and every one must realize, the plausible force with which socialistic doctrines can be pressed upon a discontented people who see real wrongs in the body politic and social.

For this reason, he takes the most conservative course in insisting on adopting measures entirely consistent with

the principle of private property in order to stamp out the
evils which have attended its abuse. There is nothing
either radical or severe in the reforms he proposes.
What is there in the tenet of private property that prevents close government regulation of the exercise of a
public franchise like that of interstate railways, or the
enactment of criminal laws or civil procedure to restrain
the evils which result from the improper use of the right
of property in combinations of capital to suppress competition and to monopolize trade, or the adjustment of tax
laws or laws of descent in such a way as to reduce the motive for accumulating fortunes so great that the power they
give their individual owners is politically dangerous?

Mr. Roosevelt believes not only in the people but also
in the individual as the unit who multiplied makes up and
gives quality to the people. He thinks that there is no
royal road to the elevation of a people but by the improvement in the intelligence and moral character of the
individual. He believes in the possibility of the individual's being honest, courageous and just and able to resist
the influence of "the money power" to wean him from
the path of duty. He believes that the people can select
individuals who may be trusted as public officers, executive,
legislative and judicial, to wield, without abuse and in the
interest of the people, the powers needed to conduct an efficient government. He has faith in the maintenance of
an honest, courageous and efficient representative popular legislature that will give the rich and poor equal protection and opportunity before the law.

Mr. Roosevelt believes in the necessity for a strong
government that can and will make both rich and poor
obey the law, and he would have the officers charged
with its maintenance render due account of their steward-
ship to their masters, the people. Mr. Roosevelt knows
no favorite in matters of lawlessness, be he rich or poor,
corporation president or member of a labor union. The
courts must be strong enough to restrain them all. Mr.

Roosevelt believes our present government the best one possible for us, and every way adapted to the genius of our people. He has the utmost confidence in the capacity of the people through their representatives and by the means provided in the Constitution by our fathers to remedy the evils that arise in our material progress.

MR. BRYAN'S THEORIES BASED ON DISTRUST.

Mr. Bryan's whole system of remedies, on the other hand, for the evils that both Mr. Roosevelt and he and many others recognize, is based on his distrust of the honesty, courage and impartiality of the individual as an agent on behalf of the people to carry on any part of government and rests on the proposition that our present system of representative government is a failure. He would have government ownership of railways because he does not believe it is possible to secure an interstate commerce commission that the "money power" cannot and will not ultimately own. He would have the initiative and referendum because he distrusts representative government and has no confidence in the ability of the people to find men who will conscientiously, and free from the influence of "the money power," represent them in preparing and voting legislation. He would take away from courts, because he distrusts the ability of judges to resist the malign influence of the "money power," the power to enforce their own orders until a jury is called to tell the court whether the order has been disobeyed, and thus, in practice, though not in theory, the jury would come to pass on the correctness and justice of the court's order.

Mr. Bryan seems to be seeking some system of administering law under which the rich wrongdoer shall be certainly restrained, while the lawless poor shall escape. He would have his judicial machinery adjusted to restrict the violations of law by a corporation but would give freedom of action to the lawless members of a labor

union.   Such a discrimination in practical legislation can
not be maintained for a moment.   Courts and judicial
procedure are made for all and must operate equally for
and against all.   The only method by which wealthy
and powerful malefactors can be restrained is by maintaining the power of the courts, and the minute the power
of the court is weakened in the supposed interest of the
lowly and unfortunate accused of wrongdoing, the lawless rich are furnished the immunity they seek.   The
wealthy wrongdoers could easily escape the restraint of
law through the rents in its meshes Mr. Bryan would
make for the benefit of those with less influence and
means.

In all his proposed reforms, Mr. Bryan seems to give
little attention to securing efficiency and force in government so that the evils he recognizes may be suppressed.
The government which his system would tend to produce would be nerveless.   Estopped by his own expressed fear of power put in the hands of any individual,
he would find difficulty in wielding it when most needed.

ABSURDITY OF NATIONAL REFERENDUM.

The representative government that has served us well
for 130 years has not been for Mr. Bryan sufficiently
expressive of the will of the people.   Election of
Senators by the people is not enough for him.   We must
call upon fourteen million electors to legislate directly.
Could any more burdensome or inefficient method be devised than this?   I believe that a referendum under certain conditions and limitations in the subdivisions of a
State on certain issues may be healthful and useful, but
as applied to our national government it is entirely impracticable.   If it is difficult for the people to use proper
judgment in the concrete question of the personality of
the representatives they are to select to carry on their
national government, as Mr. Bryan's theory assumes,
how much more difficult for them to give sufficient at-

tention to the settlement of the many questions of policy and procedure in complicated statutes which the people have always been willing to leave to the decision of their representatives, skilled in the science of legislation, whose general views on the main political issues of the day are well understood. Think of the possibility of securing a vote of fourteen million of electors on the 4,000 items of a tariff bill. The opportunity is all that the people wish and need to enforce their will.

THE PROTECTIVE TARIFF — ITS REVISION — ITS RELATION TO TRUSTS.

I come now to the question of the tariff, its revision, and its relation to the unlawful trusts. The Republican principle of protective tariff is that a tariff should be collected on all imports that compete with American products, which will at least equal the difference in the cost of production in this country and abroad, and that proper allowance should be made in this difference for reasonable profits to the American manufacturer. The claim of Protectionists, and it has been abundantly justified in the past, is that protection secures a high rate of wages and that the encouragement it gives to the home industry operating under the influence of an energetic competition between American manufacturers, induces such improvement in the methods of manufacture and such economies as to reduce greatly the price for the benefit of the American public and makes it possible to reduce the tariff without depriving the manufacturer of needed protection and a good profit.

The present business system of the country rests on the protective tariff and any attempt to change it to a free trade basis will certainly lead only to disaster.

It is the duty of the Republican party, however, to see to it that the tariff on imported articles does not exceed substantially the reasonable permanent differential between the cost of production in the foreign countries and that in the United States, and therefore when changes take place in the conditions of production likely to produce a very large reduction in the cost of production in the United States, it is time that the schedules be re-examined, and if excessive that they be reduced so as to bring them within the jurisdiction for the rule, by which the amount of tariff to be imposed under the protective system is properly determined.

Whenever the tariff imposed is largely in excess of the differential between the cost of production in the two countries, then there is formed at once a great temptation to monopolize the business of producing the particular product, and to take advantage of profit in the excessive tariff. This denies to the people altogether the economies of production that competition under a protective tariff should develop.

In the enormous progress in the manufacturing plants and the improvement in methods which have been brought about in the last ten years in this country, there is the strongest reason for thinking that in many industries the difference between the cost of production in this country and abroad, has been reduced. This is an opinion of mine formed *a priori* because I am a sincere believer in the efficiency of the protective system ultimately to cheapen the cost of production. The opinion has been confirmed by *conversation with manufacturers* and others who knew something of what they speak.

CHAPTER XXI

THE PROGRESS OF THE NEGRO

ADDRESS AT PLYMOUTH CHURCH, BROOKLYN, N. Y.,
MARCH 16, 1908

As far back as I can remember, which carries me into
the middle of the Civil War, my ideal of patriotic feeling — derived from the political attitude of my father
and mother, as I understood it — was closely associated
with the hatred of slavery and sympathy with the negro
race. Subsequently under Republican tutelage, that sympathy diffused itself into a strong political bias in favor
of the maintenance of the political rights of the negro
in the South, intensified perhaps, rather by a desire for
Republican victory, than for specific benefit to the negro
race. . . . It fell to my lot thereafter to exercise
judicial jurisdiction in two States of the South, and to
come more or less intimately face to face with the social
and political problems then presented, and to learn more
and to understand better than ever I did before, the real
attitude of both sides upon the race issue in the Southern States. .

In discussing the history of the development and
progress of the negro in this country, I think there is no
division of the topic so logical, from the standpoint of
true political science, as that which is made by the three
great war amendments to the Constitution. The taking
away from the Southern slave-owners the 5,000,000 negroes, who had been under the Constitution their property, and the making of them freemen, as they were,
without preparation for the responsibilities of freedom,

18   319

was a change so radical and a social wrench so violent that it must have been accompanied by temporary evils which for a time clouded the great beneficence of the change.   In the first place the 5,000,000 freed men, who but lately had been chattels, were 95 per cent. of them entirely illiterate.   They had never been trained to self-support or self-help.   They were dependent on others for what they wore, for what they ate, for what they did.   They were living in a country which had been dev-astated by war, and in which their former masters were themselves in a state of destitution and hopelessness, naturally embittered by the awful sufferings and trials of a four years' war, and the humiliation of defeat.   Un-der such circumstances the future of the negro, though he had attained the inestimable boon of freedom, seemed dark indeed.   It was true that in the trials of the Civil War, there had been made clear, qualities in the race which gave promise for the future.   Under the influence of their surroundings as slaves, they had long embraced the Christian religion, and though illiterate they could not but feel the influence of the civilization in which they lived.   In the history of all the peoples of the earth, there is no more uniform story of absolute fidelity to trust than that which was exhibited by the negroes of the South toward the families of their masters, when the men were gone to the war, and none but the women and children were left at home.   Though these black trustees of the hearth and home were, of course, moved deeply in sympathy with the enemies of their masters engaged in a death struggle for their freedom, they never for a moment faltered in their duty of guardianship and pro-tection.   So, too, on the other side, the negroes who were enlisted in the war for the Union and the abolition of slavery manifested courageous and warlike spirit, and a willingness to die for their country and their flag, which entitled them to share in the benefits of a common citizenship. It is necessary to mention these circumstances and race traits, in order to explain the marvelous progress that has been made out of the gloom, darkness and confusion that prevailed at the time of the adoption of the thirteenth amendment.

Whatever may be said of the reconstruction governments of the South, it is to their credit that laws were enacted instituting systems of education for the negro. Still more noteworthy is the fact that since 1880, and the passing of the political influence of the negro in the South, in the face of the bitter feeling against him which at times seems on the surface to have swept across that section, there has been spent by the Southern States in support of negro schools a sum exceeding one hundred and five millions of dollars. In the year 1900 one million colored youths attended public schools, and in the thirty-five years between 1865 and 1900, the illiteracy, which had been 95 per cent., was reduced to 47 per cent., and to-day it is not much more than 40 per cent. of the total negro population of school age. But while great progress has been made in the reduction of the illiteracy of the negro race, much remains to be done. The Southern negro schools in the country are by no means what they ought to be in many States, and the negro children are denied in many rural communities more than one or two or three months' education during the year. This it is to be hoped will improve as the revenues of the Southern States, in their present prosperity, permit larger appropriations to benefit the school, and there is room here, too, for the adding to the many generous funds — the Slater, the Peabody and the Jeannes funds — for the promotion of general education in the South. The removal of illiteracy — that is, the primary education — is indispensable in the uplift of any race. Secondary and university education are not so indispensable, but they are of the highest advantage in the instruction of the leaders of the race, and of that small proportion of professional men that the general education and industrial progress of the race make useful.

The fourteenth amendment secured the negro against any State legislation or State action which might deprive him of his right to life, liberty and property; that is, of his right to pursue happiness. It gave him protection against any effort on the part of the States to deprive him of equality of opportunity in improving his condition by self-help; and it is under this amendment and the fifteenth amendment, affecting his political rights, that one should properly consider the far-reaching influence of the education initiated by General Armstrong in the experiment of Hampton Institute.

Hampton and Tuskegee teach the dignity of labor, the value of skill, the use of the mind, and the application of the hand, and the lesson that without attention and without taking pains, without self-restraint, no progress can be made by either a man, a race or a nation.

The founders of Hampton and Tuskegee saw that the colored people needed training in the branches of human endeavor in which there was hope of real and immediate success, and made their schools accordingly. They would not decry the advantages of higher education for some of the race, and would not shut the door of opportunity to the negro in any vocation, professional or manual. But in these schools they determined to train the race in the work plainly open to the whole race, and which, in the end, must most certainly add to the economic power and influence of the negro for his uplifting.

That the policy has been abundantly justified by the event, the statistics of the negro race bear indisputable evidence.

In Virginia, in 1898, the negroes owned 978,000 acres of land. In the five years next following they had gained 326,000 acres. The total business capital of the negroes of Virginia in 1889 was $5,700,000; in 1899 this had increased to $8,800,000, and 79 per cent. of the negroes had less than $2,500 each, showing that the wealth was quite evenly distributed among them.

In Georgia, which is one of the most prosperous of the Southern States, in 1900 the negroes owned one million acres, worth upwards of $4,000,000, and the asset value of all property owned by them in that State was tax value of $15,000,000, or double that for actual value, or $30,000,000.

In 1865 the negroes were almost without homes of their own, and in 1900, thirty-five years later, there were in all the Southern States 372,000 owners of homes, and of these 225,000 were free from encumbrance.

The number of farms operated by negroes in the United States in 1900 was 746,000, and of these 287,-000 were in the South Atlantic States, and 444,000 in the South Central States. Of the Southern farms 187,-000, or 25 per cent. of all, were owned by the negroes who farmed them; 271,000 were operated by negroes who were cash tenants, and 279,000 were operated by negroes who were share tenants. Of the negroes in the South there were 1,344,000 agricultural laborers and 757,000 farmers, planters and overseers.

The agricultural wealth of the negroes of the South was estimated at $300,000,000 in 1908. Between 1890 and 1900 the number of negro farmers increased 37 per cent., and the number of farm owners increased 57 per cent. The negroes as owners or tenants cultivate one-half of all the cotton farms, one-third of all the rice farms, one-seventh of all the sugar farms, and two-elevenths of all the tobacco farms in the United States, although they form but one-eighth of the total population. Two-fifths of the cotton crop is raised on farms owned or managed by negroes. The negro population in the South is about double since the close of the war, a strong indication that, while their death rate might be higher than the whites, their conditions of bodily health and comfort are certainly greatly improving.

The increase in schools and churches among the negroes of the South demonstrates the intellectual, moral and religious progress of the race since freedom came.

The impressive weight of the statistics which I have given above cannot be minimized by a partial or prejudiced view of those who do not take a broad, comprehensive view of the situation. There are many noble white men in the South (and the number is increasing) actively interested in the spread of primary and industrial education among the negroes, from whom individual instances of the development of progressive farming and business communities among the negroes can be learned, and who, as the result of their experience and observation, believe in the ultimate success of this practical educational experiment with the race.

The immediate effect of the fifteenth amendment, with the exclusion from the franchise of those who had been engaged in the Confederacy, was to throw large political power into the hands of an electorate that had not the education properly to conduct a government. And this led to the abuses which have been held up to execration by the lurid pictures of the reconstruction days. How far those pictures have been colored beyond the truth by partisan and race prejudice it is not necessary for us to discuss, because one of the things which every lover of his country ought to refrain from doing is to say the things which are likely to stir up again the dying embers of race and sectional hatred. It is unnecessary to do so. Even the truth under such circumstances is an offense. It is enough to say that, following reconstruction days, the votes of the negroes which under State and national laws they were entitled to cast, were by fraud and violence made to count for nothing, and since 1880 the fifteenth amendment in a number of Southern States has been treated largely as a dead letter. Of recent years, however, the leaders, of the South have felt deeply the demoralization sure to follow the flouting of the law and the maintenance of a government on fraud and violence. They have seen that it was impossible to confine that lawlessness which they justified to rid themselves of what they called negro domination to the one purpose, and they have felt its degrading influence in the whole political atmosphere of the South. Hence they have attempted to make the laws of the South square with the exclusion of the negro from the ballot. They have sought to do this by acts which were in their inception an evasion of the fifteenth amendment by the use of so-called grandfather clauses, and in other ways. But ultimately after these grandfather clauses had ceased to operate, the laws upon which they have depended were laws creating educational and property qualifications for electors. It is charged, and doubtless with truth, that such laws were not intended to be enforced against the whites, but only against the blacks, and that in this way they have continued to annul the fifteenth amendment. In a population where illiteracy is proportionately very large, no one can object certainly under the Federal Constitution to the establishment of electoral educational or property qualifications. And I do not understand that the intelligent colored men of the country object to the passage and enforcement of such a law; but they do object, and have a right to object, to the partial enforcement of such a law in such a way as to exclude the ineligible black men and allow to vote the white men who are equally ignorant and ineligible.

But, my friends, I am an optimist, and as I have already said, I regard the signs in the South, changing from one method in respect to elections to another, as an indication that in the near future there will be a steady improvement toward a more and more equal and impartial enforcement of these electoral laws. I think so because it is the part of political and economical wisdom. The property and educational qualifications make utterly impossible a return to the abuses which many Southerners profess to fear. The so-called negro domination is nothing but a dream and a nightmare of the past. The fifteenth amendment, while in the past it may not have accomplished all that its author intended it should, has in it this inestimable benefit to the negro race — that it fixes a restriction upon State election laws that may be temporarily violated, but can never be removed. However the opponent of equal political rights to the negro may turn and twist, whatever devices he may invent to give a specious appearance of legality to laws intended to exclude the negro because of his race or color, he will find his purpose thwarted by the broad and generous scope of the language of the amendment. The amendment is the measure of lawfulness toward which all good movements and all progress in the South must necessarily tend. What the negro and his friends demand is equality of enforcement of the law under the Constitution, and toward that end I feel convinced that all the influence of industrial progress in the South and the closer union between the sections necessarily are making.

If the negro will make himself indispensable to the business prosperity of the South, his political influence will take care of itself. By education and the acquisition of property he will become a member of the community whose political influence, instead of being unlawfully destroyed, will be welcomed and encouraged. As the colored man becomes eligible under the laws imposing educational and property qualifications, his standing in the community will give weight to the vote he casts, and it is inevitable that in the end industrial success will bring him full political rights. But few maintain that the negro to-day has not in the South an equal chance for bettering his condition by industry and education. The demand for labor with the increased prosperity of

the South makes him more and more valuable to that
section, and if by industrial education under the influence
of the greatest of these great industrial institutions his
usefulness as a member of the community has increased,
race prejudice will fade before business necessity, and we
shall have a rapidly growing negro electorate in the
South, whose political influence will be recognized in the
States of the South as worthy of respect and as one to
be reckoned with.

I know it is the habit of many contemplating the condition of the two races in the Southern States to shake
their heads and say that the negro problem is far from
solution, and that the future in this respect is dark.
Plans have been suggested for a migration of the negroes
to some other country, where they would live by themselves and grow up by themselves, and have a society
by themselves, and create a nation by themselves. Such
a suggestion is chimerical. The negro has no desire to
go, and the people of the South would seriously object
to his going. They were brought here originally against
their will, and were kept here until they have become
Americans. They are in this country as a part of our
people, and are bound to continue to be so. They are
entitled to unceasing effort on the part of the whole people in their struggle for better things, both because it is
our duty and to our interest to secure them equal opportunity. Whenever called upon, the negro has never
failed to make sacrifices for this, the only country he has,
and the only flag he loves.

All they can ask is equal opportunity and equal enforcement of the laws in respect to them and in respect
to the white race. When they have violated the laws,
they must expect the same punishment as the white race.
It is entirely natural, because they have been subjected
so often to injustice and contumely and insult, because
of their color and their race, that they should be suspicious whenever members of their race are brought to

punishment that the presumption in favor of their inno-
cence is not as strong as it would be in favor of white
men similarly accused.   It is also natural that their racial
prejudice and sympathies can be more easily aroused in
behalf of some one of their own number than are the
race prejudices of the more numerous and more fortunate
white race.   But such tendencies are to be expected, and
should no more turn aside the deep sympathy of the well-
wishers of the race than any other tendency directly
traceable to the long history of suffering and misfortune
to which they have been in the past subjected.

The statistics which may show a large criminal class
among the negroes at the South ought to frighten no
one.   This is to be expected where there is much ignorance and illiteracy.   Among the graduates of Hampton and Tuskegee, and like institutions, you will find a
clean record of Godfearing men and women struggling
onward and upward in the interest of their race.   Industrial independence, the aim of Hampton and Tuskegee, is the basis for all real progress of the negro race,
as it is of the Filipino people.   Advancement along that
path opens up to both the possibility, indeed, the certainty of attaining all other ideals, intellectual, political
and moral.

CHAPTER XXII

POLITICAL PROBLEMS OF THE SOUTH

ADDRESS AT LEXINGTON, KY., AUGUST 22, 1907

When I go through your State, and all these beautiful nature blessed States in the solid South, the thought forces itself on me why is it that in the last 40 years this magnificent part of the country, with an intelligent, high minded community is exercising so little influence in guiding the policies of this nation? Is it because they do not have influence? No. Is it because they have not votes? No. Is it because they do not have representation in Congress and in the Senate? No. Well, why is it? It is because the South has permitted itself to be united on an idea and a fear that ought to be outlived. It ought to assert its independence of the race issue and join the Republican party, and thus when we have a Republican administration it should be entitled to its representation in the great offices. When the Northern Democracy looks to the South and says to itself, " Well, these people and these delegates are going to vote with our community and it does not make any difference what candidate we nominate or what platform we adopt," how much influence do you suppose they have even with the Northern Democracy. Still less what influence can they expect to have with the Republican administration that knows that no matter how meritorious the issues that that party is sustaining in the nation it can count on no real support from the Southern States. Now, my dear friends, that ought to be changed. We have reached a time when there ought to be a reform in that matter; when there ought to be some independence of the ghost of a past issue and when the Southern men should express themselves as they have shown themselves to believe on the great living issues of the day. . . .

I know I venture a good deal in taking up an issue in the South which has occupied so much of the attention of the thinkers and the men of that region. I am dealing with a Southern question and a Southern white man does not think that a Northern white man can understand the question or can sympathize with the South. On the other hand my colored fellow citizens are not willing to look with as much judicial impartiality as they should upon the question, from their standpoint, and remembering the wrongs and oppression which they have suffered in the history of this country are not content except when a discussion of it is accompanied by condemnation that does not help at all. I am an optimist on the race question. I think that considering the difficulties of that question as we look back upon them now toward the war we have made marvelous progress. . . . Originally it was supposed that education of a general character would clear everything. Subsequently there was borne in upon the people the feeling that what that race needed was industrial education to teach them the dignity of labor, to teach them how to labor, both skilled and unskilled, to teach them how to carry on business, how to farm and ultimately to grow up and become valuable members of the community. Now that is the *eligibility that Booker Washington* is preaching to his race and I do not care whether you are a white man with' a white man's sympathy or a black man with a black man's sympathy, you will all agree with me, if you look down in your hearts, in saying that Booker Washington is one of the great men of this century. The reason is *that he sees that the only method* by which his race can be lifted up is by lifting themselves up and making themselves valuable members of the community by their own work. When they shall have made themselves valuable to the community then the community will value them and so do away with the prejudice. . . .

The South cannot get along without the negro and the negro needs the South. What is it that you hear from all the world around? I am in a position to know because I happen to be connected with a work that is engaged in hunting twenty-five or thirty-five thousand laborers. It is a demand for labor. If we were to take the negro out of the South the South would be poor indeed. Of course as he grows to be a better laborer he becomes more valuable but when it is proposed to move him out of Mississippi I observe that there is a tremendous objection and prejudice against it even to the point of violent preventing of his going. . . .

Now the issue, as it is to-day, is a past issue so far as the control of the votes in the States of the South is concerned. Therefore why should the men of the South to-day merely because of that past issue not vote their real sentiments on the living national issues of the day?

Take first the question of protection. All through the South the manufacturers have expended in an enormous way. Do you think the Southern white men who own those factories that you see on every side as you go from Washington to New Orleans would want changed the system of protection upon which that prosperity entirely depends? Of course they do not. Why then do they vote for the party in whose platform is the statement that protection is the robbery of the many for the benefit of the few? Are the Democrats of the South in favor of free trade or protection? I do not know that as a body you can say they are for one or the other, but that there are many in the South who are just as sound protectionists as any Republican in the North, every man within the sound of my voice knows, and they ought to vote the Republican ticket on that question and on that account.

Secondly, there is the foreign policy, the policy with respect to our dependencies, Porto Rico, Cuba and the Philippines. . . . Mr. Bryan's theory is that it is contrary to the Declaration of Independence for us to remain in the Philippines. The Declaration of Independence was made to apply to a people who for 1,000 years had been hammering out the principle of self-government and who were as well fitted to construct a government as any people that ever lived, but if the construction put upon that instrument is that every person has implanted in his bosom a divine knowledge of the science of self-government then all of the beautiful ladies in my presence ought to be able to vote for Governor Wilson at the next election. Every boy or girl that walks on the street ought to have a vote and the rules of eligibility for electors never could contain any thing which looked to education or property qualifications. In other words all those things which we have in our government and which existed at the time the Declaration of Independence was penned and signed refute the proposition that every man, no matter who he be, is capable of self-government. . . . .

Now I do not believe from what I have seen in the Southern newspapers and from the conversations that I have had with Southern men that upon that question most of the South are in favor of the scuttle policy of moving out and letting the Philippines, as one distinguished statesman said, " go to hades." I believe the men of the South are in favor of our assuming the responsibility that was thrust upon us of assisting our weaker brethren to build up themselves into a self-governing nation by means of education. . . .

Then there is the question of railway regulation or government ownership. I know the men of the South are opposed to government ownership. I know they are in favor of the system which Theodore Roosevelt has inaugurated of rigid control of the railways, to see that they discharge the trust which is imposed upon them in the enjoyment of their great franchises of furnishing transportation and of furnishing it at reasonable prices with fair dealing to all. Mr. Bryan in his Madison Square speech said that he was in favor of government ownership because he did not believe that the Interstate Commerce Tribunal, or whatever other tribunal you created, could be trusted to be free from the influence of the money power. Now Mr. Roosevelt believes in an entirely different doctrine. He believes that we have men courageous enough to enforce the law without regard to the influence of the money power and we ought to regulate rather than to take the step to assume an indebtedness of fourteen billions of dollars, put in the hands of the Executive the power which if it is abused would be dangerous to the community and the Republic.

There is another question, the question of trusts. Combination is the life of our present business. The government ought not to forbid combination of capital to reduce the cost of production any more than it should forbid the assembling of part of a machine in order to reduce the cost of manufacturing that which before was made by hand. We have also combinations of labor. The laboring man found, and he was quick to find, that he could not stand alone against the great capital that was amassed for the purpose of carrying on a business, and that the only way that he could carry on the necessary strife (I mean peaceful strife between capital and labor for a division of the joint profit) was to unite with his fellow workingman so that they might organize, so that they might have some discipline among themselves, so that they might raise money with which at times when there was enforced idleness they could maintain themselves and their families and hold the capitalist and the employer to an accountability as to better terms of employment and a larger share of the profit. Therefore we have that great system of trade unions which have been of inestimable benefit to labor and the working-man. But in the discipline that is necessary to make them effective they have to repose great power in their leaders and if that great power is misused and produces lawlessness then that is to be restrained. And so it is with combinations of capital. If they go on to reduce the cost of production and then share that reduction or that benefit with the public by reducing prices they are to be encouraged. But if they take in all the plants in the production of a particular article and reduce the cost of production by the use of a greater plant and then exert that means to control and monopolize the market and so maintain or raise the price they then deny to the public the benefit that the public is entitled to have and they become unlawful trusts.

We have not reached the millennium. I wish we had. I wish we could count on every nation being for government on strictly moral principles. On that account I believe the Southerners are with us and if they voted their real sentiments there would not be any doubt as to where they stood. I shall not go on to discuss the other issues. I only want to say that it seems to me now that in the State of Kentucky is the accepted hour for beginning the great reform which I have urged. You have a good beginning, with Governor Wilson at the head, who is a member of the bar of Louisville. He will make you a high-toned, courageous governor. The time is coming for Kentucky to take her place with the Republics north of the Ohio River and to range that State under the banner and leadership of the party of efficiency, the party of courage, the party of reform and new ideas, under the banner of Theodore Roosevelt.

CHAPTER XXIII

INJUNCTIONS IN LABOR DISPUTES

Llewelyn Lewis, of Martins Ferry, Ohio, President of the Ohio Federation of Labor, on January 4, 1908, addressed to Mr. Taft a letter, requesting answers to four questions concerning the relations between labor unions on strike and the courts. This letter, and the reply to it, follow:

MARTINS FERRY, OHIO, January 4, 1908.
Hon. William H. Taft, Secretary of War, Washington,
D. C.

DEAR SIR: At present the people of our country are much interested in the nomination of a candidate for President of the United States. The selection of such candidates by and for the respective political parties is but incidental in public interest to the views of the proposed candidates on questions, which vitally affect the rights, liberties and welfare of our citizens.

You are classed by your many friends everywhere as a presidential probability. As a citizen of Ohio, and an executive officer of the Ohio Federation of Labor, an organization which represents the interests of organized labor and the laboring people throughout the State, I take the liberty of respectfully soliciting your views upon a question which is an intensely live issue amongst the laboring people everywhere. I refer to the subject of injunctions, and their use or abuse as applied to the workingman. You are aware, of course, of many of the abuses which have arisen and been embodied as law in

19   335,

the administration of this special branch of legal remedies.

You will therefore pardon me if I submit specifically for your consideration and answer the following propositions:

1st. The enactment of a specific law upon which an injunction or temporary restraining order may issue; in other words, defining in specific terms the language in which such an injunction, or restraining order, may be had.

2nd. That no temporary restraining order or injunction should be issued until after notice to the defendant and a hearing is had upon the petition.

3rd. That a final hearing and determination should be made within five or ten days from the making of the temporary restraining order.

4th. In citations for contempt for alleged violations of restraining orders or injunctions, that it should be optional with the defendant to be heard by a court other than the one issuing the temporary or permanent injunction.

Thanking you for a reply at your earliest convenience, I am,　　　　　Very respectfully yours,
　　　　　　　　　　　　LLEWELYN LEWIS.

SECRETARY TAFT'S REPLY.

WAR DEPARTMENT, WASHINGTON,
　　　　　　　　　January 6, 1908.

MY DEAR SIR: I am in receipt of your letter of January 4th in which you ask me, on behalf of the Ohio Federation of Labor, to state my views in respect to the use and abuse of injunctions in what are generally called labor disputes; and you put four specific questions on the subject for answer.

Before taking up the specific questions, and in order more completely to understand my answers to those questions, I should shortly state my opinion with the reference to the organization of labor, as I have expressed this on numerous occasions in years past. I believe it to be highly beneficial and entirely lawful for laborers to unite in their common interests. They have labor to sell, and if they stand together they are often able, all of them, to command better prices for their labor, or more advantageous terms of employment than when dealing singly, for the necessities of the single employee may compel him to accept any terms offered him. The accumulation of funds for the support of those who propose to enter into the controversy with the employer by striking, is one of the legitimate objects of such an organization. Its members have the right to appoint officers, who shall advise them as to the course to be taken by them in their relations to their employer, and if the members choose to repose such authority in any one, the officers may order members, on pain of expulsion, to join a strike. Having left their employment, they have the right, by persuasion and other peaceable means, to induce those who would take their places, to join the strike and their union. They may not do this by violence, by threats of violence, or by any other conduct equivalent to duress. It is only when the object is not betterment of the terms of their employment, or some other lawful purpose, but is for an unlawful purpose, or when the means they use are unlawful, that they can be properly restrained by law.

Coming now to the answer of your first question: You ask me what I would think of an enactment of a law defining the cases in which a temporary restraining order may issue, and defining in specific terms the language in which such orders may be framed. I see no objection to the enactment of a statute which shall define the rights of laborers in their controversies with their former employers. As this statute would fix the lawful limits of their action, it would necessarily furnish a

definite rule for determining the cases in which injunctions might issue, as well as their character and scope.
It should be said that this statute, however, if enacted
by Congress, could relate only to the District of Columbia or some place within the exclusive jurisdiction of the
Federal government, or to those employers and employees whose relations are within congressional definition
and control.

Generally, the law governing the relation between employer and employee is a State law and is only enforced
in the Federal courts when the jurisdiction arises by reason of the diverse citizenship of the parties. Speaking,
generally, however, both as to Federal and State legislation, I see no objection to a statute, which shall, so far
as possible, definite the rights of both parties in such
controversies more accurately. Indeed, the more exactly the lawful limitations on the actions of both parties
are understood, the better for them, and for the public.

Second: You ask me what I think of a provision
that no restraining order or injunction shall issue, except
after notice to the defendant and a hearing had. This
was the rule under the Federal statutes for many years,
but it was subsequently abolished. In the class of cases
to which you refer, I do not see any objection to the re-
enactment of that Federal statute. Indeed, I have taken
occasion to say in public speeches, that the power to issue injunction ex parte has given rise to certain abuses
and injustice to the laborers engaged in a peaceable
strike. Men leave employment on a strike; counsel for
the employer applies to a judge and presents an affidavit
averring fear of threatened violence and making such a
case on the ex parte statement that the judge feels called
upon to issue a temporary restraining order. The temporary restraining order is served on all the strikers; they
are not lawyers; their fears are aroused by the process
with which they are not acquainted; and, although their
purpose may have been entirely lawful, their common

determination to carry through the strike is weakened by an order which they never have had an opportunity to question, and which is calculated to discourage their proceeding in their original purpose. To avoid this injustice, I believe, as I have already said, that the Federal statute might well be made what it was originally, requiring notice, and a hearing before an injunction issues.

Third: In answer to your third question, it would seem that it is unnecessary to impose any limitation as to the time for a final hearing, if, before an injunction can issue at all, notice and hearing must be given. The third question is relevant and proper, only should the power of issuing ex parte injunctions be retained in the court. In such case, I should think it eminently proper that the statute should require the court issuing an ex parte injunction to give the person against whom the injunction was issued an opportunity to have a hearing thereon within a very short space of time, not to exceed, I should say, three or four days.

Fourth: Your fourth query is, in effect, what I would think of a provision in such cases by which the contemnor — that is, the person charged with the violation of an order of injunction — might object to the judge who issued the injunction, as the one to try the issue, whether the injunction had been violated, and to fix punishment in case of conviction, and thereby require another judge to try the issue and impose sentence, if necessary. In Federal courts in such a case it would be proper to provide that the senior circuit judge of the circuit should, upon the application of the defendant or contemnor, designate another district or circuit judge to sit and hear the issue presented. I do not think such a restriction would be unreasonable. In most cases it would be unnecessary. But I admit that there is a popular feeling that in contempt proceedings, and the very name of the proceeding suggests it, that the judge issuing the injunction has a personal sensitiveness in respect to its violation, and therefore that he does not bring to the trial of the issue presented by the charge of contempt of his order the calm, judicial mind which insures justice.

I think that this popular feeling is, in most cases, unfounded, but I believe that it is better, where it can be done without injuring the authority of the court and the efficiency of its process, to grant such a privilege to the contemnor and thus avoid an appearance of injustice, even at some inconvenience in the matter of securing another judge. There is some analogy, though it is not complete, between the exclusion of a judge from sitting in the court of appeals to review a decision of his own, which now obtains in the practice of the Federal court of appeals, by statute, and the present suggested case. It is of the highest importance that the authority of the court to enforce its own orders effectively should not be weakened and therefore I am opposed to the intervention of a.jury between the court's decree and its enforcement by contempt proceedings. It would mean long delay and greatly weaken the authority of the court.

I do not think that the permission to change the judge, however, would constitute either serious delay or injure the efficacy of the order, while it may secure greater public confidence in the justice of the court's action. The appearance of justice is almost as important as the existence of it in the administration of courts.

Sincerely yours,
WM. H. TAFT.

Llewelyn Lewis, Esq., Martins Ferry, Ohio.

CHAPTER XXIV

LABOR AND CAPITAL

COOPER UNION, NEW YORK, JANUARY 10, 1908.

ORIGIN OF INSTITUTION OF PROPERTY.

Property and capital were first accumulated in implements, in arms, and personal belongings, the value of which depended almost wholly on the labor in their making. As man's industry and self-restraint grew, he produced by his labor not only enough for his immediate necessities, but also a surplus, which he saved to be used in aid of future labor. By this means the amount which each man's labor would produce was thereafter increased. There followed at length the corollary that he whose savings from his own labor had increased the product of another's labor was entitled to enjoy a share in the joint result, and in the fixing of these shares was the first agreement between labor and capital. The certainty that a man could enjoy as his own that which he produced or that which he saved, and so could dispose of it to another, was the institution of private property and the strongest motive for industry beyond that needed merely to live.

This is what has led to the accumulation of capital in the world. It is the mainspring of human action which has raised man from the barbarism of the early ages to modern civilization.

Labor needs capital *to secure the best production*, while capital needs labor in producing anything. The more capital in use the more work there is to do, and the more work there is to do the more laborers are needed. The greater the need for laborers the better their pay per man. Manifestly, it is in the direct interest of the laborer that capital shall increase faster than the number of those who work. It follows, as a necessary conclusion, that to destroy the guaranties of property is a direct blow at the interest of the workingman.

The last two generations have witnessed a marvelous material development. It has been effected by the assembling and enforced co-operation of simple elements that previously had been separately used. Therefore the aggregation of capital, the other essential element with labor in producing anything, became an obvious means of securing economy in the manufacture of everything. The result was a great increase in the number of the corporations and the assumption of the corporate form by seven-eighths of the active capital of the country. The men who have by economic organization of capital at the same time increased the amount of the country's capital, increased the demand and price for labor, and reduced the cost of necessities are not philanthropists. Their sole motive has been one of gain, and with the destruction of private property that motive would disappear, and so would the progress of society. The very advantage to be derived from the security of private property in our civilization is that it turns the natural selfishness and desire for gain into the strongest motive for doing that without which the upward development of mankind would cease and retrogression would begin.

It is greatly in the interest of the workingman, therefore, that corporate capital should be fairly treated. Any injustice done to it acts directly upon the wage-earners that must look to corporate wealth for their employment. Take the large body of railroad employees. Any drastic legislation which tends unjustly to reduce the legitimate earnings of the railroad must in the end fall with heavy weight upon the employees of that railroad, because the manager will ultimately turn toward wages as the place

where economy can be effected.   So in respect to taxation, if the corporation is made to bear more than its
share of the public burdens, it reacts directly, first, upon
its stockholders, and then upon its employees.

The conclusion I seek to reach is that the workingman
who entertains a prejudice against the lawful capitalist
because he is wealthy, who votes with unction for the men
who are urging unjust and unfair legislation against him,
and who makes demagogic appeals to acquire popular
support in what they are doing is standing in his own
light, is blind to his own interests, and is cutting off the
limb on which he sits.   It is to the direct interest of the
workingman to use careful discrimination in approving
or disapproving proposed legislation of this kind and to
base his conclusion and vote on the issue whether the provision is fair or just, and not on the assumption that any
legislation that subjects a corporation to a burden must
necessarily be in the interest of the workingman.   What
I am anxious to emphasize is that there is a wide economic
and business field in which the interests of the wealthiest
capitalist and of the humblest laborer are exactly the same.

But while it is in the common interest of labor and
capital to increase the fruits of production, yet in determining the share of each in the product, their interests
are plainly opposed.   The organization of capital into
corporations with the position of advantage which this
gives it in a dispute with single laborers over wages,
makes it absolutely necessary for labor to unite to maintain itself.

For instance, how could workingmen dependent on each
day's wages for living dare to take a stand which might
leave them without employment if they had not by small
assessments accumulated a common fund for their support during such emergency.   In union they must sacrifice
some independence of action, and there have sometimes
been bad results from the tyranny of the majority in such
cases; but the hardships which have followed impulsive

resort to extreme measures have had a good effect to lessen them. Experience, too, is leading to classification among the members, so that the cause of the skilled and worthy shall not be leveled down to that of the lazy and neglectful. This is being done, I am told, by what is called the maximum and minimum wage.

The effect of the organization of labor, on the whole, has been highly beneficial in securing better terms for employment for the whole laboring community. I have not the slightest doubt, and no one who knows anything about the subject can doubt, that the existence of labor unions steadies wages. More than this, it has brought about an amelioration of the condition of the laborers in another way. Labor unions have given great attention to factory acts which secure a certain amount of air and provision for the safety of employees, to the safety-appliance acts in respect to railroads, to fixing the law governing the liability of railroads to their employees for injuries sustained by accident, to the restriction of child labor in factories, and to similar remedial legislation. The interest of the workingman has been more direct in these matters than even that of the philanthropists, and he has pressed the matter until in the legislation of nearly every state, the effect of his influence is seen.

What the capitalist, who is the employer of labor, must face is that the organization of labor — the labor union — is a permanent condition in the industrial world. It has come to stay. If the employer would consult his own interest, he must admit this and act on it. Under existing conditions the blindest course that an employer of labor can pursue is to decline to recognize labor unions as the controlling influence in the labor market and to insist upon dealing only with his particular employees. Time and time again one has heard the indignant expression of a manager of some great industrial enterprise, that he did not propose to have the labor union run his business;

that he would deal with his own men, and not with outsiders.

The time has passed in which that attitude can be assumed with any hope of successfully maintaining it. What the wise manager of corporate enterprise employing large numbers of laborers will do, is to receive the leaders of labor unions with courtesy and respect and listen to their claims and arguments as they would to the managers of any other corporate enterprise with whom they were to make an important contract affecting the business between them. At times some labor leaders are intoxicated with the immense power that they exercise in representing thousands of their fellow-workers and are weak enough to exhibit a spirit of arrogance. Dealing with them is trying to the patience of the employer. So, too, propositions from labor unions sometimes are so exorbitant in respect to the terms of employment as literally to deprive the manager of the control which he ought to retain over the laborers employed in his business. This is to be expected in a comparatively new movement and is not to be made a ground for condemning it.

On the other hand, the arrogance is not confined to one side. We all of us know that there are a number of employers who have the spirit of intolerance and sense of power because of their immense resources, and that their attitude is neither conciliatory nor likely to lead to an adjustment of differences. The wise men among the employers of labor and the labor leaders are those who discard all appearance of temper or sense of power and attempt by courteous consideration and calm discussion to reach a common ground. One of the great difficulties in peaceful adjustments of controversies between labor and capital is the refusal of each side to take time to understand the attitude of the other. If the leaders of the workingmen believe that the employer is considering their argument and weighing it, and the labor leaders manifest an interest in the conditions with reference to expense and profit of the employer, the possibility of an adjustment is much greater than when each occupies a stiff and resentful attitude against the other.

It goes without saying that where an adjustment can not be reached by negotiation, it is far better for the community at large that the differences be settled by submission to an impartial tribunal under an agreement to abide its judgment than to resort to a trial of resistance and endurance by lockouts and strikes.

One of the instances, most striking in the history of this country, of the possibility of bringing capital and labor together to consider the question from a standpoint of reasonableness and patriotism is the settlement of the Pennsylvania anthracite coal strike. The permanence of the settlement which was there effected is a triumphant vindication of what was done. And it illustrates the possibilities when opponents in such controversies can be brought face to face and in the presence of impartial persons be made to discuss all the circumstances surrounding the issue.

I shall not stop to cite statistics to show the enormous loss in the savings of labor as well as of capitalists which strikes and lockouts have involved. Everybody admits their destructive character and that all means should be resorted to to avoid them. Still, there are times when nothing but a strike will accomplish the legitimate purpose of the laborer.

And, now, what is the right of the labor union with respect to the strike? I know that there has been at times a suggestion in the law that no strike can be legal. I deny this. Men have the right to leave the employ of their employer in a body in order to impose on him as great an inconvenience as possible to induce him to come to their terms. They have the right in their labor unions to delegate to their leaders the power to say when to strike. They have the right in advance to accumulate by contribution from all members of the labor union a fund which shall enable them to leave during the pendency of the strike.   They have the right to use persuasion with all other laborers who are invited to take their places, in order to convince them of the advantage to labor of united action.   It is the business of courts and of the police to respect these rights with the same degree of care that they respect the right of owners of capital to the protection of their property and business.   A resort to violence, or other form of lawlessness, on behalf of a labor union, properly merits and receives the sharpest condemnation from the public, and is quite likely to lose the cause of labor its support in the particular controversy.

It would be a very insufficient consideration of the relations of labor and capital if I did not take up the abuses, lawlessness, and infractions of others' rights, of which some of the combiners of capital and some of the wage-earners — members of labor unions — have been from time to time guilty and did not consider further the remedy for the restraint of these evils.

Let us deal first with industrial corporations.   The temptation to the managers, when the enterprises become very large, is to suppress competition and maintain prices, and thus to deny to the public its proper share in the benefit sought to be attained and to appropriate to the corporate owners all the profit derived from improved facilities of production.

The railway and transportation companies have misused their great powers to promote the unlawful purpose of these industrial combinations.   The largest concerns controlling enormous shipments have induced and sometimes coerced the railway companies into giving them either secret rates or open public rates so deftly arranged with a view to the conditions of the larger concern, as to make it impossible for its would-be business competitors to live. The rebate of a very small amount per hundredweight

of goods shipped by any one of the great industrial corporations will pay enormous dividends on the capital invested. The evils of railroad management can be
summed up in the words "unjust discrimination."

Wage-earners are not injuriously affected in their terms
of employment directly by such violations of law by combinations of capital. But they are very seriously affected
in another way. The maintenance of such unlawful
monopolies is for the purpose of keeping up the prices
of the necessities of life, and this necessarily reduces the
purchasing power of the wages which the wage-earners
receive. This is a serious detriment to them and a real
reason why they should condemn such corporate abuses
and sympathize with the effort to stamp them out.

In rare instances corporate managers have entered into
a course of violence to maintain their side of a labor controversy. They have justified it on the ground that they
were simply fighting fire with fire, and that if the labor
union proceeded to use dynamite they would use dynamite
in return. I can not too strongly condemn this course
or this argument. No amount of lawlessness on the part
of the labor striker will justify the lawlessness on the
part of the employer. Such a course means a recurrence
of civil war and anarchy.

A second abuse which employers are sometimes guilty
of is what is technically known as blacklisting, by which
laboring men, solely because they may have been advocates of a strike, or have been against a compromise in
a labor dispute, are tagged by one employer of labor, and
all other employers are forbidden on penalty of business
ostracism to give them a means of livelihood. This is
unlawful and should be condemned. It is the counterpart of the boycott, or indeed it is itself a boycott in one
form.

What are the abuses which not infrequently proceed
from some of the members of united labor? They are,
first, open violence and threats of violence to prevent the

employment of other workingmen in the places which such members have left on a strike. If there are other laborers available, then there are only two ways by which the strikers can accomplish their purpose, either by actual or threatened violence to those who would take their places, or by persuading them in the interest of all labor that they should join their union, receive the benefits of the common fund for support during enforced idleness, and join in the refusal to aid the employer in his extremity. Violence and threatened violence are of course unlawful and are strongly to be condemned. Persuasion not amounting in effect to duress is lawful.

Another method by which wage-earners sometimes attempt to coerce their employer into acquiescence in their demands is what is called a boycott. This is a cruel instrument and has been declared to be unlawful in every court with whose decisions I am familiar. The Anthracite Strike Commission, which had upon it such a distinguished jurist as Judge George Gray, of Delaware, and Mr. Clark, the president of one of the great labor organizations of the country, and other men entirely indifferent as between labor and capital — men selected by agreement between the employers and the employees in that great controversy — used the following language in respect to the boycott:

" What is popularly known as the boycott (a word of evil omen and unhappy origin) is a form of coercion by which a combination of many persons seek to work their will upon a single person or upon a few persons by compelling others to abstain from social or beneficial business intercourse with such person or persons. Carried to the extent sometimes practiced in aid of a strike, and as was in some instances practiced in connection with the late anthracite strike, it is a cruel weapon of aggression, and its use immoral and antisocial."

To say this is not to deny the legal right of any man or set of men voluntarily to refrain from social intercourse or business relations with any persons whom he or they, with or without good reason, dislike. This may sometimes be un-Christian, but it is not illegal. But when it is a concerted purpose of a number of persons not only to abstain themselves from such intercourse, but to render the life of their victim miserable by persuading and intimidating others to refrain, such purpose is malicious, and the concerted attempt to accomplish it is a conspiracy at common law, and merits and should receive the punishment due to such a crime.

I may add that the same Commission visited blacklisting with similar condemnation.

What are the remedies by which a person injured may be protected against the illegal acts of combinations of capital and of combinations of labor? First, if the injury sought to be inflicted is one which will be inadequately compensated for in money damages, one can apply to a court of equity to prevent the injury from being done, and that court can, in advance of the proposed violation of the plaintiff's rights, determine exactly what those rights are and advise the defendant accordingly; or he can wait until the acts are performed and then, by suit for damages, he can make himself whole if he can.

In cases of unlawful combinations of capital, as well as of such combinations of labor, the method in equity by securing an injunction seems to be preferred by those who are about to be injured. In every statute which has been enacted to denounce the improper use of capital to secure illegal restraints of trade and illegal monopolies, a specific provision has been inserted enabling those who are injured or affected to bring an equity proceeding to enjoin the carrying on of the improper methods about to be attempted. In the same way, when labor unions or members of labor unions or workingmen on a strike resort to methods destructive of the business of their employer and his property, the employer deems it the most convenient method of defending himself to apply to a court of equity for an injunction against those who give indication of their intention to carry on such methods.

This remedy by injunction has been very severely denounced and criticised, on the ground that it places in the hands of a judge legislative, judicial, and executive powers; that it enables him to make the law for one case against a particular individual and if he does not abide by it to try him and punish him. When this objection is analyzed it is found to be unjust.

An injunction suit does not differ in the slightest degree from a suit brought after the event, so far as the function of the court is concerned in declaring the law, except that the court declares the law in respect of anticipated facts rather than in respect of those which have happened. He has no authority to make law. In an injunction suit, as in any other suit, he merely interprets the law and applies it to the circumstances. His judgment in the one case involves exactly the same precedents and the same rules of law as in the other. In order to save the party plaintiff from having to bring suit to recover for an injury that he is going to suffer, he says, "This is an unlawful injury; and as you threaten to do it I enjoin you from doing it."

Certainly, prevention is better than cure, and it is no wonder that a man who is about to have his business injured or his property destroyed prefers to prevent the injury rather than to allow it to occur. Neither a suit in damages nor a criminal prosecution is likely to bring him back his property or to restore his loss. Moreover, in cases of boycott, in many States, there is no provision for criminal prosecution.

I wish to invite attention to this writ of injunction, which is one of the most beneficial remedies known to the law, and to trace its history and show how useful it has been in the past for the purpose of preventing injustice.

Originally, in England, from which we get our pro-

20

cedure and most of our law, the King was supposed to decide cases through his judges of the King's bench or of the common pleas. The common law was rather rigid and severe, especially in holding persons to the letter of their contracts, and judgments went for the plaintiff on this strict interpretation that really shocked the conscience. And so, after a while, the people began to appeal to the King to save them from the severity of his own courts. He turned the matter over to the lord keeper of the great seal, and said, "Work out equity in this case." The way the lord keeper worked it out was not to issue any direction to the court of King's bench or the common pleas; but he took hold of the plaintiff in the suit and threatened him with excommunication if he did not stop the suit and do that justice which equity required.

In other words, he enjoined the plaintiff from proceeding with the suit in the court of the King's bench or of the common pleas, as the case might be, and brought him into what grew to be a court of equity known as the court of chancery. As the lord keeper in those days was an ecclesiastic, he exercised power over the consciences of the litigants, and the threat of excommunication was generally sufficient to enforce what he wished. Subsequently, the lord keeper ceased to be a bishop and became known as the lord chancellor, and after the court of equity had been established, violation of the injunction was punished by imprisonment instead of excommunication.

Let me take a case that illustrates the usefulness of the writ of injunction. At common law, when a man wished to borrow $500 on his farm which was worth $10,000 he gave a mortgage to secure it. The mortgage was a conveyance of the title to the land with the condition that the title should become absolute if the money was not paid on the date mentioned in the mortgage. If the money was not paid, the creditor should put the debtor out of possession by suit and for $500 become the owner of a farm which was worth $10,000. In such a case the lord keeper said to the plaintiff:

"Here, you are trying to get this farm for $500 when it is worth $10,000. That is not equitable, and I will not let you do it. I will enjoin you from continuing that suit, because you are after something that is unjust, and I will make you come in before me and settle this, and if the defendant is not able to pay the $500 and interest we will sell the farm and pay you the $500 and interest and turn over the balance to the defendant."

That was an equitable decision, and it was made effective by the power of injunction.

A man leases a farm, with a row of beautiful trees, to a tenant. The tenant advises him that he is going to cut the trees down during his tenancy. What is the landlord to do? Is he to let the tenant cut his trees down and then sue him for the value of the trees? No. Equity suggests the remedy that he go into court and enjoin the man and prevent injury which could not be compensated for in damages.

A man owns a lucrative business and a numerous set of people conceive a prejudice against him or a desire to injure him, and institute a boycott against him and threaten that they will withdraw their patronage, which is valuable, from anybody that has anything to do with him. In that way he loses a lot of customers. Now, is not it better that he should apply to the court to enjoin them from taking that course and inflicting injury on him that he cannot measure in damages than that they should be permitted to destroy his business and he should have the burden of a lawsuit afterwards with all the uncertainty as to damages and the doubt about getting his money even if he secured a judgment?

So, too, where a body of strikers by continued acts of violence, trespass, constituting a nuisance, attempt to stop

his business, the injury he suffers, it is peculiarly difficult
for him to estimate, and a judgment for money would be
a very inadequate remedy.

But it is said that the writ of injunction has been
abused in this country in labor disputes, and that a number of injunctions have been issued that ought never to
have been issued. I agree that there has been abuse in
this regard. I think it has grown chiefly from the practice of issuing injunctions *ex parte;* that is, without giving
notice or hearing to the defendant. The injustice that
is worked is in this wise: Men leave employment on a
strike intending to conduct themselves peaceably and
within the law. The counsel for the employer visits a
judge, presents an affidavit in which an averment is made
that violence is threatened, injury to property and injury
to business. And accordingly on this affidavit the judge
issues a temporary restraining order *ex parte* against the
defendants who are named in the petition or bill. The
broadest expressions are used in the writ — frequently
too broad. The defendants are workingmen, not lawyers. They are not used to the processes of the court.
The expressions of the writ are formidable. A doubt
arises in their minds as to the legality of what they are
about to do. The stiffening is taken out of the strike,
the men drop back, and the strike is over, and all before
they have had a chance in court to demonstrate, as they
might, that they had no intention of doing anything unlawful or doing any violence.

Under the original Federal judiciary act, it was not
permissible for the Federal courts to issue an injunction
without notice. There had to be notice and, of course,
a hearing. I think it would be entirely right in this class
of cases, to amend the law and provide that no temporary
restraining order should issue at all until after notice and
a hearing. Then the court could be advised by both
sides with reference to the exact situation, and the danger

of issuing a writ too broad or of issuing a writ without good ground would generally be avoided.

There is another objection made, and that is that the judge who issues the writ has a personal sensitiveness in respect to its violation that gives him a bias when he comes to hear contempt proceedings on a charge of disobedience to the order which makes it unfair for him to impose a punishment if conviction follows. I think few judges on the bench would allow such a consideration to affect them, but I agree that there is a popular doubt of the judge's impartial attitude in such a case. For that reason, I would favor a provision allowing the defendant in contempt proceedings to challenge the judge issuing the injunction, and to call for the designation of another judge to hear the issue. I don't think it would seriously delay the hearing of the cause, and it would give more confidence in the impartiality of the decision. It is almost as important that there should be the appearance of justice as that there should be an actual administration of it.

If, whenever a court issues an injunction that is improperly worded, that goes too far, or that ought never to have been granted, the labor union interested will take the matter up to the court of last resort, it will secure a series of decisions that will prevent the issue of injunctions such as some of those they now complain of. The labor union has a fund, and it could not be devoted to a better purpose than fixing the law exactly as it should be under the decision of the court of last resort. I should not object at all to the definition of the rights of employer and of the withdrawing employee in labor controversies by statute. I should think that an excellent way of making clear what is lawful and what is unlawful. But until that course is pursued, the rights of the parties to such controversies should be carefully defined by courts of last resort, and when this is done courts of first instance will keep within lawful bounds.

There is a class of capitalists who look upon labor unions as *per se* vicious and a class of radical labor unionists who look upon capital as labor's natural enemy. I believe, however, that the great majority of each class are gradually becoming more conciliatory in their attitude, the one toward the other. Between them is a larger class, neither capitalist nor labor unionist, who are without prejudices, and I hope I am one of those. I earnestly hope that a more conservative and conciliatory attitude on both sides may avoid the destructive struggles of the past.

CHAPTER XXV

QUESTIONS AND ANSWERS

At the conclusion of Secretary Taft's formal address
on "Labor and Capital" at Cooper Union, an opportunity was given the audience to ask the speaker any
questions germane to the subject he had discussed. The
following is from a stenographic report of the proceedings:

> Query: Do you think that the laborer of
> to-day gets sufficient compensation for his labor?

Well, I don't know what compensation he gets and I
don't know what his labor is. I think some laborers do
not get sufficient compensation, and I think some get
more than they ought to have. (Laughter and applause.)

> Query: What caused Mr. Taft to change his
> attitude towards the workmen and unions as the
> one he had while on the bench of the Ohio court?
(Laughter.)

Judge Alec Humphries of Louisville, is one of the
best lawyers in the Sixth Circuit, and I asked him once
whether he didn't find that lawyers are the poorest witnesses. Well, he said he thought he did. He said that
the best witness he ever had was a distiller, a wealthy
man of Louisville named J. M. Atherton. He had
represented him in a number of cases and in a number
of cases where the feeling was pretty heated between him
and the other side. A great many of the questions that

357

were put were of the form of the question that I have
just read, and the way he used to begin to answer those
questions was this: I will first answer the insinuation
in your question, and then I will try to answer what you
may not be asking for. (Laughter.) Now I will tell
you. You cannot find a word in this address that I have
delivered to-night that is not supported by every opinion
that I ever rendered in an injunction suit — you hire lawyers and try to find it. I have never changed my attitude a particle on the subject, and everything I have
said to-night has been exactly in accord with my attitude in respect to the rights of labor, the necessity for
maintaining the law, the necessity for maintaining the
rights of property on the one hand and the necessity of
maintaining the rights of persons on the other. (Applause.)

　　Query: How can you make out that the policy
　　of a property right in the boycott case is parallel to
　　the cutting of the trees and the mortgage?

Well, let me illustrate a case. When I was on the
bench in Ohio, to which reference has heretofore been
made, I tried a case of this character — it was a jury
case, a suit for damages brought by Moores & Company,
lime dealers, against the Bricklayers' Union No. 3 for
a boycott that had arisen in this wise: Bricklayers'
Union No. 3 had a member who was a brother of a boss
bricklayer, and they got into a controversy. I don't
know just what the merits of that controversy were.
But they were such that the Bricklayers' Union declared
a boycott against the boss bricklayer and notified everybody in the material business that anybody that gave him
material they would in turn boycott. Moores & Company went to the boss bricklayer and said, "We have
got a contract with you, but we want to avoid trouble,
and we would like you to let us off this contract." He
said, "All right, I will get my lime." So he used to

send his wagon down to the freight car in the station and get his lime just out of the door and pay for it at that point. But some one of the labor union saw him, reported it, and so they imposed a boycott on Moores & Company. Moores & Company suffered a destruction of their business nearly, and then they brought suit on the ground that this was a boycott and they were entitled to recover damages from the Bricklayers' Union. It was tried by a jury, with a Knight of Labor on the jury, and the jury brought in quickly a verdict of $2,500. Moores & Company have since been working fifteen years trying to collect the $2,500, and they haven't got a cent of it.

Now I ask you, doesn't that present very much the case of the trees or the mortgage? Isn't it a case of inadequacy of remedy, and isn't it a case where, therefore, it would have been better to have an injunction issue against that Bricklayers' Union and have the union stop the unlawful injury to the business of Moores & Company? (Applause.)

> Query: Is there any redress in law for a disinterested public when capitalists and laborers insist on keeping up a struggle that is disastrous to the community?

Well, I don't know of any except you can keep up a good deal of thinking, and you can express your opinion through the press, and after all, the effect of public opinion is the one which restrains both the labor community and the capitalists in the end. It is the public opinion in a Republic like ours that maintains it, that saves us from destruction. You take a city government that is corrupt as hell, and yet the public opinion will keep it measurably within the law. (Applause.)

> Query: What do you advise the workingmen who are out of work for a considerable time and

who are starving with their families on account of the present crisis to do?

God knows. They have my deepest sympathy. If they can't get work, of course there is the charity in the community of New York and the country over that will aid them. But it is an awful case, an awful case, when a man who is willing to work, who scorns to be on the charity of anybody, is put in this condition. (Applause.)

Query: If injunctions are an equity safeguard, why should they not issue on behalf of labor unions when their industrial rights are threatened?

One of the uncomfortable features of administering justice from a court is that you get a great many more of one kind of cases than you do of another, and men with capital are able to go into court and men who haven't capital are afraid of it. Now, one of the difficulties in respect to these controversies is that the labor unions don't go into court as much as I wish they did. The courts will protect their industrial rights with all the care that they can possibly summon. It is a gratification to sit in a case of that sort so as to demonstrate the impartiality of courts. (Applause.)

I am asked whether government ownership of mines, railroads, and so forth, would not render disputes between operators and owners easier to adjust.

I don't think so. I think we would have the same discussions, the same political controversies. And if we had government ownership of railroads and mines, have you ever thought of the tremendous power that you are putting in the hands of a few men in Washington? The Lord knows that the powers are sufficiently concentrated there now, so much indeed that it is hard to get the business properly conducted. And you put all the railroads and all the mines under the direction of one man in Washington or a set of men, and you create a power there that may well make you tremble for the safety of the Republic. (Applause and cheers and cries of Good.)

Query: Do you believe that the Sherman law offers an adequate remedy against interstate industrial combinations?

Well, I think that we are working it out so that it will. The difficulty about the Sherman law, I don't hesitate to say, is that it was enacted at a time when Congress didn't fully understand what the evil was that it was legislating against and, therefore, put the law in such general terms that the burden has been thrown upon the courts of construing it and putting specifications into it so as to make it practicable to say that it can be used to restrain the evils that Congress was directing its legislation against. My own judgment is that the time has come now, because I think the law has been evolved sufficiently, to draft a law to substitute for the Sherman law in which specifications shall be put so that members of the business community may know with greater clearness the line between lawfulness and illegality and keep their business within that. (Applause.)

Query: Why should not a blacklisted laborer be allowed an injunction as well as a boycotted capitalist?

He ought to be, and if I were on the bench I would give him one mighty quick.

Query: In how much, Mr. Taft, or in how far do you consider the undoubted influence of trusts have gained upon legislators, and do you believe there is not sufficient remedy against this undue influence and, if so, which?

Well, I think that within the last two or three years we have had an awakening. I do not believe there are many legislators that are allowing it to be known that trusts are influencing them to-day, and that is the force of public opinion to which I referred.   There has been a great moral awakening throughout this country, and men have had to show up and say whether they are on the side of underground influence or whether they stand for justice and for preserving the rights of the people on the one side and the rights of private property and person on the other.   (Applause.)

CHAPTER XXVI

THE POLITICAL EFFECT OF CHRISTIAN MISSIONS

ADDRESS BEFORE THE LAYMEN'S MISSIONARY MOVEMENT, AT CARNEGIE HALL, NEW YORK, APRIL 20, 1908

Mr. Chairman, Ladies and Gentlemen:

I have known a good many people who were opposed to foreign missions. I have known a good many regular attendants at church — consistent members, that religiously, if you choose to use that term, refused to contribute to foreign missions. I confess that there was a time when I was enjoying a snug provincialism, that I hope has left me now, when I rather sympathized with that view. Until I went to the Orient, until there were thrust upon me the responsibilities with reference to the extension of civilization in those far distant lands, I did not realize the immense importance of foreign missions. The truth is, we have got to wake up in this country. We are not all there is in the world. There are lots of people besides us that are entitled to our effort and our money and our sacrifice to help them on in the world. Now no man can study the movement of modern civilization from an impartial standpoint, and not realize that Christianity and the spread of Christianity are the only basis for hope of modern civilization in the growth of popular self-government. The spirit of Christianity is pure democracy. It is the equality of man before God — the equality of man before the law, which is, as I understand it, the most God-like manifestation that man has been able to make.

363

I am not here to-night to speak of foreign missions
from a purely religious standpoint. That has been done
and will be done. I am here to speak of them from the
standpoint of political governmental advancement, the
advancement of modern civilization, and I think I have
had some opportunity to know how dependent we are on
the spread of Christianity for any hope we may have of
uplifting the peoples whom Providence has thrust upon us
for our guidance.

Foreign missions began a long time ago. In the Philippines in 1565 to 1571 there were five Augustinian friars
that came out by direction of Felipe Second, charged with
the duty under Legaspi of Christianizing those islands.
By the greatest good luck they reached there just before
the time when the Mohammedans were thinking of going into the same place, and they spread Christianity
through those islands with no violence but in the true
spirit of Christian missionaries. They taught the natives
of those islands agriculture. They taught them peace
and the arts of peace, and so it came about that the only
people as a body that are Christians in the whole Orient
are the Filipino people of the Christian provinces of the
Philippines, seven million souls. I dwell upon this because it is the basis of the whole hope of success that we
have in our problem in those islands. It is true that
those people were not developed beyond the point of
Christian tutelage. Those old missionaries felt that it
was not wise to oppose these people to the temptations of
the knowledge which European Christians have, and so
they were kept in a state of ignorance, but nevertheless
they were Christians, and for three hundred years have
been under that influence.

In this condition of Christian tutelage, their ideals
are western, their ideals are European, their ideals are
Christian, and they understand us. When we attempt
to unfold to them the theories and the doctrine of self-
government, of democracy, they are fit material, to make,

in two or three generations, because they are Christians, a self-governing people. We have the opportunity to know, because we have got a million non-Christians there — we have 400,000 or 500,000 Mohammedans, and they don't understand republican government. They don't understand popular government. They welcome a despotism, and they never will sustain popular self-government until they have been converted to Christianity.

I suppose I ought not to go into the discussion here of our business in the Philippines, but I never can take up that subject without pointing the moral. It is my conviction that our nation is just as much charged with the obligation to help the unfortunate peoples of other countries that are thrust upon us by fate, onto their feet to become a self-governing people, as it is the business of the wealthy and fortunate in a community to help the infirm and the unfortunate of that community.

It is said that there is nothing in the Constitution of the United States that authorizes national altruism of that sort. Well, of course there is not; but there is nothing in the Constitution of the United States that forbids it. What there is in the Constitution of the United States is a breathing spirit that we are a nation with all the responsibilities that any nation ever had, and therefore when it becomes the Christian duty of a nation to assist another nation, the Constitution authorizes it because it is part of national well-being.

We went into the Cuban war, and we did not go into it for conquest. We went in because we thought there was an international scandal that ought to be ended, and that we had some responsibility with respect to that scandal, if we could end it and did not do so. We passed a self-denying ordinance with respect to Cuba but we found those other countries on our hands. I have been at the head of the Philippines, and I know what I am talking about when I say that the hope of those islands depends upon the development of the power of the churches that are there. One of the most discouraging things to-day is the poverty-stricken condition of the Roman Catholic Church, which has the largest congregations in those islands, and every man, be he Protestant or Catholic, must in his soul hope for the prosperity of the Roman Catholic Church in those islands, in order that it may do the work that it ought to do in uplifting those people. Protestant missions in those islands are doing a grand and noble work. It may be that their congregations will not be as large as that of the Roman Catholic Church. It is not to be expected; but the spirit of Christian emulation, if I may use that term, of competition between the representatives of the churches there, has the grandest effect upon such agents of all the churches, and so indirectly upon the people; that is, the influence of the church upon a people as ignorant as they are, and of these churches that hold up the hands of the civil governor, charged with the responsibility of maintaining peace and order, of inducing them to educate their children, and to go on upward on the path toward self-government. I am talking practical facts — about the effect of religion on political government. I know what I am talking about.

Foreign missions accomplish — I did not know it until I went into the Orient — a variety of things. They have reached the conclusion that in order to make a man a good Christian you have got to make him useful in the community and teach him something to do and give him some sense and intelligence. So, connected with every successful foreign mission is a school, ordinarily an industrial school. You have also got to teach him that cleanliness is next to Godliness, and that one business of his is to keep himself healthful. So in connection with every good foreign mission they have hospitals and doctors, and the mission makes a nucleus of modern civilization, with schools and teachers, a physician and a church. In that way, having educated the native, having taught him how to live, then they are able to be sure that they have made him a consistent Christian.

Of course, it is said there are a great many rice Christians in China. Doubtless there are. Chinese don't differ from other people, and they are quite willing to admit a conversion they don't feel, in order that they may fill their stomachs; but the real fact is that every mission in China is a nucleus for the advancement of modern civilization. China is in a state of transition. China is looking forward to progress. China is to be guided by whom? It is to be guided by the young Christian students and scholars that either learn English or some other foreign language at home, or are sent abroad to be instructed, and who come back, and whose words are listened to by those who exercise influence at the head of the government. Therefore it is that these frontier posts of civilization are so much more important than the mere numerical account of those who are converted, or those who yield allegiance to the foreign missions seems to make them, and I speak from the standpoint, as I say, of political civilization in such a country as China. They have I think some 3,000 missionaries in China. The number of students last year was 35,000. They go out into the neighborhood, and they cannot but have a good effect throughout that great Empire, large as it is, to promote the ideas of Christianity and the ideas of civilization.

Two or three things make one impatient when he understands the facts. One is the criticism that the missionary is constantly involving governments in trouble and constantly bringing about war. The truth is that western civilization in trade is pressing into the Orient, and the agents that are sent forward, I am sorry to say, are not the best representatives of western civilization. The Americans and Englishmen and others who live in the Orient are many of them excellent, honest, God-fearing men, but there are in that set of advance agents of west-

21

ern civilization gentlemen who left the west for the good
of the west, and because their history in the west might
prove embarrassing at home. More than that, where
there are honest, hardworking tradesmen and merchants
attempting to push business into the Orient, their minds
are constantly on business. It is not human nature that
they should resist the temptations that not infrequently
present themselves, to get ahead of the Oriental brother
in business transactions. They generally are quite out of
sympathy with a spirit of brotherhood toward the Oriental native. Even in the Philippines that spirit is shown,
for while I was there I quite remember hearing on the
streets a song of a gentleman who did not agree with
my view of what we ought to do by the Filipinos, "He
may be a brother of William H. Taft, but he ain't no
brother of mine." That is the spirit that we are too
likely to find among the gentlemen who go into the east
for the mere purpose of extending trade.

Then I am bound to say that the restraints of public
opinion that one finds at home to keep men in the straight
and narrow path are loosened in the Orient, and we find
a number of foreigners not the models that they ought
to be in probity and morality. They look upon the native as inferior, and they are too likely to treat him with
contumely and insult. Hence it is that in the progress
of civilization we must move on as trade moves on and
as the foreign missions move on.

It is through the foreign missions that we must expect
to have the true picture of Christian brotherhood presented to those natives, the true spirit of Christian sympathy. In the progress of civilization you can not over-
estimate the immense importance of Christian missions.
If in China to-day you try to find out what the conditions
are in the interior, you consult in Pekin the gentlemen
who are supposed to know, and where do you go? You
go at once to the missionaries, the men who have spent
their lives far advanced into the nation, far beyond the

point of safety if an uprising takes place, and who have learned by association with the natives, by living with them, by bringing them into their houses, by helping them on their feet, what the secret of Chinese life is. Therefore it is that the only reliable books that you can read telling you exactly the condition of Chinese civilization, are written by these foreign missionaries who have been so much blamed for involving us in foreign wars. It is said that the Boxer war was due to the interference of the missionaries and the feeling of the Chinese against the Christian religion as manifested and exemplified by the missionaries. That is not true. It is true that the first outbreak was against the missionaries, because the outbreak was against foreign interferences, and it was easiest to attack those men who were furthest in the Chinese nation. But that which really aroused the opposition of the Chinese was that feeling that all of us Christian nations were sitting around waiting to divide up the Middle Kingdom and waiting to get our piece of the pork. Now that is the feeling that the Chinese have, and I am not prepared to say that there was not some ground for the suspicion.

I have described to you the character of some Americans in the cities of the Orient, in Shanghai and in others. It has improved. Our consular system has been greatly improved, and then we established a circuit court of the United States, for China. A man was put in there as judge who had been Attorney-General in the Philippine Islands. He found an Augean stable that needed cleaning out, so far as the Americans were concerned, and I think perhaps in this audience I would be able to call on witnesses who could testify to the condition of immorality that was carried on there under the protection of the American flag. He went to work and before he got through the American flag floated over a moral community and in so doing he had the sympathy of the foreign missionaries who were in that neighborhood. With this change in our diplomatic relations with China, and by doing what was a plain, honest thing to do, and which as between nations seems to be a little more exceptional perhaps than between individuals — by agreeing to return the money that we really ought not to have taken, the Boxer indemnity, by the influence of our own foreign missionaries there, and by the belief in China that we are not there for our exploitation or to appropriate jurisdiction territorially or otherwise, I think we stand well in China to-day. I think we stand in such a position that such a movement as this, in order to raise money to increase the number of missionaries and the number of nuclei of Christianity and of civilization in that teeming population of 450,000,000 is better to-day than it ever was.

Therefore such a movement as this must enlist the sympathy and aid of all who understand the great good that these self-denying men who go so far to accomplish their good are doing. You can read books (I have read them) in which the missions are described as most comfortable buildings, and it is said that they are living much more luxuriously than they are at home, and therefore that they don't call for our support or sympathy. It is true that there are a good many mission buildings that are handsome buildings. I have seen them. It is true that they are comfortable, but they ought to be comfortable. One of the things that you have got to do with the Oriental is to fill his eye with something that he can see, and if you erect a great missionary building he deems the coming of the missionary into that community as of some importance and the missionary societies that are doing that and are building their own buildings for their missionaries are following a very much more sensible course than is the United States in denying to its representatives anything to shelter them.

But it is not a life of ease; it is not a life of comfort and luxury. I don't know how many have felt that thing I think physicians call " nostalgia." I don't know whether you have experienced that sense of distance from home, that being surrounded by an alien people, that impression that if you could only have two hours of association with your old friends at home, if you could only get into a street car and sit down or hang by a strap, in order to be near your friends. I tell you when you come back after an absence of five or ten years, even the strap seems a dear old memory. Those men are doing a grand good work. I don't mean to say that there are not exceptions among them, that sometimes they don't make mistakes and sometimes they don't meddle in something which it would be better for them from a political standpoint to keep out of, but I mean as a whole, those 3,000 missionaries in China and those thousands in other countries worthily represent the best Christian spirit of this country, and worthily are doing the work that you have sent them out to do.

CHAPTER XXVII

THE REPUBLICAN PARTY

ADDRESS BEFORE THE YOUNG MEN'S REPUBLICAN CLUB,
KANSAS CITY, MO., FEBRUARY 10, 1908

Fellow-Republicans:

We meet to-day to celebrate the memory of Abraham Lincoln. One of the bases for the everlasting gratitude which the country owes him is the part he took in the successful establishment in national political control of the Republican party. Lincoln was a party man, as all men must be who expect to leave their individual impress upon the political character of the Nation.

A modern government of a people of 80,000,000 is complicated under any system. The difficulties of its management are not lessened when we commit its control to all males over the age of twenty-one, and call it a Republic. How is it possible to reduce the varying views of the entire population to one resultant executive force which shall carry on this machine of government in the public interest and for the public weal? The problem has been solved by the institution of parties. A party cannot be useful unless those who are members of it yield their views on some issues and unite with respect to the main policies to be pursued. The resultant solidarity is necessary to secure efficacy. The sense of responsibility for the continued successful operation of the government must furnish cohesive power. The party is the more efficient, in which the members are more nearly united on the great principles of governmental action. Though a party has its platform, and on the faith of it has been elected to power, many issues may unexpectedly arise in the course of an administration not controlled by the party's declared principles. The disposition of such issues must depend on the ability and courage of the party leaders. A party may divide on a new issue until by a process of education the sounder view prevails, and the party becomes united again in the enforcement of the new principle. As a party shows itself homogeneous, able to grasp the truth with respect to new issues, able to discard unimportant differences of opinion, sensitive with respect to the successful maintenance of government, and highly charged with the responsibility of its obligation to the people at large, it establishes its claim to the confidence of the public and to its continuance in political power. We are apt to deny to parties characteristics and traits like those of a person, but I venture to think that a history of political parties in which the description is clothed with life and truth must always treat them as having some personal attributes.

The course of the Republican party since its organization in 1856, and its real assumption of control in 1861, down to the present day, is remarkable for the foresight and ability of its leaders, for the discipline and solidarity of its members, for its efficiency and deep sense of responsibility for the preservation and successful maintenance of the government, and for the greatest resourcefulness in meeting the various trying and difficult issues which a history of now a full half century has presented for solution. It was born of a desire to maintain inviolate the union of the States. Its essence was that of nationalism, and its spirit was that of sacrifice, no matter how great, to maintain the integrity of our whole country. The federalism of Washington, Marshall and Hamilton was the guide of its constitutional construction, and it did not hesitate, when the issue was presented, to submit its view of the great fundamental instrument of our government to the arbitrament of a long and bloody war. The leader of the Republican party during the Civil War was Abraham Lincoln. In all the varieties of controversy with which it has since had to deal, it has never lost the inspiration of his leadership.

When the Republican party entered upon the war in 1861, the only issue it was willing to fight out was that of the preservation of the Union. It did not then assume the burden of the complete abolition of slavery. There were many in its ranks who pressed for such a declaration, but the time had not come. The course of war made abolition inevitable, and Mr. Lincoln, who was the greatest politician of his age, led his party a long way by the Emancipation Proclamation. Even as he did this, he created a division in his party. It was one of the first instances in which the party showed its own power of self-preservation by gradually convincing the minority of the righteousness of the new issue.

After the martyrdom of Lincoln came the period of reconstruction and the adoption of the so-called War Amendments. The Thirteenth Amendment gave to the negro the boon of freedom, but it left as children in the world four or five millions of people, not 5 per cent. of whom could read or write, and all of whom had been dependent upon others for what they ate and wore and did. Their emancipation was, of course, the first great step in their elevation as a race, but it involved at first great hardship and suffering and discouragement, as all great changes in existing conditions must. Still the Thirteenth Amendment has accomplished its purpose.

The Fourteenth Amendment secured to the negro the equal protection of the laws of the State in which he lived. This is the amendment which, second to his emancipation, has become the most important in his development. The opportunity of the Southern negro lay, first, in education; second, in the skill of his hands as a laborer and in his industry as a tiller of the soil; and, third, in his capacity to save from his earnings sufficient to enable him to accumulate capital to buy land and establish his economic independence. Thus could he make himself useful to the community in which he lived and secure the respect which would certainly come to one showing himself indispensable to the growth and prosperity of the South. Thus would flow all the incidents of power and influence to which he aspired. When we regard the history of the forty years through which the colored man of this country has been obliged to struggle, the progress which he has made, material and educational, is wonderful.

The third great War Amendment — the Fifteenth — forbade any State to deprive the negro of his vote on account of his color or previous condition of servitude. The operation of this amendment has not been as successful as that of the Thirteenth and Fourteenth. Nor is this surprising. Consider the condition of things immediately after the war. Here was a masterful people, who had been used to a social condition in which the negro occupied a servile status, brought by law to face the prospect of sharing political control with the poor, ignorant, and bewildered masses, who, but the day before, had been their property. Declarations of equality and popular rights and universal suffrage offer but a feather's weight against the inevitable impulses of human nature. . . .

While I fully recognize the fact that the Fifteenth Amendment has not accomplished all that it was intended to accomplish, and that for a time it seemed to be a dead letter, I am confident that in the end it will prove to be a bulwark equally beneficial with that of the Thirteenth and Fourteenth Amendments to an unfortunate, downtrodden, struggling race, to whom, in view of the circumstances under which they were brought to this country and the conditions of bondage in which they were continued for more than two centuries, we owe every obligation of care and protection. That which has been done for the benefit of the negro race is the work of the Republican party. It is one of those great issues presented by the exigencies of the war which the party has had the firmness and courage to meet. The party has not yet been entirely successful in fully working out the problem, but nearly all that has been done has been done at its instance or with its aid.

Another issue which the Republican party found itself pursued by as an outgrowth of the war was the question of money, and on that the party showed a marked capacity for reaching a unanimous and sound conclusion after much controversy within its ranks. In order to maintain the government during the dark days of the war, we departed from the gold and silver monetary medium and issued as currency paper promises of the Government to pay. We found ourselves at the end of the war with a great volume of greenback currency and no means of redeeming it. For a time many members of the Republican party seemed to think that the wise course to pursue was to reduce the evil by increasing our irredeemable obligations. They imbibed the theory of fiat currency, that the government might create money and pay all its debts by merely printing promises to pay. Gradually the greenback heresy was eliminated. The Republican party sloughed off its diseased members and took the firm, solid and righteous position that it would redeem every dollar of its bonds and of its other indebtedness in coin of the United States. On the 1st of January, 1878, specie payments were resumed and the paper of the government became as good as gold.

In the decade between 1880 and 1890, the greater production of silver had cheapened the metal in comparison with gold, and quack remedies for financial troubles, in the form of the greater use of silver money, seized a large part of the electorate, both Republicans and Democrats. The silver question was fought out for twelve or fifteen years, and in that time many of the Republican leaders supported doctrines which now would seem heretical.

Gradually, however, the lines were formed. The Democracy under Mr. Bryan advanced the theory that the free coinage of silver, which was in effect repudiation of half of every debt, was the solution of all our difficulties, while the Republican party, gradually and reluctantly, took its position in favor of the single gold standard and against any depreciation of it to make easier payment of debts. In the great battle of 1896 the Republican party again stood for the maintenance of the integrity of the nation. The fight was against odds produced by a great industrial depression, and against the most sophistical arguments. The Republican party maintained a campaign of education among the wage-earners and the farmers, which ultimately led to the complete defeat of this second financial heresy which had threatened the integrity of our business structure.

One of the great policies to which the Republican party has been pledged from the beginning has been the protective system, by which industries have been diversified and domestic manufactures and farm productions have been enormously developed. Our whole business structure rests on the system, and the wage-earners dependent on it are myriad. The system has continued without a break from the time of the Morrill Tariff in 1861 until the present day, except that during the second administration of Mr. Cleveland an attempt was made to pass a revenue tariff, which failed, but resulted in the passage of a tariff which illustrated no theory of taxation at all and only brought disaster. There was put in force by the Republicans a new tariff in 1890, called the McKinley Tariff, which was repealed by the Gorman-Wilson Tariff in 1893, which in turn was repealed by the Dingley Tariff of 1897. In the ten years which has elapsed since the enactment of the Dingley Tariff, the conditions have so changed as to make a number of the schedules under that tariff too high and some too low. This renders it necessary to re-examine the schedules in order that the tariff shall be placed on a purely protective basis. By that I mean it should properly protect, against foreign competition, and afford a reasonable profit to all manufactures, farmers and business men, but should not be so high as to furnish a temptation to the formation of monopolies to appropriate the undue profit of excessive rates.

In 1898 came the war with Spain. While both parties lent their aid in Congress and there was an outburst of patriotism in all sections, the war, for which we were so little prepared, had to be conducted by the Republican Party. Whatever efficiency was displayed in its maintenance was due to that party, and the ability with which it could meet a new issue. After the Spanish War, comparatively so short and bloodless in its extent, there have developed national questions for settlement of greater importance than any save those of the great Civil War. The Republican Party has marched up to their solution with the same courage, the same skill and the same persistence that it has shown in respect to all the questions arising in its history. After peace with Spain was signed, Congress left to McKinley to pioneer in respect to the government of Porto Rico, Cuba and the Philippines, imposing only as to the Cuban policy the condition that there should be an early date for turning over that island to the people of Cuba in accordance with the self-denying ordinance known as the Teller resolution. Congress did not interfere in the Philippines for a full four years, and in that time McKinley had worked out a policy which substantially received the full confirmation of Congress and to which the Republican Party is to-day pledged. The policy of expansion is what distinguishes the administration of McKinley and adds another to the list of patriotic victories of the Republican Party. By this policy the United States has become a world power. In the course of it we have built up a navy, not large enough as yet, but large enough to be respectable and to make our influence felt for peace and good international morals the world over.

In every one of these policies which I have thus enumerated — in the war for the Union — the building up and protection of the negro race with the war amendments — in the maintenance of the sacredness of our promises to pay contained in the greenbacks and in the national bonds — in our maintenance of the national integrity by an adherence to the gold standard and a refusal to enter upon the free coinage of silver — in the support of a policy of protection under which our manufacturers and our farm productions have found a prosperity never before known in the world — in the policy of expansion and the development of the unfortunate peoples entrusted to our care by Providence — and in our progress toward world-wide influence — we have encountered the official and persistent opposition of the Democratic Party. At times we have been beaten. Only twice, however, in all that remarkable history of 48 years have we lost the confidence of the people of the United States to the point of their turning over the government to a Democratic executive. I venture to say that neither in this nor any other country can be disclosed such a remarkable record of arduous deeds done as in that history of half a century of the Republican Party.

By reason of circumstances I need not detail, the influence of the Republican Party has been little felt south of Mason and Dixon's line. It is true that in Maryland, West Virginia, Kentucky and Missouri the Republican Party has been often in the majority, but in the other Southern States a contest has seemed hopeless. The time has come, in my judgment, when it is the duty of our party to make an earnest effort to win to our support the many Southerners who think with us on every living national issue and have only been kept from our ranks by the ghost of the past.

During the present administration the Republican

Party has been called again to meet a great national need and to save the country from a growing danger. In the enormous industrial development and the accumulation of capital, due to the combination in corporate form of the wealth of the country, there have arisen abuses which have threatened to undermine our whole business fabric. The intense desire for gain, stimulated by the prospect of enormous profits, produced a reckless spirit with reference to the methods of acquisition. Official investigations have disclosed a lack of business integrity on the part of some charged in a fiduciary capacity with the custody and management of great accumulations of capital. Other official investigations showed the eagerness with which certain industrial combinations were willing to use their patronage to induce or compel railroad companies to grant to them unjust and secret discriminations and rebates. The fact that the Interstate Commerce law was violated with perfect impunity became known to the public at large, and a conviction seized the people that there were many engaged in the management of corporate wealth who regarded the statutes of their country as dead letters and themselves as a privileged class. Their corrupting influence in politics and in respect of State and national legislation was naturally becoming greater and greater as their wealth grew and their associations spread. We were passing into a regime of an irresponsible plutocracy. During the last four years there has been a great moral awakening to this danger among the people and a popular demand that the lawbreakers — no matter how wealthy or how high or powerful their position — shall be made to suffer. Under the leadership of Theodore Roosevelt the Republican Party has not faltered in its determination to meet the requirements of this situation and to enact such legislation as may be necessary to bring to a close this period of illegitimate corporate immunity.

At the instance of the President, Congress was called upon to pass an amendment to the Interstate Commerce law, known as the Rate Bill. What has been the effect of the Rate Bill? Everyone who knows anything about the management of railroads knows that there has been a revolution in respect to their obedience to the law. No longer are special privileges granted to the few — no longer are secret rebates extended to build up the monopoly of the trusts. The railroads are operating within the law, and the railroad directors and officers and stockholders ought to rise up and call blessed the men who are responsible for the passage of the Rate Bill. It may be that it has not reduced rates where it was expected. It may be that it has not furnished local relief, as it was hoped, at various points, but it has put the railroad business in this country on an honest basis, has eliminated from the operation of the railroads privilege and discrimination, and has enabled railroad men to look their fellows in the face without a consciousness that they are conducting a business in violation of law. It has put every railroad man in the country on his good behavior, and created a complete change of attitude on the part of him and of his subordinates in respect to the statutes of his country.

I am not now speaking of what may be accomplished, but what has been accomplished — not what the result of litigation under a new law has been or will be, but I am speaking of the result of the movement which found expression in the passage of the Rate Law.

Another policy proposed as a means of regulating railway rates is that of the improvement of our national waterways. Much money has been spent on sea harbors and the mouths of our rivers at the sea, but comparatively little upon the internal waterways which nature has furnished to the country, and which form highways of travel from one border of it to the other. The call from the country for the development of a well-thought-out plan for the improvement of all these waterways is so emphatic that it cannot longer be resisted. That which has been done is largely piece work. What is needed now is the consistent development of this method of inter-communication, so that a certain amount a year can be assigned to the execution of the plan. The direct effect in the transportation of merchandise will doubtless be most beneficial, while the indirect effect of regulating and reducing excessive railroad rates will be even of greater benefit.

Other corporate abuses have been made manifest besides discrimination in rates. They consist in using the corporate form of investment to float bonds and stocks whose par value is far in excess of the real money value invested in the enterprise — a practice which, in addition to deceiving and defrauding the public, involves consequences with reference to reckless corporate management that are most demoralizing. Legislation looking to the restraint in this regard of interstate commerce railways has been recommended to, and doubtless will receive, the careful consideration and approval of the National Legislature.

Under the stimulus of the revelations in respect to the illegal combinations of wealth for purposes of monopoly, prosecution under the Interstate Commerce law and the anti-trust law by the Executive has been important and effective, and the whole weight of the Republican Administration has been thrown in favor of holding up to a strict compliance with the anti-trust law those who in times past had regarded it as of no effect.

In the midst of this reform movement for the elimination from our business methods of illegal monopoly and discrimination, our country has been visited by a severe financial panic. The panic was doubtless chiefly due to the exhausting of the free capital of the world by reason of the over-investment in enterprises that have not been as productive as expected. The enormous industrial expansion had at last tied up nearly all the world's capital which was available and the new investments had to halt. This result was world-wide. In addition to this general condition, the revelations concerning the management of a number of our large corporations affected the confidence of European investors in our whole business fabric. Then our monetary system is not of such an elastic nature as to meet the emergency produced by sudden fright on the part of the holders of money, who withdraw it from business uses and hoard it against disaster. The result has been an industrial depression which we all hope and believe from the conditions prevailing will be of short duration. But those who have been made to feel the lash of public criticism by this moral awakening have been quick to seize upon and hold up the panic as a result of the measures taken or agitated to stamp out corporate abuses and illegality, and they have not been slow most unjustly to attack the Republican Administration, and Mr. Roosevelt at its head, as the responsible authors of this industrial depression. There are those who have been members of the Republican Party who differ with Mr. Roosevelt in respect to the proper course to be taken in stamping out these abuses of corporate wealth. The great bulk of the Republican Party, however, stands solidly at his back in the work which he and the representatives of the party in Congress are doing.

Vigorous action and measures to stamp out existing abuses and effect reforms are necessary to vindicate society as at present constituted. Otherwise, we must yield to those who seek to introduce a new order of things on a socialistic basis.

The Republican Party follows the Administration upon this social and moral reform — approves its attitude in favor of vested rights, of maintaining the power of the courts, of rendering more equal by legislation the basis of dealing between employer and employee, of strengthening the regulative power over railroads and other interstate corporations, and of prosecuting those law breakers who continue to defy public opinion. Roosevelt leads his party as Lincoln led his — as McKinley led his — to

22

meet the new issues presented, to arm our present civilization, and fit it with a bold front to resist the attacks of
socialism, and to transmit to the coming generations un-
harmed, the great institutions of civil liberty inherited
from our fathers.

CHAPTER XXVIII

THE REPUBLICAN NATIONAL CONVENTION

The 14th Republican National Convention, which met in Chicago on June 16th, nominated Mr. Taft for the Presidency, and chose as his running mate Representative James S. Sherman of New York.

The voluntary retirement of President Roosevelt from consideration as a Presidential possibility had thrown the field open and resulted in a larger number of candidates than had contested for the Republican nomination in any campaign for years.

Mr. Taft had from the first the support of Mr. Roosevelt, and it was evident several weeks before the Convention met that he would be nominated.

The Convention was called to order at noon on June 16th with Senator J. C. Burrows of Michigan as temporary chairman. Nothing but routine business was transacted that day, and immediately after the appointment of the usual committees the Convention adjourned. A tentative draft of the platform to be adopted by the Convention had been prepared in Washington by friends of President Roosevelt and Mr. Taft, and after consultation with them. This draft was submitted to the Committee on Resolutions, and after a long discussion it was adopted, practically entire, with very little modification. In the main it is a very strong indorsement of the Roosevelt administration and policies and an emphatic pledge of the intention of the Republican party to continue to carry out the work Mr. Roosevelt had begun.

This is entirely in accord with the desire of Mr. Taft.

The main fight in the Committee on Resolutions was over the plank discussing the procedure in Federal courts regarding the issuance of the writ of injunction. As the plank was finally adopted it expresses Mr. Taft's idea in almost the exact language which he has used in several speeches in discussing the relations of labor and capital.

The second day of the Convention was devoted to perfecting the permanent organization and the discussion of a resolution looking to a reorganization of the representation in future Conventions. This would have based future representation upon the number of Republican votes cast in a district, and was aimed at the reduction of the Southern influence in Republican Conventions. It was defeated after an interesting contest. The Committee on Resolutions not being yet ready to report the platform, the Convention then adjourned until Thursday, June 18th.

The first business at the Thursday session was the adoption of the platform, which was done unanimously. Immediately thereafter the roll of the states was called for nomination of candidates for the Presidency. Six states responded: Indiana naming Vice-President Fairbanks; Illinois, Speaker Cannon; New York, Gov. Hughes; Pennsylvania, Senator Knox; Wisconsin, Senator LaFollette, and Ohio, Secretary Taft and Senator Foraker.

There had been a great outburst of cheering for President Roosevelt during the second day's session, the applause continuing for fully three-quarters of an hour. At the close of the nominating speeches, and just before the beginning of the roll call on the ballot there was another prolonged outburst of Roosevelt cheers. The delegates, however, had taken the President at his word, and were not disturbed by this attempt to stampede them to Roosevelt. As the roll call proceeded it became evident to all the spectators that the country as represented by the delegates was really for Taft. State after state gave him its solid vote and the result of the ballot was his nomination by the overwhelming vote of 702 out of a total of 980, over 200 more than was necessary to nominate.   He had votes from every State in the Union but one.   Immediately upon the announcement of the vote, representatives of all the other candidates moved to make the nomination unanimous, which was done with a great shout.   The Convention then adjourned until Friday morning.

The question of the Vice-Presidency had been an open one, and there were nearly a score of candidates.   The sentiment of the delegates converged rapidly upon Mr. Sherman, despite the fact that it was known that the administration had favored the nomination of a western man. When the Convention reassembled on Friday morning, June 19th, the feeling among the delegates for Mr. Sherman had grown to such proportions that his nomination was already assured.   It took but one ballot to accomplish it, and he received over 800 votes.   The nomination was immediately made unanimous and the Convention adjourned.

CHAPTER XXIX

JAMES S. SHERMAN, CANDIDATE FOR VICE-PRESIDENT

History has again repeated itself in the placing of a New Yorker on the ticket of national candidates headed by a man from Ohio. As Hayes and Wheeler, Garfield and Arthur and McKinley and Roosevelt, respectively, represented Ohio and New York, so now Taft and Sherman are the candidates hailing from the same two states. Ability and availability may be credited with controlling the choice of the running mate of Secretary Taft. Mr. Sherman is widely known as a national figure, having been a Representative in Congress for nearly a score of years, serving on important committees and representing the Republican party on many notable occasions. An eloquent speaker, a master of parliamentary tactics, an able and aggressive campaign manager, a successful business man and banker, as well as a lawyer, in the prime of life and a popular man, with hosts of friends both in his native state and at the national capital, he is regarded as an ideal candidate.

James Schoolcraft Sherman is in his fifty-third year and is a native of Utica, of which city he is regarded as one of the foremost citizens. His parents were Richard U. and Mary Frances Sherman, and the date of his birth was October 24, 1855. He studied in the Utica schools and went to Hamilton College, at Clinton, N. Y., near his home, and was graduated as a Bachelor of Arts in 1878, the same year that Secretary Taft was graduated from Yale. He decided on the same profession, the law, and was admitted to the bar in 1880. He entered at once on

JAMES SCHOOLCRAFT SHERMAN
Copyright, 1908, by Harris & Ewing.

WILLIAM JENNINGS BRYAN
Copyright 1908 by Harris & Ewing

the practice of his profession at Utica, and at the same time began to take an interest in public affairs. He was soon made President of the Utica Trust and Deposit Company, a post he still retains. From speaking in campaigns he developed a desire for public life, and in 1883 was Chairman of the Oneida County Republican Committee. In 1884, when only twenty-nine years old, he was elected Mayor of his native city. After holding this post two years he accepted a nomination for Congress in the 23d New York District, and was elected and re-elected, serving from 1887 to 1891. For one term he was then out of the House, but in 1893 he was elected from the 25th District, and by successive re-elections represented it for ten years. He then became the Representative from the 27th District, being seated in 1902, and re-elected in 1904 and 1906. He is now Chairman of the Committee on Indian Affairs.

A great personal friend of Speaker Cannon, Mr. Sherman has been repeatedly called on to preside over the deliberations of the House, and especially when it has been in committee of the whole has he occupied the chair. He was an aspirant for the Speakership when Thomas B. Reed retired from it nearly ten years ago, but David B. Henderson was elected. The office of General Appraiser of the Port of New York was offered to Mr. Sherman by President McKinley in 1899, but a mass meeting of his fellow citizens of Utica was called to protest against his acceptance, and he decided to decline after his nomination had been confirmed.

Mr. Sherman widely extended his political friendships as the Chairman of the Republican Congressional Committee in the campaign of 1906, and was manager of the proceedings to re-elect the substantial Republican majority in the House of Representatives. He was the originator of the plan of calling for dollar subscriptions from all Republicans, and the sobriquet was attached to him of " Dollar Jim." The plan was successful in raising a large fund for the purposes of the campaign, and the success attendant on his efforts made Mr. Sherman's reputation as a campaign manager.   He is a man of genial temperament and known among his associates as " Jim. "   He is hearty and companionable and has much energy and enthusiasm.   There was more or less talk before the National Convention that in case Governor Hughes declined renomination Mr. Sherman might be a candidate for the Republican nomination for Governor the coming fall, and there was also mention of his name for the seat in the Senate now occupied by Mr. Platt.   But when the New York delegates got together on the way to Chicago it was found that of the possible aspirants for the nomination for Vice-President from that state Sherman's name led all the rest, and it was decided to make a united effort to secure for him a place on the ticket, which proved successful. Although Mr. Sherman is a man of stout build he is quick and active on his feet.   His good nature is one of his chief characteristics.   As a speaker he is eloquent and forceful, and he has an especial faculty of making friends wherever he goes.   The post of Secretary of the Senate was offered to him in 1900, but he declined it to remain in the lower House, but now his opportunity has come to preside over the deliberations at the other end of the Capitol.

Mr. Sherman has a beautiful home in Utica.   Connected with it are large gardens and greenhouses, in which he takes great delight, but to which he is not able to give much time on account of the many demands of his political and business life.   Mr. Sherman's wife, Mrs. Carrie Babcock-Sherman, is a daughter of the late Lewis H. Babcock, who was a prominent member of the Oneida County Bar.   Mrs. Sherman's mother lives with the Congressman at his Utica home.

Mr. and Mrs. Sherman have three sons — Sherill, aged twenty-six, who is engaged in the banking business with his father; Richard Updike, aged twenty-four, professor of mathematics at Hamilton College, and Thomas Moore, aged twenty-two, who is Secretary and Treasurer of the Smyth-Despard Company. Mr. Sherman's diversions, owing to the many demands upon his time, are few. He greatly enjoys games with his family when he is able to be at home and is a devotee of golf.

Mr. Sherman is largely interested in affairs in his home city. As President of the Utica Trust and Deposit Company, to which recently he has devoted much time and attention, and Vice-President of the Utica City National Bank he has large influence in local financial matters. He is President of the New Hartford Canning Company, the Utica Ice Company and is interested in various other industrial enterprises of this region.

CHAPTER XXX

REPUBLICAN NATIONAL PLATFORM ADOPTED BY THE REPUBLICANS AT CHICAGO CONVENTION, JUNE 18, 1908

Once more the Republican party, in national convention assembled, submits its cause to the people. This great historic organization that destroyed slavery, preserved the Union, restored credit, expanded the national domain, established a sound financial system, developed the industries and resources of the country and gave to the nation her seat of honor in the councils of the world, now meets the new problems of government with the same courage and capacity with which it solved the old.

In this, the greatest era of American advancement, the Republican party has reached its height of service under the leadership of Theodore Roosevelt.

His administration is an epoch in American history. In no other period since national sovereignty was won under Washington, or preserved under Lincoln, has there been such mighty progress in those ideals of government which make for justice, equality and fair dealing among men. The highest aspirations of the American people have found a voice. Their most exalted servant represents the best aims and worthiest purpose of all his countrymen.

American manhood has been lifted to a nobler sense of duty and obligation. Conscience and courage in public station and higher standards of right and wrong in private life have become cardinal principles of political faith; capital and labor have been brought into closer relations of confidence and interdependence, and the abuse of wealth, the tyranny of power and all the evils of privileges and favoritism have been put to scorn by the simple, manly virtues of justice and fair play.

The great accomplishments of President Roosevelt have been first and foremost a brave and impartial enforcement of the law

394

and the prosecution of illegal trusts and monopolies, punishment of evil doers in the public service, the more effective regulation of rates and service of the great transportation lines, the complete overthrow of preferences, rebates and discriminations and the arbitration of labor disputes; the amelioration of the condition of wage workers everywhere, the conservation of the natural resources of the country; the forward step in the improvement of the inland waterways, and always the earnest support and defense of every wholesome safeguard which has made more secure the guaranties of life, liberty and property.

These are the achievements that will make for Theodore Roosevelt his place in history, but more than all else the great things he has done will be an inspiration to those who have yet greater things to do. We declare our unfaltering adherence to the policies thus inaugurated, and pledge their continuance under a Republican administration of the Government.

EQUALITY OF OPPORTUNITY.

Under the guidance of Republican principles the American people have become the richest nation in the world. Our wealth today exceeds that of England and her colonies, and that of France and Germany combined.

When the Republican party was born the total wealth of the country was $16,000,000,000. It has leaped to $110,000,000,000 in a generation, while Great Britain has gathered but $60,000,-000,000 in 500 years. The United States now owns. one-fourth of the world's wealth and makes one-third of all modern manufactured products.

In the great necessities of civilization, such as coal, the motive power of all activity; iron, the chief basis of all industry; cotton, the staple foundation of all fabrics; wheat, corn, and all the great products that feed mankind, American supremacy is undisputed. And yet her great natural wealth has been scarcely touched.

We have a vast domain of 3,000,000 square miles, literally bursting with latent treasure, still waiting the magic of capital and industry to be converted to the practical uses of mankind; a country rich in soil and climate, in the unharnessed energy of its rivers and in all the varied products of the field, the forest and the factory.

With gratitude for God's bounty, with pride in the splendid productiveness of the past, and with confidence in the plenty and prosperity of the future, the Republican party declares for the principle that in the development and enjoyment of wealth so great and blessings so benign there shall be equal opportunity for all.

REVIVAL OF BUSINESS.

Nothing so clearly demonstrates the sound basis upon which our commercial industry and agricultural interests are founded, and the necessity of promoting the present continued welfare through the operation of Republican policies as the safe passage of the American people through a financial disturbance, which, if appearing in the midst of Democratic rule or the menace of it, might have equaled the familar Democratic panics of the past.

We congratulate the people upon this renewed evidence of American supremacy, and hail with confidence the signs now manifest of a complete restoration of business prosperity in all lines of trade, commerce and manufacturing.

REPUBLICAN LEGISLATION.

Since the election of William McKinley in 1896 the people of this country have felt anew the wisdom of intrusting to the Republican party through decisive majorities the control and direction of national legislation. The many wise and progressive measures adopted at recent sessions of Congress have demonstrated the patriotic resolves of Republican leadership in the legislative department to keep step in the forward march to better government.

Notwithstanding the indefensible filibustering of a Democratic minority in the House of Representatives during the last session, wholesome and progressive laws were enacted, and we especially commend the passage of the emergency currency bill, the appointment of the National Monetary Commission, the employers' and Government liability laws, the measures for the greater efficiency of the army and navy, the widows' pension bills, the child labor law for the District of Columbia, the new statutes for the safety of railroad engineers and firemen, and many other acts conserving the public welfare.

THE TARIFF.

The Republican party declares unequivocally for a revision of the tariff by a special session of Congress immediately following the inauguration of the next President, and commends the steps already taken to this end in the work assigned to the Appropriations Committee of Congress, which is now investigating the operation and effect of existing schedules.

In all tariff legislation the true principle of protection is best maintained by the imposition of such duties as will equal the difference between the cost of production at home and abroad, together with a reasonable profit to American industries. We favor the establishment of maximum and minimum rates to be administered by the President under limitations fixed in the law, the maximum to be available to meet discriminations by foreign countries against American goods entering their markets and the minimum to represent the normal measure of protection at home, the aim and purpose of the Republican policy being not only to preserve, without excessive duties, that security against foreign competition to which American manufacturers, farmers and producers are entitled, but also to maintain the high standard of living of the wage earners of this country, who are the most directly benefited by the protective system.

Between the United States and the Philippines we believe in a free interchange of products with such limitations as to sugar and tobacco as will afford adequate protection to domestic interests.

CONCERNING CURRENCY.

We approve the emergency measures adopted by the Government during the recent financial disturbance, and especially commend the passage by Congress at the last session of the law designed to protect the country from a repetition of such stringency.

The Republican party is committed to the development of a permanent currency system responding to our greater needs, and the appointment of the National Monetary Commission by the present Congress, which will impartially investigate all proposed methods, insures the early realization of this purpose.

The present currency laws have fully justified their adoption, but an expanding commerce, a marvelous growth in wealth and population multiply the centers of distribution, including the demand for movement of crops in the West and South and entailing periodic changes in monetary conditions disclose the need of a more elastic and adaptable system. Such a system must meet the requirements of agriculturists, manufacturers, merchants and business generally; must be automatic in operation, minimizing the fluctuation in interest rates, and, above all, must be in harmony with that Republican doctrine which insists that every dollar shall be based upon and as good as gold.

POSTAL SAVINGS.

We favor the establishment of a postal savings bank system for the convenience of the people and the encouragement of thrift.

ABOUT THE TRUSTS.

The Republican party passed the Sherman anti-trust law over Democratic opposition and enforces it after Democratic dereliction.

It has been a wholesome instrument for good in the hands of a wise and fearless Administration. But experience has shown that its effectiveness can be strengthened and its real objects better attained by such amendments as will give to the Federal Government greater supervision and control over, and secure greater publicity in the management of that class of corporations engaged in interstate commerce having power and opportunity to effect monopolies.

RAILROAD LAWS.

We approve the enactment of the railroad rate law and the vigorous enforcement by the present Administration of the statutes against rebates and discriminations, as a result of which the advantages formerly possessed by the large shipper over the small shipper have substantially disappeared, and in this connection we commend the appropriation by the present Congress to enable the Interstate Commerce Commission to thoroughly investigate and give publicity to the accounts of interstate railroads.

We believe, however, that the interstate commerce law should be further amended so as to give railroads the right to make and publish traffic agreements, subject to the approval of the commission, but maintaining always the principle of competition between naturally competing lines and avoiding the common control of such lines by any means whatever. We favor such national legislation and supervision as will prevent the future overissue of stocks and bonds by interstate carriers.

EMPLOYERS' LIABILITY.

The enactment at the present session of Congress of the employers' liability law, the passage and enforcement of the safety appliance statutes, as well as the additional protection secured for engineers and firemen, the reduction in the hours of labor of train-men and railroad telegraphers, the successful exercise of the powers of mediation and arbitration between interstate railroads and their employees and the law making a beginning in the policy of compensation for injured employees of the Government are among the most commendable accomplishments of the present Administration.

But there is further work in this direction yet to be done, and the Republican party pledges its continued devotion to every cause that makes for safety and the betterment of conditions among those whose labor contributes so much to the progress of the country.

WAGE EARNERS.

The same wise policy which has induced the Republican party to maintain protection to American labor; to establish an eight-hour day on the construction of all public works; to increase the list of employees who shall have preferred claims for wages under the bankruptcy laws; to adopt a child labor statute for the District of Columbia; to direct an investigation into the condition of working women and children, and later, of employees of telephone and telegraph companies engaged in interstate business; to appropriate $150,000 at the recent session of Congress in order to secure a thorough inquiry into the causes of catastrophes and loss of life in the mines, and to amend and strengthen the law prohibiting the importation of contract labor, will be pursued in every legitimate direction within Federal authority to lighten the burdens and increase the opportunity for happiness and advancement of all who toil.

The Republican party recognizes the special needs of wage workers generally, for their well being means the well being of all.

But more important than all other considerations is that of good citizenship, and we especially stand for the needs of every American, whatever his occupation, in his capacity as a self-respecting citizen.

AS TO INJUNCTION.

The Republican party will uphold at all times the authority and integrity of the Courts, state and Federal, and will ever insist that their powers to enforce their processes, to protect life, liberty and property, shall be preserved inviolate.

We believe, however, that the rules of procedure in the Federal

Courts with respect to the issuance of writ of injunction should be more accurately defined by statute, and that no injunction or temporary restraining order should be issued without notice, except where irreparable injury would result from delay, in which case a speedy hearing thereafter should be granted.

THE AMERICAN FARMER.

Among those whose interests are vital to the welfare of the whole country, as is that of the wage earner, is the American farmer.

The prosperity of the country rests peculiarly upon the prosperity of agriculture.

The Republican party during the last 12 years has accomplished extraordinary work in bringing the resources of the National Government to the aid of the farmer, not only in advancing agriculture itself, but in increasing the conveniences of rural life. Free rural mail delivery has been established; it now reaches millions of our citizens, and we favor its extension until every community in the land receives the full benefits of the postal service.

We recognize the social and economic advantages of good country roads, maintained more and more largely at public expense and less and less at the expense of the abutting owner.

In this work we commend the growing practice of state aid, and we approve the efforts of the National Agricultural Department, by experiments and otherwise, to make clear to the public the best methods of road construction.

RIGHTS OF THE NEGRO.

The Republican party has been for more than 50 years the consistent friend of the American negro. It gave him freedom and citizenship.

It wrote into the organic law the declarations that proclaim his civil and political rights, and it believes to-day that his noteworthy progress of intelligence and good citizenship has earned the respect and encouragement of the nation.

We demand equal justice for all men, without regard to race or color; we declare once more, and without reservation, for the enforcement in letter and spirit of the Thirteenth, Fourteenth and Fifteenth Amendments to the constitution, which were designed for the protection and advancement of the negro, and we condemn all devices that have for their real aim his disfranchisement for reasons of color alone, as unfair, un-American and repugnant to the supreme law of the land.

NATURAL RESOURCES.

We indorse the movement inaugurated by the Administration for the conservation of natural resources; we approve all measures to prevent the waste of timber; we recommend the work now going on for the reclamation of arid lands and reaffirm the Republican policy of free distribution of the available areas of the public domain to the landless settler. No obligation of the future is more insistent and none will result in greater blessings to posterity.

In line with this splendid undertaking is the further duty, equally imperative, to enter upon a systematic improvement upon a large and comprehensive plan, just to all portions of the country, of the waterways, harbors and great lakes, whose natural adaptability to the increasing traffic of the land is one of the greatest gifts of a benign Providence.

ARMY AND NAVY.

The Sixtieth Congress passed many commendable acts, increasing the efficiency of the army and navy, making the militia of the states an integral part of the national establishment, authorizing joint maneuvers of army and militia, fortifying new naval bases and completing the construction of coaling stations, instituting a female nurse corps for naval hospitals and ships, and adding two new battle ships, ten torpedo boat destroyers, three steam colliers and eight submarines to the strength of the navy.

Although at peace with all the world, and secure in the consciousness that the American people do not desire and will not provoke a war with any other country, we, nevertheless, declare our unalterable devotion to a policy that will keep this republic ready at all times to defend her traditional doctrines and assure her appropriate part in promoting permanent tranquillity among the nations.

PROTECTION OF CITIZENS.

We commend the vigorous efforts made by the Administration to protect American citizens in foreign lands, and pledge ourselves to insist upon the just and equal protection of all our citizens abroad. It is the unquestionable duty of the Government to procure for all our citizens, without distinction, the rights of travel and sojourn in friendly countries, and we declare ourselves in favor of all proper efforts tending to that end.

EXTENSION OF COMMERCE.

Under the Administration of the Republican party the foreign commerce of the United States has experienced a remarkable growth and good will with all the nations of the world.

MERCHANT MARINE.

We adhere to the Republican doctrine of encouragement to American shipping and urge such legislation as will revive the merchant marine prestige of the country, so essential to national defense, the enlargement of foreign trade and the industrial prosperity of our own people.

VETERANS OF THE WAR.

Another Republican policy, which must be ever maintained, is that of generous provision for those who have fought the country's battles, and for the widows and orphans of those who have fallen.

We commend the increase in the widows' pensions made by the present Congress and declare for a liberal administration of all pension laws, to the end that the people's gratitude may grow deeper as the memories of heroic sacrifice grow more sacred with the passing years.

CIVIL SERVICE.

We reaffirm our former declaration that the Civil Service laws, enacted, extended and enforced by the Republican party, shall continue to be maintained and obeyed.

PUBLIC HEALTH.

We commend the efforts designed to secure greater efficiency in national public health agencies, and favor such legislation as will effect this purpose.

BUREAU OF MINES.

In th. interest of the great mineral industries of our country, we earnestly favor the establishment of a Bureau of Mines and Mining.

ISLAND POSSESSIONS.

The American Government, in Republican hands, has freed Cuba, given peace and protection to Porto Rico and the Philippines, under our flag, and begun the construction of the Panama Canal.

The present conditions in Cuba vindicate the wisdom of maintaining, between that republic and this, imperishable bonds of mutual interest, and the hope is now expressed that the Cuban people will soon again be ready to assume complete sovereignty over their land.

In Porto Rico the Government of the United States is meeting loyal and patriotic support; order and prosperity prevail, and the well-being of the people is in every respect promoted and conserved.

We believe that the native inhabitants of Porto Rico should be at once collectively made citizens of the United States, and that all others properly qualified under existing laws, residing in said island, should have the privilege of becoming naturalized.

In the Philippines insurrection has been suppressed, law established and life and property made secure.

Education and practical experience are there advancing the capacity of the people for government, and the policies of McKinley and Roosevelt are leading the inhabitants, step by step, to an ever increasing measure of home rule.

Time has justified the selection of the Panama route for the great isthmian canal, and events have shown the wisdow of securing authority over the zone through which it is to be built. The work is now progressing with a rapidity far beyond expectation until it has a present annual valuation of approximately $3,000,000, and gives employment to a vast amount of labor and capital which would otherwise be idle.

It has inaugurated, through the recent visit of the Secretary of State to South America and Mexico, a new era of pan-American commerce and comity, which is bringing us into closer touch with our 20 sister American republics, having a common historical heritage, a republican form of government, and offering us a limitless field of legitimate commercial expansion.

ARBITRATION AND TREATIES.

The conspicuous contributions of American statesmanship to the great cause of international peace, so signally advanced in

The Hague conferences, are an occasion for just pride and gratification.

At the last session of the Senate of the United States 11 Hague conventions were ratified, establishing the rights of neutrals, laws of war on land, restriction of submarine mines, limiting the use of force for the collection of contractual debts, governing the opening of hostilities, extending the application of Geneva principles, and in many ways lessening the evils of war and promoting the peaceful settlement of international controversies.

At the same session 12 arbitration conventions with great nations were confirmed, and extradition, boundary and neutralization treaties of supreme importance were ratified.

We indorse such achievements as the highest duty a people can perform, and proclaim the obligation of further strengthening the bonds of friendship, and already the realization of the hopes of centuries has come within the vision of the near future.

NEW MEXICO AND ARIZONA.

We favor the immediate admission of the territories of New Mexico and Arizona as separate states in the Union.

LINCOLN'S CENTENARY.

February 12, 1909, will be the one hundredth anniversary of the birth of Abraham Lincoln, an immortal spirit whose fame has brightened with the receding years and whose name stands among the first of those given to the world by the great republic. We recommend that this centennial anniversary be celebrated throughout the confines of the nation by all the people thereof, and especially by the public schools as an exercise to stir the patriotism of the youth of the land.

DEMOCRATIC INCAPACITY.

We call the attention of the American people to the fact that none of the great measures here advocated by the Republican party could be enacted and none of the steps forward here proposed could be taken under a Democratic administration or under one in which party responsibility is divided. The continuance of present policies, therefore, absolutely requires the continuance in power of that party which believes in them and which possesses the capacity to put them into operation.

FUNDAMENTAL DIFFERENCES.

Beyond all platform declarations there are fundamental differences between the Republican party and its chief opponent which make the one worthy and the other unworthy of public trust.

In history the difference between Democracy and Republicanism is that the one stood for debased currency, the other for honest currency; the one for free silver, the other for sound money; the one for free trade, the other for protection; the one for the contraction of American influence, the other for its expansion; the one has been forced to abandon every position taken on the great issues before the people, the other has held and vindicated all.

In experience, the difference between Democracy and Republicanism, is that one means adversity, while the other means prosperity; one means low wages, the other means high; the one means doubt and debt, the other means confidence and thrift.

In principle the difference between Democracy and Republicanism is that one stands for vacillation and timidity in government, the other for strength and purpose; one stands for obstruction, the other for construction; one promises, the other performs; one finds fault, the other finds work.

The present tendencies of the two parties are even more marked by inherent differences. The trend of Democracy is toward Socialism, while the Republican party stands for a wise and regulated individualism.

Socialism would destroy wealth. Republicanism would prevent its abuse. Socialism would give to each an equal right to take; Republicanism would give to each an equal right to earn. Socialism would offer an equality of possession which would soon leave no one anything to possess; Republicanism would give equality of opportunity which would assure to each his share of a constantly increasing sum of possession.

In line with this tendency the Democratic party of to-day believes in Government ownership, while the Republican party believes in Government regulation. Ultimately, Democracy would have the nation own the people, while Republicanism would have the people own the nation.

Upon this platform of principles and purposes, reaffirming our adherence to every Republican doctrine proclaimed since the birth of the party, we go before the country, asking the support not only of those who have acted with us heretofore, but of all our fellow citizens, who, regardless of past political differences, unite in the desire to maintain the policies, perpetuate the blessings and make secure the achievements of a greater America.

www.ingramcontent.com/pod-product-compliance
Lightning Source LLC
Chambersburg PA
CBHW080951020726
47505CB00009B/2157